John Charles Ryle

Hymns for the Church on Earth

Being three hundred Hymns and Spiritual Songs

John Charles Ryle

Hymns for the Church on Earth
Being three hundred Hymns and Spiritual Songs

ISBN/EAN: 9783337081799

Printed in Europe, USA, Canada, Australia, Japan

Cover: Foto ©Andreas Hilbeck / pixelio.de

More available books at **www.hansebooks.com**

HYMNS FOR THE CHURCH ON EARTH.

BEING THREE HUNDRED

HYMNS AND SPIRITUAL SONGS.

(FOR THE MOST PART OF MODERN DATE.)

SELECTED AND ARRANGED

BY THE REV. J. C. RYLE, B. A.,

CHRIST CHURCH, OXFORD,

RECTOR OF HELMINGHAM, SUFFOLK.

" Whoso offereth praise glorifieth me."—*Psalm* l. 23.

" Where is God my Maker, who giveth songs in the night?"—Job xxxv. 40.

NEW YORK:

ANSON D. F. RANDOLPH,

No. 770 BROADWAY, COR. OF NINTH STREET.

1865

EDWARD O. JENKINS,
Printer & Stereotyper,
No. 20 North William St.

PREFACE.

In sending forth a new collection of Hymns, I feel it necessary to preface the work by a few words of explanation. I am anxious that no purchaser should misunderstand the nature of its contents.

The first hundred hymns in this collection have already appeared in a separate form, under the title of "Spiritual Songs."* The remaining two hundred hymns have been added to the former selection; and the whole three hundred are now sent forth (to prevent confusion) under the new title of "HYMNS FOR THE CHURCH ON EARTH."

* This edition was reprinted in the small form, some years ago, and the success which has attended its publication has led the American publisher to reproduce the present volume.

Some explanatory account of the whole collection will now, perhaps, not be thought out of place.

I wish it then to be distinctly understood, that the volume now in the reader's hands, does not profess to be a complete collection of all the best English hymns. The old familiar compositions of Watts, Wesley, Newton, Cowper, Toplady, &c., with which every lover of Christian psalmody is acquainted, are, for the most part, purposely excluded from its pages. It contains, with a few exceptions, no hymns which are not comparatively of modern date. The greater proportion of the hymns in this volume are either very little known, or at any rate are not to be found in most of the hymn-books commonly used. It is a collection of the best modern hymns, and of a few old hymns, which are not so well known as they deserve to be.

Furthermore, I wish it to be understood, that this collection is not primarily intended for *congregational* use. Many of the hymns, no doubt, are admirably adapted for singing in the congregation. Many others, however, from their highly experimental character, are better suited for private reading; while many are shut out from public usefulness by their peculiar and irregular metres. The comfort of invalids and the edification of Christians in private, have been the two principal objects I have had in view in preparing this collection. I hold strongly, that holy thoughts often abide for ever in men's memories under the form of poetry, which pass away and are forgotten under the form of prose.

In compiling this hymn-book, I have availed myself of all the best modern collections which I have been able to obtain, whether of English, Scotch, Irish, or American origin; and I have laid no British or Irish authors under contribution without first seeking their permission. To the following writers I desire especially to express my grateful acknowledgments, and to thank them for the kindness and courtesy with which they have acceded to my applications for leave to use their hymns:—Dr. Bonar, of Kelso, N. B.;—Rev. R. Macduff;—Miss Catherine Winkworth, translator of the German hymns entitled " Lyra Germanica;" —R. Massie, Esq., translator of the German hymns by Spitta, entitled " Lyra Domestica;"—the translator of the German hymns entitled " Hymns from the Land of Luther;"—A. L. W., author of "Hymns and Meditations;"—J. T., author of "Woodsorrel;"—the author of "The Christian Life in Song;"—and Rev. C. T. Astley, author of "Songs in the Night." I desire also to express my thanks to Messrs. Longman & Co., the well-known publishers, for their permission to insert some hymns from the first series of "Lyrics Germanica," and from "Lyra Domestica," in the copyright of both which works they have a beneficial interest.

I must frankly confess, that I have been unable to discover the authorship of many of the hymns which I have inserted in this collection, and have consequently been unable to ask the permission of the writers to use them. If, therefore, any living authors of hymns should happen to see their compositions used without leave in this volume, I can only ask them to acquit me of any intentional discourtesy, and to believe, that I would have asked their permission, if I had known where to apply.

The subjects of the hymns in this collection.

are of wide range. I have purposely excluded all hymns which can only interest some one particular section of the Church of Christ. I have specially endeavoured to include those which come home to the hearts of all true Christians, of every name, and people, and tongue. Hymns full of Jesus Christ, whether living, dying, rising, interceding, sympathizing, or coming again,—hymns full of the experience of believers, their conflicts, crosses, hopes, fears, sorrows, and joys,—such hymns are always useful. Of such, the Church can never have too many. Of such, I venture to think the present volume contains a rich store.

Of the general value of hymns, it is needless to say anything. The children of the world may regard psalm-singing, or hymn-writing, with indifference, or ill-disguised contempt. But the true-hearted servants of that Saviour, who "sung a hymn" before He went out to the Mount of Olives, have ever loved, in every age, to "teach and admonish one another in psalms, and hymns, and spiritual songs." (Coloss. iii. 19.) The Bible, on which they love to feed daily, abounds in hymns of praise. The Heaven, which they hope to in habit one day, will be the abode of eternal praise. A thankful, hymn-singing spirit has always marked the days of a Church's spiritual prosperity. It is a pleasant thought, that, however much Christians may disagree in pulpits, on platforms, and in prose writing, they are generally of one heart, and one mind, in praise and prayer.

If the three hundred hymns, which I now send forth, shall do good to the weakest lamb in Christ's flock, and shall comfort, cheer, stablish, or build up one suffering member of Christ's mystical body, the labour which I have expended in collecting them will be more than repaid.

J. C. RYLE.

Helmingham Rectory, Suffolk,
DECEMBER, 1860.

INDEX TO FIRST LINES.

(9)

1

2*

SPIRITUAL SONGS.

1.

Colossians i. 19.

1. I LAY my sins on Jesus,
   The spotless Lamb of God ;
He bears them all, and frees us
   From the accursed load.
I bring my guilt to Jesus,
   To wash my crimson stains,
White in His blood most precious,
   Till not a spot remains.

2. I lay my wants on Jesus ;
   All fulness dwells in Him :
He heals all my diseases,
   He doth my soul redeem.
I lay my griefs on Jesus,
   My burdens and my cares ;
He from them all releases,
   He all my sorrow shares.

3.   I rest my soul on Jesus,
     This weary soul of mine;
  His right hand me embraces,
     I on his breast recline.
  I love the name of Jesus,
     Immanuel, Christ, the Lord;
  Like fragrance on the breezes
     His name abroad is poured.

4.   I long to be like Jesus,
     Meek, loving, lowly, mild;
  I long to be like Jesus,
     The Father's holy child.
  I long to be with Jesus
     Amid the heavenly throng,
  To sing with saints His praises,
     To learn the angels' song.

H. BONAR.

———

2.   1 *Corinthians* vi. 19–20.

1.   WHEN this passing world is done,
     When has sunk yon glaring sun,
  When we stand with Christ in glory,
  Looking o'er life's finished story,
  Then, Lord, shall I fully know,—
  Not till then,—how much I owe.

2. When I hear the wicked call
   On the rocks and hills to fall,
   When I see them start and shrink,
   On the fiery deluge brink,
   Then, Lord, shall I fully know,—
   Not till then,—how much I owe.

3. When I stand before the throne,
   Dress'd in beauty not my own,
   When I see Thee as Thou art,
   Love Thee with unsinning heart,
   Then, Lord, shall I fully know,—
   Not till then,—how much I owe.

4. When the praise of heav'n I hear,
   Loud as thunders to the ear,
   Loud as many waters' noise,
   Sweet as harp's melodious voice,
   Then, Lord, shall I fully know,—
   Not till then,—how much I owe.

5. Chosen not for good in me,
   Waken'd up from wrath to flee,
   Hidden in the Saviour's side,
   By the Spirit sanctified,
   Teach me, Lord, on earth to show,
   By my love, how much I owe.

6.   Oft I walk beneath the cloud,
Dark as midnight's gloomy shroud ;
But when fear is at the height,
Jesus comes, and all is light.
Blessed Jesus ! bid me show
Doubting saints how much I owe.

R. M. M'CHEYNE.

---

3.   1 *Peter* v. 7.

1.   LORD, it belongs not to my care,
     Whether I die or live ;
To love and serve Thee is my share,
     And this Thy grace must give.

2.   If life be long, I will be glad,
     That I may long obey ;
If short, yet why should I be sad
     To soar to endless day ?

3.   Christ leads me through no darker rooms
     Than He went through before ;
He that unto God's kingdom comes,
     Must enter by His door.

4.   Come, Lord, when grace has made me meet
     Thy blessed face to see ;
For if Thy work on earth be sweet,
     What will Thy glory be ?

5. Then shall I end my sad complaints,
    And weary sinful days,
  And join with the triumphant saints,
    Who sing Jehovah's praise.

6. My knowledge of that life is small,
    The eye of faith is dim ;
  But 't is enough that Christ knows all,
    And I shall be with Him.

R. BAXTER.

4. *John* vi. 37.

1. JUST as I am, without one plea,
    But that Thy blood was shed for me,
  And that Thou bid'st me come to Thee,—
      O Lamb of God, I come !

2. Just as I am,—and waiting not
  To rid my soul of one dark blot,
  To thee, whose blood can cleanse each spot,
      O Lamb of God, I come !

3. Just as I am,—though toss'd about
  With many a conflict, many a doubt,
  With fears within and wars without—
      O Lamb of God, I come !

3

4. Just as I am,—poor, wretched, blind,—
Sight, riches, healing of the mind,
Yea, all I need, in thee to find,—
O Lamb of God, I come!

5. Just as I am,—Thou wilt receive,
Wilt welcome, pardon, cleanse, relieve,—
Because Thy promise I believe,
O Lamb of God, I come!

6. Just as I am,—Thy love unknown
Has broken every barrier down,
Now to be thine, yea, Thine alone,—
O Lamb of God, I come!

-----

5.   *Isaiah* xxvi. 15.

1. GIVE to the winds thy fears,
Hope, and be undismay'd
God hears thy sighs, and counts thy tears,
God shall lift up thy head.

2. Through waves, and clouds, and storms,
He gently clears the way;
Wait thou His time; so shall this night
Soon end in joyous day.

3. Still heavy is thy heart ?
        Still sink thy spirits down ?
    Cast off the weight, let fear depart,
        And ev'ry care be gone.

4. What though thou rulest not ?
        Yet heaven, and earth, and hell,
    Proclaim God sitting on the throne,
        And ruling all things well.

5. Leave to His sovereign sway
        To choose and to command ;
    So shalt thou, wond'ring, own His way,
        How wise, how strong His hand !

6. Far, far above thy thought,
        His counsel shall appear,
    When fully He the work hath wrought
        That caused thy needless fear.

---

6.   *Psalm* **xxxi. 15.**

1. OUR times are in Thy hand,
        O God, we wish them there ;
    Our life, our friends, our souls we leave
        Entirely to Thy care.

2.　Our times are in Thy hand,
　　　　Whatever they may be,—
　　Pleasing or painful, dark or bright,
　　　　As best may seem to Thee.

3.　Our times are in Thy hand;
　　　　Why should we doubt or fear?
　　A father's hand will never cause
　　　　His child a needless tear.

4.　Our times are in Thy hand,
　　　　Jesus the crucified;
　　The hand our many sins have pierc'd,
　　　　Is now our guard and guide.

5.　Our times are in Thy hand;
　　　　We'll always trust in Thee,
　　Till we have left this weary land,
　　　　And all Thy glory see.

———

7.　　　　　*Hebrews* xii. 2.

1.　WHEN along life's thorny road
　　　　Faints the soul beneath the load,
　　By its cares and sins opprest,
　　Finds on earth no peace or rest,—

When the wily tempter's near,
Filling us with doubts and fear,
Jesus, to Thy feet we flee,
Jesus, we will look to Thee.

2. Thou, our Saviour, from the throne,
List'nest to Thy people's moan ;
Thou, the living Head, dost.share
Ev'ry pang Thy members bear.
Full of tenderness Thou art ;
Thou wilt heal the broken heart :
Full of power, thine arm shall quell
All the rage and might of hell.

3. By Thy tears o'er Lazarus shed,
By Thy power to raise the dead,
By Thy meekness under scorn,
By Thy stripes and crown of thorn,
By that rich and precious blood,
That hath made our peace with God,—
Jesus, to Thy feet we flee,
Jesus, we will cling to Thee.

4. Mighty to redeem and save,
Thou hast overcome the grave ;
Thou the bars of death hast riven,
Open'd wide the gates of heaven ;

3*

Soon in glory Thou shalt come
Taking Thy poor pilgrims home;
Jesus, then we all shall be,
Ever—ever—Lord, with Thee.

---

8.   1 *Thessalonians* iv. 17.

1.   FOR ever with the Lord !
          Amen, so let it be !
      Life from the dead is in that word,
          'T is immortality.

2.   Here in the body pent,
          Absent from Him I roam,
      Yet nightly pitch my moving tent
          A day's march nearer home.

3.   My Father's house on high,
          Home of my soul, how near
      At times to faith's illumin'd eye
          Thy golden gates appear !

4.   My thirsty spirit faints
          To reach the land I love,
      The bright inheritance of saints,
          Jerusalem above.

5. Yet clouds will intervene,
    And all my prospect flies;
    Like Noah's dove, I flit between
    Rough seas and stormy skies.

6. Anon the clouds depart,
    The winds and waters cease,
    While sweetly o'er my gladden'd hea
    Expands the bow of peace.

Romans viii. 1.

1. NO condemnation! O my soul,
        'Tis God that speaks the word;
    Perfect in comeliness art thou,
        In Christ thy glorious Lord.

2. In heaven His blood for ever speaks
        In God the Father's ear;
    His church, the jewels, on His heart
        Jesus will ever bear.

3. No condemnation! precious word!
        Consider it, my soul;
    Thy sins were all on Jesus laid,
        His stripes have made thee whole.

4. Teach us, O God, to fix our eyes
        On Christ, the spotless Lamb,

So shall we love Thy gracious will,
  And glorify Thy name.

------

10.   2 *Corinthians* v. 14, 15.

1. O LORD, who now art seated
      Above the heavens on high,
  The gracious work completed,
      For which thou cam'st to die,
  To Thee our hearts are lifted,
      While pilgrims wand'ring here,
  For Thou alone art gifted
      Our ev'ry weight to bear.

2. We know that Thou hast bought us,
      And wash'd us in Thy blood :
  We know Thy grace has brought us
      As kings and priests to God :
  We know that soon the morning,
      Long look'd for, hasteth near,
  When we, at Thy returning,
      In glory shall appear.

3. O Lord, Thy love 's unbounded,
      So full, so sweet, so free !
  Our thoughts are all confounded,
      Whene'er we think on Thee :

For us Thou cam'st from heaven,
   For us to bleed and die,
That, purchased and forgiven,
   We might ascend on high.

4.   O let this love constrain us
     To give our hearts to Thee ;
Let nothing henceforth pain us,
     But that which paineth Thee ;
Our joy, our one endeavour,
     Through suffering, conflict, shame,
To serve Thee, gracious Saviour,
     And magnify Thy name.

---

11.   *Isaiah* iii. 10.

1.   WHAT cheering words are these !
     Their sweetness who can tell ?
In time and to eternal days
     " 'T is with the righteous well."

2.   In ev'ry state secure,
     Kept as Jehovah's eye,
'T is well with them while life endures,
     And well when called to die.

3.   Well when they see His face,
     Or sink beneath the flood ;--

Well in affliction's thorny maze,
    Or on the mount with God.

4.   'T is well when joys arise,
      'T is well when sorrows flow,
    'T is well when darkness veils the sk.es,
      And strong temptations grow.

5.   'T is well when Jesus calls,
      And bids from earth arise,
    To join the host of ransom'd souls,
      Made to salvation wise.

---

12.   *Matthew* xiv. 28, 29.

1. HE bids us come ; His voice we know,
    And boldly on the waters go,
      To Him our Lord and God ;
We walked on life's tempestuous sea,
For He who died to set us free,
      Hath call'd us by His word.

2.   Secure from troubled waves we tread,
Nor all the storms around us heed,
      While to our Lord we look ;
O'er every fierce temptation bound,
The billows yield a solid ground,
      The wave is firm as rock.

3. But if from Him we turn our eye,
   And see the raging floods run high,
      And feel our fears within;
   Our foes so strong, our flesh so frail,
   Reason and unbelief prevail,
      And sink us into sin.

4. Lord, we our unbelief confess,
   Our little spark of faith increase,
      That we may doubt no more;
   But fix on Thee a steady eye,
   And on Thine outstretched arm rely,
      Till all the storm is o'er.

---

13.   2 *Corinthians* iv. 16.

1. FAINT not, Christian! though the road
      Leading to thy blest abode,
   Darksome be, and dangerous too —
   Christ, thy guide, will bring thee through.

2. Faint not, Christian! though in rage
   Satan would thy soul engage;
   Gird on faith's anointed shield,
   Bear it to the battle-field.

3. Faint not, Christian! though the world
   Has its hostile flag unfurl'd;

Hold the cross of Jesus fast,
Thou shalt overcome at last.

4. Faint not, Christian! though within
There's a heart so prone to sin ;
Christ the Lord is over all,
He 'll not suffer thee to fall.

5. Faint not, Christian! though thy God
Smite thee with His chast'ning rod ;
Smite He must, with father's care,
That He may His love declare.

6. Faint not, Christian! Jesu's near ;
Soon in glory He 'll appear ;
And His love will then bestow
Power over every foe.

7. Faint not, Christian! look on high,
See the harpers in the sky ;
Patient wait, and thou wilt join—
Chant with them of love divine.

---

14.   *Proverbs* xviii. 10.

1. REJOICE, ye saints, rejoice and praise
The blessings of redeeming grace :
Jesus, your everlasting tower,
Can shield you from the tempest's power.

2   His love 's a refuge ever nigh,
His watchfulness as mountains high,
His name 's a rock, which winds above,
And waves below, can never move.

3.   While all things change, He changes not;
He ne'er forgets, though oft forgot ;
His love's unchangeably the same,
And as enduring as His name.

4.   Rejoice, ye saints, rejoice and praise
The blessings of this wondrous grace ;
Jesus, your everlasting tower,
Can bear unmov'd the tempest's power.

15.   *John* xiv. 1, 2.

1.   AWAY with our sorrow and fear !
We soon shall have enter'd our home ;
The city of saints shall appear,
The day of eternity come ;
From earth we shall quickly remove,
To dwell in our native abode,
In mansions of glory above,
Prepar'd by our Father and God.

2.   Ah ! who upon earth can conceive
The bliss that in heaven they 'll share ?

4

And who this dark world would not leave,
  And cheerfully seek to be there ?—
Where Christ is the light and the sun,
  And we by reflection shall shine,
With Him everlastingly one,
  And bright in effulgence divine.

3.   'T is good at Thy word to be here,
       'T is better in Thee to be gone,
   And see Thee in glory appear,
       And rise to a share in Thy throne :
   All tears will be wiped from our eyes,
       When Thee we behold in the cloud,
   And echo the joys of the skies,
       And shout to the trumpet of God.

———

16.   1 *Corinthians* xv. 10.

1.   A LL that I was, my sin, my guilt,
        My death, was all my own :
   All that I am I owe to Thee,
       My gracious God alone.

2.   The evil of my former state
       Was mine, and only mine ;
   The good in which I now rejoice
       Is Thine, and only Thine.

3. The darkness of my former state,
    The bondage,—all was mine ;
    The light of life in which I walk,
    The liberty is Thine.

4. Thy grace first made me feel my sin,
    And taught me to believe ;
    Then, in believing, peace I found,
    And now I live, I live.

5. All that I am, e'en here on earth,
    All that I hope to be,
    When Jesus comes, and glory dawns,
    I owe it, Lord, to Thee.

---

17. 1 *Peter* ii. 7.

1. WE'LL sing of Christ, no matter who
    Should disapprove the theme :
    When He is precious to our view,
    We can't but sing of Him.

2. And He is precious in the sight
    Of all who know His voice :
    'T was He who brought them to the light,
    And taught them to rejoice.

3. 'T is He who cheers them by His smile,
    And guards them by His power ;

Who keeps them safe from force and guile,
In every trying hour.

4. 'T is He who will conduct them home,
Beyond the reach of ill,
Where all the ransom'd people come,
Where saints for ever dwell.

5. Then let His people make their boast
Of Him, and Him alone,
Who come from heaven to save the lost:
The praise be His alone!

---

18. *Isaiah* xlii. 16.

1. WHEN we cannot see our way,
Let us trust and still obey;
He who bids us forward go,
Cannot fail the way to show.

2. Though the sea be deep and wide,
Though a passage seem denied,
Fearless let us still proceed,
Since the Lord vouchsafes to lead.

3. Though it seems the gloom of night,
Though we see no ray of light,
Since the Lord Himself is there,
'T is not meet that we should fear.

4. Night with him is never night,
   Where He is, there all is light;
   When He calls us, why delay?
   They are happy who obey.

5. Be it our's then, while we're here,
   Him to follow without fear,
   Where He calls us, there to go,
   What He bids us, that to do.

---

19.   *Hebrews* x. 37.

1. "A LITTLE while!"—Our Lord shall come,
   And we shall wander here no more;
   He'll take us to our Father's home,
   Where He for us has gone before.

2. "A little while!"—He'll come again;
   Let us the precious hours redeem;
   Our only grief to give Him pain,
   Our joy to serve and follow Him.

3. "A little while!"—'T will soon be past;
   Why should we shun the promised cross?
   O let us in His footsteps haste,
   Counting for Him all else but loss.

4*

4. " A little while !"—Come, Saviour, come !
    For Thee Thy bride has tarried long ;
    Take Thy poor wearied pilgrims home,
    To sing the new eternal song.

20,   *Matthew* xviii. 20.

1. IN Thy name, O Lord, assembling,
        We, Thy people, now draw near ;
    Teach us to rejoice with trembling ;
        Speak, and let thy servants hear,
            Hear with meekness,
    Hear Thy word with godly fear.

2. While our days on earth are lengthen'd,
        May we give them, Lord, to Thee ;
    Cheer'd by hope, and daily strengthen'd,
        May we run, nor weary be ;
            Till Thy glory
    Without clouds in heaven we see.

3. Then in worship, purer, sweeter,
        Thee Thy people shall adore,
    Tasting of enjoyment greater
        Far than thought conceived before,
            Full enjoyment,
    Full, unmix'd and evermore.

21.   2 *Peter* iii. 12.

1. O HASTE away, my brethren dear,
        And come to Canaan's shore;
    We'll meet and sing for ever there,
        When all our toils are o'er.

    O that will be joyful, joyful, joyful,
        O that will be joyful!
        To meet to part no more,
        To meet to part no more,
        On Canaan's happy shore;
    And there sing hallelujah
    With the friends that have gone before.

2. How sweet to hear the hallow'd theme
        That saints shall ever sing,
    To hear their voices all proclaim,
        "Salvation to the King."

                O that will be, etc.

3. Around His throne all cloth'd in white,
        Will all His saints appear,
    And, shining in His glory bright,
        Will see our Saviour there.

                O that will be, etc.

4. Through heav'n the shouts of angels ring
   When sons to God are born ;
O what a company will sing
   On the millennial morn !

        O that will be, etc.

5. Through one eternal day we 'll sing,
   And bless His sacred name,
With hallelujah to the King,
   And " Worthy is the Lamb."

        O that will be, etc.

---

22.   *Revelations* xxii. 20.

1. THE church has waited long
   Her absent Lord to see ;
And still in loneliness she waits,
   A friendless stranger she.
Age after age has gone,
   Sun after sun has set,
And still in weeds of widowhood
   She weeps a mourner yet.

        Come then, Lord Jesus, come !

2. Saint after saint on earth
   Has liv'd, and lov'd, and died ;

And as they left us one by one,
  We laid them side by side;
We laid them down to sleep,
  But not in hope forlorn;
We laid them but to ripen there,
  Till the last glorious morn.

> Come then, Lord Jesus, come!

3. The serpent's brood increase,
      The powers of hell grow bold,
    The conflict thickens, faith is low,
      And love is waxing cold.
    How long, O Lord our God,
      Holy, and true, and good,
    Wilt thou not judge thy suffering church,
      Her sighs, and tears, and blood?

> Come then, Lord Jesus, come!

4. We long to hear Thy voice,
      To see Thee face to face,
    To share thy crown and glory then,
      As now we share Thy grace.
    Should not the loving Bride
      The absent Bridegroom mourn?
    Should she not wear the weeds of grief
      Until her Lord return?

> Come then, Lord Jesus, come!

5.   The whole creation groans,
        And waits to hear that voice
     That shall restore her comeliness,
        And make her wastes rejoice.
     Come, Lord, and wipe away
        The curse, the sin, the stain,
     And make this blighted world of ours
        Thine own fair world again.

                 Come then, Lord Jesus, come !

                                    H. BONAR.

————

23.   *Canticles* viii. 5.

1.   O HOLY Saviour ! Friend unseen !
        Since on Thine arm Thou bid'st us lean,
     Help us throughout life's changing scene
        By faith to cling to Thee !

2.   Bless'd with this fellowship divine,
     Take what Thou wilt, we'll not repine :
     For, as the branches to the vine,
        We only cling to Thee !

3.   Though far from home, fatigued, opprest,
     Here we have found a place of rest,
     As exiles still, yet not unblest,
        Because we cling to Thee !

4. What though the world deceitful prove,
    And earthly friends and hopes remove?
    With patient uncomplaining love
        Still can we cling to Thee!

5. Though oft we seem to tread alone
    Life's dreary waste with thorns o'ergrown,
    Thy voice of love, in gentlest tone,
        Whispers, " Still cling to me!"

6. Though faith and hope are often tried,
    We ask not, need not, aught beside,
    So safe, so calm, so satisfied,
        The souls that cling to Thee!

7. They fear not Satan, nor the grave,
    They know Thee near, and strong to save;
    With Thee all danger they can brave,
        Because they cling to Thee!

8. Bless'd is our lot whate'er befal;
    Who can affright, or who appal?—
    Since as our strength, our Rock, our all,
        Jesus, we cling to Thee.

24.   *Galatians* vi. 14.

1. LET worldly minds the world pursue ;
      What are its charms to me ?
    Once I admired its trifles too,
      But grace has set me free.

2. Its pleasures now no longer please,
      No more content afford,
    Far from my heart be joys like these,
      Now I have seen the Lord.

3. As by the light of opening day,
      The stars are all conceal'd,
    So earthly pleasures fade away,
      When Jesus is reveal'd.

4. Creatures, no more divide my choice ;
      I bid you all depart ;
    His name, and love, and gracious word,
      Have fix'd my roving heart.

---

25.   *Galatians* iii. 13.

1. BLESSED be God, for ever blest,
      And glorious be His name !
    His Son He gave, our souls to save
      From everlasting shame.

2   Had I worn sackcloth, and in dust
    Cast myself humbly down,
Cover'd my miserable head
    With ashes for a crown :

3.   This could not save me from the curse,
    Nor end the endless pain,
Nor quench the fire, nor ease the heart,
    Nor wipe away one stain.

4.   Th' eternal Life His life laid down,—
    Such was the wondrous plan,—
And God, the blessed God, was made
    A curse for cursed man.

5.   Our flesh He took, our sins He bore,
    Himself for us He gave ;
His woes were our's, and we with Him
    Were buried in one grave.

6.   With Him we rose, with Him we live,
    With Him we sit above ;
With Him for ever we shall share
    The Father's boundless love.

7.   Bless, then, Jehovah's blessed name,
    And bless our blessed King ;
And songs of glad deliverance
    For ever, ever sing !

   5

26.   *Matthew* xi. 28.

1.   I HEARD the voice of Jesus say,
         Come unto me and rest ;
     Lay down, thou weary one, lay down
         Thy head upon my breast.
     I came to Jesus as I was,
         Weary, and worn, and sad,
     I found in Him a resting-place,
         And He has made me glad.

2.   I heard the voice of Jesus say,
         Behold, I freely give
     The living water,—thirsty one,
         Stoop down, and drink, and live.
     I came to Jesus, and I drank
         Of that life-giving stream,
     My thirst was quench'd, my soul reviv'd,
         And now I live in Him.

3.   I heard the voice of Jesus say,
         I am this dark world's light,
     Look unto me, thy morn shall rise,
         And all thy day be bright.
     I look'd to Jesus, and I found
         In Him my Star, my Sun ;
     And in that light of life I'll walk,
         Till travelling days are done.

                                        H. BONAR.

27. *Ephesians* v. 30.

1. L ORD Jesus, are we one with Thee?
       O height, O depth of love!
    With Thee we died upon the tree,
       In Thee we live above.

2. Such was Thy grace, that for our sake
       Thou did'st from heav'n come down,
    Our mortal flesh and blood partake,
       In all our misery one.

3. Our sins, our guilt, in love divine,
       Were borne on earth by Thee;
    The gall, the curse, the wrath were Thine,
       To set Thy members free.

4. Ascended now in glory bright,
       Still one with us Thou art,
    Nor life, nor death, nor depth, nor height,
       Thy saints and Thee can part.

5. Soon, soon shall come that glorious day,
       When, seated on Thy throne,
    Thou shalt to wond'ring worlds display
       That Thou with us art one.

28.   *Proverbs* xiv. 32.

1.   AH ! I shall soon be dying,
        Time swiftly glides away ;
But, on my Lord relying,
    I hail the happy day,
The day when I shall enter
    Upon a world unknown ;—
My helpless soul I'll venture
    On Jesus Christ alone.

2.   He once a spotless victim,
        Upon Mount Calvary bled,
Jehovah did afflict Him,
        And bruise Him in my stead :
Hence all my hope arises,
        Unworthy as I am ;
My soul most surely prizes
        The sin-atoning Lamb.

3.   Soon with thy saints in glory
        The grateful song I'll raise ;
And chant my blissful story
        In high seraphic lays.
Free grace, redeeming merit,
        And sanctifying love,
Of Father, Son, and Spirit,
        I'll sing in realms above.

29. *Philippians* i. 21.

1. REJOICE for a brother deceas'd :
    Our loss is his infinite gain ;
A soul out of prison releas'd
    And freed from its bodily chain :
With songs let us follow his flight,
    And mount with his spirit above,
Escap'd to the mansions of light,
    And lodg'd in the Eden of love.

2. Our brother the haven hath gain'd,
    Out-flying the tempest and wind ;
His rest he hath sooner obtain'd
    And left his companions behind,
Still toss'd on a sea of distress,
    Hard toiling to make the blest shore,
Where all is assurance and peace,
    And sorrow and sin are no more.

3. There all the ship's company meet,
    Who sail'd with the Saviour beneath ;
With shouting each other they greet,
    And triumph o'er trouble and death :
The voyage of life 's at an end,
    Their mortal affliction is past ;
The age that in heaven they spend,
    For ever and ever shall last.

C. WESLEY

5*

30.   *Revelations* xiv. 13.

1.   HOW blest is our sister, bereft
            Of all that could burden her mind!
      How easy the soul that has left
            This wearisome body behind!
      This earth is affected no more
            With sickness, or shaken with pain:
      The war in the members is o'er,
            And never shall vex her again.

2.   This languishing head is at rest,
            It's thinking and aching are o'er;
      This quiet immoveable breast
            Is heaved by affliction no more:
      This heart is no longer the seat
            Of trouble and torturing pain;
      It ceases to flutter and beat,
            It never shall flutter again.

3.   The eyes she so seldom could close,
            By suff'ring forbidden to sleep,
      Seal'd up in their mortal repose,
            Have strangely forgotten to weep:
      She is dwelling with Jesus in light,
            Where sickness and death are unknown,
      Faith and hope are at last chang'd for sight,
            And her cross is laid down for a crown.

                                        C. WESLEY.

31.   *Romans* viii. 31.

1. IS God for me ? what is it
       That man can do to me ?—
Oft as my God I visit,
    All woes give way and flee.
If God be my salvation,
    My refuge in distress,
What earthly tribulation
    Can shake my inward peace ?

2. The ground of my profession
       Is Jesus and His blood ;
He gives me the possession
    Of everlasting good.
In me and in my doing
    Is nothing on this earth ;
What Jesus is bestowing
    Alone is truly worth.

3. For me there is provided
       A city fair and new ;
To it I shall be guided,—
    Jerusalem the true !
My portion there is lying,
    A destined Canaan lot ;
Though I am daily dying,
    My Canaan withers not.

4.   My heart within me leapeth,
        And cannot down be cast ;
      In sunshine bright it keepeth
        A never-ending feast.
      The sun which smiling lights me,
        Is Jesus Christ alone ;
      And what to sing invites me,
        Is heaven on earth begun.

---

32.   *2 Kings* iv. 23.

1.   THROUGH the love of God our Saviour,
        All will be well ;
      Free and changeless is His favour,
        All, all is well ;
      Precious is the blood that heal'd us ;
      Perfect is the grace that seal'd us ;
      Strong the hand stretch'd out to shield us ;--
        All must be well.

2.   Though we pass through tribulation,
        All will be well ;
      Our's is such a full salvation,
        All, all is well.
      Happy, still to God confiding,
      Fruitful, if in Christ abiding,
      Holy, through the Spirit's guiding,
        All must be well.

3.   We expect a bright to-morrow,—
        All will be well ;
Faith can sing through days of sorrow,
        All, all is well.
On our Father's love relying,
Jesus ev'ry need supplying,
Or in living or in dying,
        All must be well.

---

33.   *Matthew* xiv. 27.

1.   WHEN waves of sorrow round me swell,
        My soul is not dismay'd ;
I hear a voice I know full well,
     " 'T is I, be not afraid."

2.   When black the threat'ning clouds appear,
        And storms my path invade,
That voice shall tranquilize each fear,
     " 'T is I, be not afraid."

3.   There is a gulf that must be cross'd,—
        Saviour ! be near to aid ;
Whisper, when my frail bark is toss'd,
     " 'T is I, be not afraid."

4.   There is a dark and fearful vale
        Death hides within its shade ;
     O say, when flesh and heart shall fail,
        " 'Tis I, be not afraid."

————

34.   *John* xvii. 24.

1.   LET me be with Thee where Thou art,
        My Saviour, my eternal rest ;
     Then only will this longing heart
     Be fully and for ever blest.

2.   Let me be with Thee where Thou art,
     Thy unveil'd glory to behold ;
     Then only will this wandering heart
     Cease to be false to Thee and cold.

3.   Let me be with Thee where Thou art,
     Where spotless saints Thy name adore ;
     Then only will this sinful heart
     Be evil and defiled no more.

4.   Let me be with Thee where Thou art,
     Where none can die, where none remove,
     There neither death nor life will part
     Me from Thy presence and Thy love.

35.　　　　　*Matthew* xxvi. 42.

1.　MY God, my Father, while I stray,
　　　　Far from my home, on life's rough way,
　　O teach me from my heart to say,
　　　　　　　" Thy will be done."

2.　If Thou should'st call me to resign
　　What most I prize,—it ne'er was mine ;—
　　I only yield Thee what was Thine !—
　　　　　　　" Thy will be done."

3.　Should pining sickness waste away
　　My life in premature decay,
　　My Father, still I'll strive to say,
　　　　　　　" Thy will be done.'

4.　If but my fainting heart be blest
　　With Thy sweet Spirit for its guest,
　　My God, to Thee I leave the rest,—
　　　　　　　" Thy will be done."

5.　Renew my will from day to day,
　　Blend it with Thine, and take away
　　All that now makes it hard to say,
　　　　　　　" Thy will be done."

6.　Then, when on earth I breathe no more
　　The prayer oft mix'd with tears before,
　　I'll sing upon a happier shore,
　　　　　　　" Thy will be done."

36.   *Romans* viii. 28.

1. WHEN I by faith the Saviour's death
        Behold, and know Him mine,
    Sweetly my rising hours advance,
        And peacefully decline.

2. I cannot doubt His bounteous love,
        So full, so free, so kind ;
    To His unerring, gracious will
        Be ev'ry wish resign'd.

3. Good when He gives, supremely good,
        Nor less when He denies ;
    Afflictions from His gracious hand
        Are blessings in disguise.

4. Inscrib'd in Thy fair book of life,
        O may I read my name !
    There let it fill some humble place,
        'Midst those around the Lamb !

---

37.   *Revelations* v. 12.

1. GLORY to God on high !
        Let heaven and earth reply,
        Praise ye His name :

His love and grace adore,
Who all our sorrows bore ;
Sing aloud evermore,
    " Worthy the Lamb !"

2.   Jesus, our Lord and God,
Bore sin's tremendous load :
    Praise ye His name :
Tell what His arm hath done,
What spoils from death He won ;
Sing His great name alone ;
    " Worthy the Lamb !"

3.   Join, all ye ransom'd race,
Our Lord and God to bless ;
    Praise ye His name :
In Him we will rejoice,
And make a cheerful noise,
Shouting with heart and voice,
    " Worthy the Lamb !"

4.   What though we change our place,
Yet we shall never cease
    Praising His name :
To Him our songs we bring,
Hail Him our gracious King,
And without ceasing sing,
    " Worthy the Lamb !"

6

5.   Let all the hosts above
Join in one song of love,
     Praising His name :
To Him ascribed be
Honour and majesty,
Through all eternity :
     " Worthy the Lamb !"

----

38.   *Psalm* cxxxiv. 1.

1.   STAND up, and bless the Lord,
     Ye people of His choice :
Stand up, and bless the Lord your God,
     With heart, and soul, and voice.

2.   Though high above all praise,
     Above all blessing high,
Who would not fear His holy name,
     And laud and magnify ?

3.   O for the living flame,
     From His own altar brought,
To touch our lips, our minds inspire,
     And wing to heav'n our thought !

4.   God is our strength and song,
     And His salvation ours :

Then be His love in Christ proclaim'd,
With all our ransom'd powers.

5. Stand up, and bless the Lord,
   The Lord your God adore ;
Stand up, and bless His glorious name,
   Henceforth for evermore.

MONTGOMERY.

---

39. *Luke* xxi. 28.

1. AWAKE, ye saints, and raise your eyes,
      And lift your voices high ;
Extol the sovereign love that shows
   Our full redemption nigh.

2. Fast on the wings of time it flies,
      Its coming nought can stay :
It speeds with each revolving year,
   With each declining day.

3. Not many years their rounds shall run,
      Not many mornings rise,
E'er all its glories stand reveal'd
   To our admiring eyes.

4. Then let the wheels of nature roll
      Yet onward to decay :

We long to hail the rising sun,
That brings th' eternal day.

DODDRIDGE.

———

40.   1 *John* iv. 19.

1.   WE love Thee, Lord, because when we
        Had erred and gone astray,
Thou didst recall our wand'ring souls
    Into the homeward way ;
When helpless, hopeless, we were lost
    In sin and sorrow's night,
Thou didst send forth a guiding ray
    Of Thy benignant light :—

2.   Because when we forsook Thy ways,
        Nor kept Thy holy will,
Thou wert not an avenging Judge,
    But a gracious Father still ;
Because we have forgot Thee, Lord,
    But Thou hast not forgot,—
Because we have forsaken Thee,
    But Thou forsakest not :—

3.   Because, O Lord, Thou lovedst us
        With everlasting love ;
Because Thou gav'st Thy Son to die,
    That we might live above ;

Because when we were heirs of wrath,
Thou gav'st the hopes of heaven ;
We love because we much have sinn'd,
And much have been forgiven.

---

41.   1 *John* ii. 1.

1. O THOU, the contrite sinner's Friend,
       Who loving, lov'st them to the end,
    On this alone my hopes depend,
                That Thou wilt plead for me.

2. When weary in the Christian race,
    Far off appears my resting place,
    And, fainting, I mistrust Thy grace,
                Then, Saviour, plead for me.

3. When I have err'd and gone astray,
    Afar from Thine and wisdom's way,
    And see no glimm'ring, guiding ray,
                Still, Saviour, plead for me.

4. When Satan, by my sins made bold,
    Strives from Thy cross to loose my hold,
    Then with pitying arms enfold,
                And plead, O plead for me.
                6*

5.　And when my dying hour draws near,
　　Darken'd with conflict, pain, and fear,
　　Then to my fainting sight appear
　　　　　　Pleading in heav'n for me.

6.　When the full light of heav'nly day
　　Reveals my sins in dread array,
　　Say Thou hast wash'd them all away,—
　　　　　　O say, Thou plead'st for me !

WESLEY.

42.　　　　　*Romans* v. 1.

1.　I THOUGHT upon my sins, and I was sad,
　　　My soul was troubled sore and fill'd with
　　　　　　pain ;
　　But then I thought on Jesus, and was glad,
　　　My heavy grief was turn'd to joy again.

2.　I thought upon the law, the fiery law,
　　　Holy, and just, and good in its decree ;
　　I look'd to Jesus, and in Him I saw
　　　That law fulfilled, its curse endured for me.

3.　I thought I saw an angry, frowning God,
　　　Sitting as Judge upon the great white
　　　　　　throne ;

My soul was overwhelm'd—then Jesus shew'd
His gracious face, and all my dread was
gone.

4. I saw my sad estate, condemn'd to die;
Then terror seiz'd my heart, and dark de-
spair;
But when to Calvary I turn'd my eye,
I saw the cross, and read forgiveness there.

5. I saw that I was lost, far gone astray,
No hope of safe return there seem'd to be;
But then I heard that Jesus was the way,
A new and living way prepar'd for me.

6. Then in that way, so free, so safe, so sure,
Sprinkled all o'er with reconciling blood,
Will I abide, and never wander more,
Walking along in fellowship with God.

H. BONAR.

—————

43. *Isaiah* xliv. 22.

1. MY sins are blotted out,
    Since Jesus died for me;
My times are in a Father's hand,
My steps in His decree.

2.   Jesus in heaven appears,
       For me to intercede ;
   And countless benefits proclaim,
       " The Lord is ris'n indeed."

3.   A little child is free
       From carefulness and guile,
   Rests in a mother's guardian love,
   And waits a father's smile.

4.   Father of spirits, hear,
       Make me this little child ;
   May I delight myself in Thee,
   By no mistrust defil'd.

---

44.   *Revelations* xxii. 17–20

1.   THE Spirit in our hearts
       Is whispering, Sinner, Come !
   The bride, the Church of Christ, proclaims
   To all His children, Come !

2.   Let him that heareth, say
       To all about him, Come !
   Let him that thirsts for righteousness,
       To Christ, the fountain, Come !

3. Yes ! whosoever will,
      O let him freely Come,
    And freely drink the stream of life ;
      'T is Jesus bids him Come.

4. Lo ! Jesus, who invites,
      Declares, " I quickly come ;"
    Lord, even so ! I wait Thy hour :
      Jesus, my Saviour, Come !

---

45.   *2 Peter* i. 19.

1. HOPE of our hearts, O Lord, appear,
      Thou glorious star of day !
    Shine forth, and chase the dreary night,
      With all our tears, away.

2. Strangers on earth, we wait for Thee ;
      O leave the Father's throne ;
    Come with a shout of victory, Lord,
      And claim us as Thine own.

3. O bid the bright archangel now
      The trump of God prepare,
    To call Thy saints—the quick, the dead,
      To meet Thee in the air.

4. No resting place we seek on earth,
      No loveliness we see ;

Our eye is on the royal crown,
    Prepar'd for us and Thee.

5.   But, dearest Lord, however bright
    That crown of joy above,
    What is it to the brighter hope
    Of dwelling in Thy love?

6.   What to the joy, the deeper joy,
    Unmingled, pure, and free,
    Of union with our living Head,
    Of fellowship with Thee?

7.   This joy e'en now on earth is our's,
    But only, Lord, above
    Our heart without a pang shall know
    The fulness of Thy love.

8.   There, near Thy heart, upon the throne,
    Thy ransom'd Bride shall see,
    What grace was in the bleeding Lamb,
    Who died to make her free.

---

46.   *Acts* ii. 2.

1.   SPIRIT divine! attend our prayer,
    And make this house Thy home;
    Descend with all Thy gracious power,
    O come, great Spirit, come!

2. Come as the light,—to us reveal
   Our emptiness and woe ;
   And lead us in those paths of life,
   Where all the righteous go.

3. Come as the fire,—and purge our hearts
   Like sacrificial flame ;
   Let our whole souls an offering be
   To our Redeemer's name.

4. Come as the dew,—and sweetly bless
   This consecrated hour ;
   May barren minds be taught to own
   Thy fertilizing power.

5. Come as the dove,—and spread Thy wings,
   The wings of peaceful love ;
   And let the Church on earth become
   Blest as the Church above.

---

47.   1 *Corinthians* iii. 22.

1. IF God is mine, then present things,
      And things to come are mine ;
   Yea Christ, His Word, and Spirit too,
   And glory all divine.

2. If He is mine, then from His love
   He every trouble sends ;
   All things are working for my good,
   And bliss His rod attends.

3. If He is mine, I need not fear
   The rage of earth and hell ;
   He will support my feeble power,
   And every foe repel.

4. If He is mine, let friends forsake,
   Let wealth and honour flee,—
   Sure He who giveth me Himself,
   Is more than these to me.

5. If He is mine, I 'll boldly pass
   Through death's dark, gloomy vale ;
   He is solid comfort, when
   All other comforts fail.

6. O tell me, Lord, that Thou art mine ;
   What can I wish beside ?
   My soul shall at the fountain live,
   When all the streams are dried.

48.   *Revelations* v. 9.

1. SING we the song of those who stand
      Around th' eternal throne,
   Of every kindred, clime, and land,
      A multitude unknown.

2. Life 's poor distinctions vanish here ;—
      To-day the young, the old,
   Our Saviour and His flock appear,
      One Shepherd and one fold.

3. Toil, trial, suffering still await
      On earth the pilgrim throng ;
   Yet learn we in our low estate
      The Church triumphant's song.

4. Worthy the Lamb for sinners slain !
      Cry the redeem'd above,
   Blessing and honour to obtain,
      And everlasting love.

5. Worthy the Lamb ! on earth we sing,
      Who died our souls to save ;
   Henceforth, O death, where is thy sting ?
      Thy victory, O grave ?

6. Then hallelujah ! power and praise
      To God in Christ be given ;
   May all who now this anthem raise,
      Renew the strain in heaven !

MONTGOMERY.

7

49.   *Revelations* xiv. 4.

1.   A PILGRIM through this lonely world,
         The blessed Saviour pass'd ;
     A mourner all His life was He,
         A dying Lamb at last.

2.   That tender heart that felt for all,
         For all its life blood gave ;
     It found on earth no resting-place
         Save only in the grave.

3.   Such was our Lord,—and shall we fear
         The cross, with all its scorn ?
     Or love a faithless, evil world,
         That wreath'd His brow with thorn ?

4.   No ! facing all its frowns or smiles,
         Like Him obedient still,
     We homeward press through storm or calm,
         To Zion's blessed hill.

———

50.   *Luke* xxii. 42.

1.   ONE prayer I have,—all prayers in one,
         When I am wholly Thine,
     Thy will, my God, Thy will be done,
         And let that will be mine.

2. All-wise, Almighty, and all-good,
    In Thee I firmly trust ;
Thy ways, unknown or understood,
    Are merciful and just.

3. May I remember, that to Thee
    Whate'er I have I owe ;
And back in gratitude from me
    May all Thy bounties flow.

4. Thy gifts are only then enjoyed,
    When used as talents lent ;
Those talents only well employed,
    When in Thy service spent.

5. And though Thy wisdom takes away,
    Shall I arraign Thy will ?
No ! let me bless Thy name and say,
    " The Lord is gracious still."

6. A pilgrim through the earth I roam,
    Of nothing long possess'd ;
And all must fail when I go home,
    For this is not my rest.

7. Write but my name upon the roll
    Of Thy redeem'd above ;
Then, heart, and mind, and strength, and soul,
    I 'll love Thee for Thy love.

51.   1 *Peter* ii. 25.

1. I WAS a wand'ring sheep,
        I did not love the fold ;
    I did not love my Shepherd's voice,
        I would not be controll'd.

2. I was a wayward child,
        I did not love my home ;
    I did not love my Father's voice,
        I lov'd afar to roam.

3. The Shepherd sought His sheep,
        The Father sought His child ;—
    They follow'd me o'er vale and hill,
        O'er desert, waste, and wild.

4. They found me nigh to death,
        Famish'd, and faint, and lone ;
    They bound me with the bands of love,
        They sav'd the wand'ring one.

5. They wash'd my filth away,
        They made me clean and fair ;
    They brought me to my home in peace,—
        The long-sought wanderer.

6. Jesus my Shepherd is,—
        'T was He that lov'd my soul,

'T was He that wash'd me in His blood,
 'T was He that made me whole.

7. 'T was He that sought the lost,
  That found the wand'ring sheep,
 'T was He that brought me to the fold,
  'T is He that still doth keep.

8. I was a wand'ring sheep,
  I would not be controll'd :
 But now I love my Shepherd's voice,
  I love, I love the fold !

9. I was a wayward child,
  I once preferr'd to roam ;
 But now I love my Father's voice,—
  I love, I love His home !

H. BONAR.

---

52.   *Luke* xxii. 32.

1. THOU, who did'st for Peter's faith
  Kindly condescend to pray,
Thou, whose loving-kindness hath
 Kept me to the present day,
   Kind Conductor,
Still direct my devious way !
  7*

2. When a tempting world in view
    Gains upon my yielding heart,
When its pleasures I pursue,
    Then one look of pity dart,—
            Teach me pleasures
Which the world can ne'er impart.

3. When I listen to Thy word,
    In Thy temple cold and dead ;
When I cannot see Thee, Lord,
    All faith's little day-light fled,—
            Sun of glory,
Beam again around my head.

4. When Thy statutes I forsake,
    When my graces dimly shine ;
When my covenant I break,
    Jesus, then remember Thine,—
            Check my wanderings,
By a look of love divine.

5. When Thy heav'nly dew distils,
    And my views, O Lord, are clear,
Clear and bright from Zion's hills,—
    Temper joys with holy fear,—
            Keep me watchful,
Safe alone when Thou art near.

6.   When afflictions cloud my sky,
     When the tide of sorrow flows,
  When Thy rod is lifted high,
     Let me on Thy love repose,—
            Stay the rough wind,
  When Thy chilling east wind blows.

7.   When the vale of death appears,
     Faint and cold this mortal clay,
  Kind Forerunner, soothe my fears,
     Light me through the darksome way—
            Break the shadows,
  Usher in eternal day.

                              J. TAYLOR.

———

53.   *Psalm* cxxi. 1.

1.   WELCOME, days of solemn meeting!
     Welcome, days of praise and prayer!
  Far from earthly scenes retreating,
     In your blessings we would share,—
          Sacred seasons,
     In your blessings we would share.

2.   Be Thou near us, blessed Saviour,
     Still at morn and eve the same;

Give us faith that cannot waver,
   Kindle in us heaven's own flame,—
       '   Blessed Saviour,
   Kindle in us heaven's own flame.

3. When the fervent prayer is glowing,
    Holy Spirit, hear that prayer:
  When the song of praise is flowing,
    Let that song Thine impress bear,—
      Holy Spirit,
    Let that song Thine impress bear.

———

54.   *Revelations* v. 6.

1. EARTH has engross'd my love too long,
    'T is time I lift mine eyes
  Upwards, dear Father, to Thy throne,
    And to my native skies.

2. There the blest man, my Saviour sits,
    The God! how bright He shines!
  And scatters infinite delights
    On countless happy minds.

3. Seraphs with elevated strains
    Compass the throne around,
  And move and charm the starry plains
    With an immortal sound.

4. Jesus, the Lord, their harps employs;
  Jesus, my God, they sing !
Jesus, the life of both our joys,
  Sound sweet from ev'ry string.

5. Now let me mount and join their song,
  And be an angel too :
My heart, my ear, my hand, my tongue,
  Here's joyful work for you.

6. I would begin the music here,
  And so my soul should rise :
O for some heav'nly notes to bear
  My praises to the skies !

7. There ye that love my Saviour sit,
  There I would fain have place,
Among your thrones, or at your feet,
  So I might see His face.

WATTS.

---

55.   *Psalm* cxlviii. 14.

1. NEARER, my God, to Thee,—
    Nearer to Thee ;
E'en though it be a cross
    That raiseth me ;
Still all my song shall be,
Nearer, my God, to Thee,
    Nearer to Thee !

2. Though like a wanderer,
        The sun gone down,
    Darkness comes over me,
        My rest a stone,
    Yet in my dreams I'd be
    Nearer, my God, to Thee,
        Nearer to Thee!

3. There let my way appear
        Steps unto heav'n,
    All that Thou sendest me
        In mercy giv'n,
    Angels to beckon me
    Nearer, my God, to Thee,
        Nearer to Thee!

4. Then with my waking thoughts
        Bright with Thy praise,
    Out of my stony griefs
        Bethel I'll raise;
    So by my woes to be
    Nearer, my God, to Thee,
        Nearer to Thee.

5. And when on joyful wing,
        Cleaving the sky;
    Sun, moon, and stars forgot,
        Upward I fly;

Still all my song shall be,
Nearer, my God, to Thee,
   Nearer to Thee!

---

56.   *Psalm* xxiii. 4.

1. THERE is an hour when I must part
   With all I hold most dear ;
 And life, with its best hopes, will then
  As nothingness appear.

2. There is an hour when I must sink
  Beneath the stroke of death ;
 And yield to Him who gave it first,
  My struggling vital breath.

3. There is an hour when I must stand
  Before the judgment seat ;
 And all my sins, and all my foes,
  In awful vision meet.

4. There is an hour when I must look
  On one eternity ;
 And nameless woe, or blissful life,
  My endless portion be.

5. O Saviour, then. in all my need,
  Be near, be near to me ;
 And let my soul, by steadfast faith,
  Find life and heaven in Thee.

57.   *Acts* xxi. 13.

1.   WHEN the spark of life is waning
    Weep not for me:
When the languid eye is straining,
    Weep not for me.
When the feeble pulse is ceasing,
Start not at its swift decreasing,
'T is the fettered soul 's releasing;
    Weep not for me.

2.   When the pangs of death assail me,
    Weep not for me:
Christ is mine,—He cannot fail me,—
    Weep not for me.
Yes! though sin and doubt endeavour
From His love my soul to sever,
Jesus is my strength for ever;
    Weep not for me.

---

58.   *2 Timothy* iv. 6.

1.   I 'M going to leave all my sadness,
    I 'm going to change earth for heaven,
There, there all is peace, all is gladness,
    There pureness and glory are given.
Friends, weep not in sorrow of spirit,
    But joy that my time here is o'er;

I go the good part to inherit,
    Where sorrow and sin are no more.

2.   The shadows of evening are fleeing,
    Morn breaks on the city of light;
This moment day starts into being,
    Eternity bursts on my sight.
The first-born redeem'd from all trouble,
    (The Lamb that was slain in the throng)
Their ardour in praising redouble : —
    Breaks not on the ear the new song ?

3.   I 'm going to tell their glad story,
    To share in their transports of praise ;
I 'm going in garments of glory,
    My voice to unite with their lays.
Ye fetters corrupted, then leave me ;
    Thou body of sin, droop and die ;
Pains of earth, cease ye ever to grieve me,
    From you 't is for ever I fly.

---

59.   *John* xxi. 16.

1.   DO not I love Thee, O my Lord ?
    Behold my heart, and see !
And cast each hated idol down,
    That dares to rival Thee.

8

2. Do not I love Thee from my soul ?
        Then let me nothing love ;
    Dead be my heart to every joy,
        When Jesus cannot move.

3. Is not Thy name melodious still,
        To mine attentive ear ?
    Does not each pulse with pleasure bound
        My Saviour's voice to hear ?

4. Thou know'st I love Thee, gracious Lord,
        But O, I long to soar
    Far from the sphere of mortal joys,
        And learn to love Thee more.

                                    DODDRIDGE.

---

60.   *Exodus* xiv. 15.

1. PRESS forward and fear not; the billows
        may roll,
    But the power of Jesus their rage can control ;
    Though waves rise in anger, their tumult shall
        cease,
    One word of His bidding shall hush them to
        peace.

2. Press forward and fear not; though trial be
        near,
    The Lord is our refuge,—whom then shall we
        fear ?

His staff is our comfort, our safe-guard His
 rod ;
Then let us be steadfast, and trust in our God.

3. Press forward and fear not ; be strong in the
 Lord,
 In the pow'r of His promise, the truth of His
 word ;
 Through the sea and the desert our pathway
 may tend,
 But He who hath sav'd us will save to the
 end.

4. Press forward and fear not ; we'll speed on
 our way ;
 Why should we e'er shrink from our path in
 dismay ?
 We tread but the road which our Leader has
 trod ;
 Then let us press forward, and trust in our
 God.

---

61.   *Psalm* cvii. 1, 2.

1. L ET sinners sav'd give thanks and sing
     Of mercies past, of joys to come ;
    The Lord their Saviour is and King,
    The cross their hope, and heav'n their home.

2. Let sinners sav'd give thanks and sing,—
    Sweet is the subject of their song,—
    Who, made the children of a King,
    Expect to sit in heav'n ere long.

3. Let sinners sav'd give thanks and sing,—
    The Lord has kept in dangers past;
    And oh! sweet thought, the Lord will bring
    His people safe to heav'n at last.

4. Let sinners sav'd give thanks and sing,
    Of Jesus sing through all their days;
    In heav'n their golden harps they 'll string,
    And then for ever sing His praise.

---

62.   *Hebrews* xi. 16.

1. I HAVE a home above,
        From sin and sorrow free;
    A mansion which eternal love
        Design'd and form'd for me.

2. My Father's gracious hand
        Has built this sweet abode;
    From everlasting it was plann'd;
        My dwelling-place with God.

3. My Saviour's precious blood
      Has made my title sure:
    He pass'd through death's dark raging flood,
      To make my rest secure.

4. The Comforter is come,
      The earnest has been given;
    He leads me onward to the home,
      Reserved for me in heaven.

5. Bright angels guard my way,
      His ministers of power,
    And watching round me night and day,
      Preserve in danger's hour.

6. Lov'd ones are gone before,
      Whose pilgrim days are done;
    I soon shall greet them on that shore
      Where partings are unknown.

7. Thy love, most gracious Lord,
      My joy and strength shall be,
    Till Thou shalt speak the gladdening word
      That bids me rise to Thee.

8. And then through endless days,
      Where all Thy glories shine;
    In happier, holier strains I' ll praise
      The grace that made me Thine.

8*

63.   *2 Kings* iv. 26.

1.   BELOVED, "it is well!"
     God's ways are always right;
And perfect love is o'er them all,
     Tho' far above our sight.

2.   Beloved, "it is well!"
     Tho' deep and sore the smart,
The hand that wounds knows how to bind,
     And heal the broken heart.

3.   Beloved, "it is well!"
     Tho' sorrow clouds our way,
'T will only make the joy more dear
     That ushers in the day.

4.   Beloved. "it is well!"
     The path that Jesus trod,
Tho' rough, and strait, and dark it be,
     Leads home to heaven and God.

---

64.   *2 Thessalonians* i. 7.

1.   I HEAR a voice at dawn of day,
     And to my heart it seems to say,
When sorrow dims hope's brightest ray,
       "There 's rest in heaven."

2. I hear it at the evening tide,
   When fitful shadows round us glide,
   Still whispering gently at my side,
       "There 's rest in heaven."

3. E'en at noon's busy hour I hear
   The same sweet word accost my ear,
   With power to stay the rising tear,--
       "There 's rest in heaven."

4. Blest words! which tell of nought but joy,
   Of endless rest without alloy,
   Well may they oft our thoughts employ—
       "There 's rest in heaven."

5. Spirit of life and love divine,
   Subdue my heart and make it Thine,
   That I may dwell upon as mine,
       That "rest in heaven."

———

65.   *Philippians* iv. 6.

1. PRAYER is the breath of God in man,
       Returning whence it came;
   Love is the sacred fire within,
       And prayer the rising flame.

2. It gives the burdened spirit ease,
      And soothes the troubled breast,
    Yields comfort to the mourning soul,
      And to the weary rest.

3. The prayers and praises of the saints,
      Like precious odours sweet,
    Ascend and spread a rich perfume
      Around the mercy-seat.

4. When God inclines the heart to pray,
      He hath an ear to hear;
    To Him there 's music in a groan,
      And beauty in a tear.

5. The humble suppliant cannot fail
      To have his wants supplied,
    Since He for sinners intercedes,
      Who once for sinners died.

                                     BEDDOME.

66.   *Psalm* xviii. 1.

1. THEE will I love, my strength, my tower;
      Thee will I love, my joy, my crown;
    Thee will I love with all my power,
      In all Thy works, and Thee alone:

Thee will I love till sacred fire
Fills my whole soul with pure desire.

2. Ah ! why did I so late Thee know,
        Thee lovelier than the sons of men ?
    Ah ! why did I no sooner go
        To Thee, the only ease in pain ?
    Ashamed I sigh and inly mourn,
    That I so late to Thee did turn.

3. In darkness willingly I strayed ;
        I heard Thee, yet from Thee I roved ;
    Far wide my wandering thoughts were spread ;
        Thy creatures more than Thee I loved :
    And now, if more at length I see,
    'T is through Thy light, and comes from Thee.

4. I thank Thee, uncreated Sun,
        That Thy bright beams on me have shined ;
    I thank Thee, who hast overthrown
        My foes, and healed my wounded mind ;
    I thank Thee, whose enlivening voice
    Bids my free'd heart in Thee rejoice.

5. Uphold me in the upward race,
        Nor suffer me again to stray ;
    Strengthen my feet with steady pace
        Still to press forward in Thy way :

Let all my powers, with all their might,
In Thy sole glory now unite.

6.   Thee will I love, my joy, my crown ;
        Thee will I love, my Lord, my God ;
    Thee will I love, beneath Thy frown,
        Or smile,—Thy sceptre, or Thy rod ;
    What though my flesh and heart decay,
    Thee shall I love in endless day.

                                        WESLEY.

67.   *Galatians* vi. 1.

1.   LOOK thou with pity on a brother's fall,
        But dwell not with stern anger on his
                fault ;
    The grace of God alone holds thee, holds all ;
    Were that withdrawn, thou too would'st
                swerve and halt.

2.   Lead back the wanderer to the Saviour's fold ;
    That were an action worthy of a saint ;
    But not in malice let the crime be told,
    Nor publish to the world the evil taint.

3.   The Saviour suffers when His children slide ;
    Then is His holy name by men blasphem'd,
    And He afresh is mocked, and crucified
    Even by those His bitter death redeemed.

4. Rebuke the sin, but yet in love rebuke,
   Feel as one member in another's pain ;
   Win back the soul that His fair path forsook,
   And mighty and eternal is the gain.

---

68.   *Psalm* cxix. 105.

1. WOULD'ST thou be wise, and know the
               Lord ?
   Would'st thou believe aright ?
   Make the blest volume of His word
     Thy rule, thy guide, thy light.

2. Here is the spring where waters flow
     To quench our heat of sin ;
   Here is the tree where truth doth grow,
     To lead our lives therein.

3. Here is the Judge that stints the strife,
     When men's devices fail ;
   Here is the bread that feeds the life
     Which death cannot assail.

4. The tidings of salvation dear
     Come to our ears from hence ;
   The fortress of our faith is here,
     Our shield, and our defence.

5. Read not this book in any case
      But with a single eye;
    Read not but first desire God's grace
      To understand thereby.

6. Pray still in faith with this respect,
      To fructify therein;
    That knowledge may bring this effect,
      To mortify thy sin.

7. Then happy thou in all thy life,
      Whatso to thee befalls;
    Yea! doubly happy shalt thou be,
      When God by death thee calls.

                              GRESSOP.   A. D. 1550.

———

69.   *2 Thessalonians* iii. 13.

1. BREAST the wave, Christian, when it is
            strongest;
    Watch for day, Christian, when the night's
            longest;
    Onward and onward still be thine endeavour,
    The rest that remaineth will be for ever.

2. Fight the fight, Christian, Jesus is o'er thee;
    Run the race, Christian, heaven is before thee;

He who hath promised faltereth never;
The love of eternity flows on for ever.

3. Raise the eye, Christian, just as it closeth;
Lift the heart, Christian, ere it reposeth;
Thee from the love of Christ nothing shall
    sever,
Mount when thy work is done,—praise Him
    for ever.

———

70.   *Ezekiel* xi. 16.

1. JESUS our Lord! to thee we call,
    Thou art our life, our hope, our all;
And we have nowhere else to flee,
No sanctuary, Lord, but Thee.

2. Whatever foes or fears betide,
In Thy dear presence let us hide;
And while we rest our souls on Thee,
Do Thou our sanctuary be.

3. Quickly the day of light draws nigh,
Or we may bow our heads and die;
But oh! what joy this witness gives!
Jesus, our sanctuary, lives.

9

4. He from the grave our dust will raise,
    We in the heavens shall sing His praise :
    And when in glory we appear,
    He'll be our sanctuary there.

———

71.   *Ecclesiastes* xi. 6.

1. SOW in the morn thy seed,
        At eve hold not thine hand ;
    To doubt and fear give thou no heed,—
        Broad-cast it o'er the land.

2. Beside all waters sow,
        The highway furrows stock ;
    Drop it where thorns and thistles grow,
        Scatter it on the rock.

3. The good, the fruitful ground,
        Expect not everywhere ;
    O'er hill and dale, by plots, 't is found ;
        Go forth then everywhere.

4. Thou know'st not which may thrive,
        The late or early sown ;
    Grace keeps the precious germ alive,
        When and wherever strown ;

5.   And duly shall appear,
  In verdure, beauty, strength,
 The tender blade, the stalk, the ear,
  And the full corn at length.

6.   Thou can'st not toil in vain ;
  Cold, heat, and moist, and dry,
 Shall foster and mature the grain,
  For garners in the sky.

7.   Thence, when the glorious end,
  The day of God is come,
 The angel reapers shall descend,
  And heaven cry, " Harvest home."

MONTGOMERY.

---

72.   1 *Samuel* vii. 12.

1. A ND are we yet alive,
  And see each other's face !
 Glory and praise to Jesus give
  For His redeeming grace !

2. Preserv'd by power divine,
  To full salvation here,
 Again in Jesus' praise we join,
  And in His sight appear.

3.   What troubles have we seen,
    What conflicts have we past,
Fightings without and fears within,
    Since we assembled last !

4.   But out of all the Lord
    Hath brought us by His love ;
And still He doth his help afford,
    And hides our life above.

5.   Then let us make our boast
    Of His redeeming power,
Which saves us to the uttermost,
    Till we can sin no more.

6.   Let us take up the cross,
    Till we the crown obtain ;
And gladly reckon all things loss,
    So we may Jesus gain.

WESLEY.

---

73.   *Luke* xviii. 1.

1.   PRAYER was appointed to convey
    The blessings God designs to give ;
Long as they live should Christians pray,
For only while they pray they live.

2. The Christian's heart his prayer indites,
   He speaks as prompted from within;
   The Spirit his petition writes,
   And Christ receives and gives it in.

3. And wilt thou in dead silence lie,
   When Christ stands waiting for thy prayer?
   My soul, thou hast a Friend on high;—
   Arise and try thy interest there.

4. If pains afflict or wrongs oppress,
   If cares distract or fears dismay,
   If guilt deject, if sin distress,
   The remedy 's before thee,—pray.

5. 'T is prayer supports the soul that's weak,
   Though thought be broken, language lame;
   Pray if thou canst or canst not speak;
   But pray with faith in Jesus' name.

6. Depend on Him, thou canst not fail;
   Make all thy wants and wishes known;
   Fear not, His merits must prevail;
   Ask what thou wilt, it shall be done.

   HART.

74.   *Romans* xiii. 12.

1. SOON and for ever the breaking of day
    Shall chase all the night-clouds of sor-
       row away ;
Soon and for ever we 'll see as we 're seen,
    And know the deep meaning of things that
       have been,—
Where fightings without and conflicts within
    Shall weary no more in the warfare with
       sin,—
Where tears, and where fears, and where
       death shall be never,
    Christians with Christ shall be soon and
       for ever.

2. Soon and for ever,—such promise our trust,—
    Though ashes to ashes, and dust be to dust,
Soon and for ever our union shall be
    Made perfect, our glorious Redeemer, in
       Thee ;
When the cares and the sorrows of time shall
       be o'er,
    Its pangs and its partings remembered no
       more,
Where life cannot fail and where death can-
       not sever,
    Christians with Christ shall be soon and
       for ever.

8. Soon and for ever the work shall be done,
   The warfare accomplished, the victory won;
Soon and for ever the soldier lay down
   The sword for a harp, the cross for a crown:
Then droop not in sorrow, despond not in
      fear,
   A glorious to-morrow is brightening and
      near,
When—blessed reward for each faithful en-
      deavour,—
   Christians with Christ shall be soon and
      for ever!

---

75.   *Psalm* lxxiii. 25, 26.

1. PASS away earthly joy,
      Break every mortal tie,
         Jesus is mine!
   Dark is the wilderness;
   Distant the resting-place;
   Jesus alone can bless:—
         Jesus is mine!

2. Tempt not my soul away,
   Here would I ever stay,
         Jesus is mine!

Perishing things of clay,
Born but for one brief day,
Pass from my heart away,
    Jesus is mine !

3.   Fare ye well, dreams of night,
Mine is a dawning bright,
    Jesus is mine !
All that my soul has tried
Left but a dismal void ;
Jesus has satisfied,—
    Jesus is mine !

4.   Farewell mortality,
Welcome eternity,
    Jesus is mine !
Welcome ye scenes of rest,
Welcome ye mansions blest,
Welcome a Saviour's breast,
    Jesus is mine !

---

76.   *Psalm* lxv. 2.

1. THERE is an eye that never sleeps
    Beneath the wing of night ;
There is an ear that never shuts,
   When sink the beams of light.

2. There is an arm that never tires,
 When human strength gives way;
There is a love that never fails,
 When earthly loves decay.

3. That eye is fix'd on seraph throngs;
 That arm upholds the sky;
That ear is fill'd with angel songs;
 That love is thron'd on high.

4. But there's a power which man can wield,
 When mortal aid is vain,
That eye, that arm, that love to reach
 That listening ear to gain.

5. That power is prayer; which soars on high
 Through Jesus to the throne,
And moves the hand which moves the world,
 To bring salvation down.

---

77.   *Ezekiel* xxxiv. 23.

1. O GRACIOUS Shepherd! bind us
 With cords of love to Thee,
And evermore remind us
 How mercy set us free.

O may Thy Holy Spirit
Set this before our eyes,
That we Thy death and merit
Above all else may prize.

2. We are of our salvation
Assured through Thy love;
Yet oh! on each occasion
How faithless do we prove!
Thou hast our sins forgiven,—
Then leaving all behind,
We would press on to heaven,
Bearing the prize in mind.

3. Grant us henceforth, dear Saviour,
While in this vale of tears,
To look to Thee and never
Give way to anxious fears.
Thou, Lord, wilt not forsake us,
Though we are oft to blame;
Oh! let Thy love then make us
Hold fast Thy faith and name.

----

78.   1 *John* i. 7.

1. WALK in the light! so shalt thou know
That fellowship of love,

His Spirit only can bestow
Who reigns in light above.

2. Walk in the light! and thou shalt find
    Thy heart made truly His,
Who dwells in cloudless light enshrined,
    In whom no darkness is.

3. Walk in the light! and sin abhorr'd
    Shall ne'er defile again ;
The blood of Jesus Christ the Lord
    Shall cleanse from every sin.

4. Walk in the light! and e'en the tomb
    No fearful shade shall wear ;
Glory shall chase away its gloom,
    For Christ hath conquer'd there.

5. Walk in the light! and thou shalt see
    Thy path, tho' thorny, bright,
For God by grace shall dwell in thee
    And God Himself is light.

---

79.   1 *Peter* ii. 21, 22, 23.

1. WHAT grace, O Lord, and beauty shone
        Around Thy steps below !
What patient love was seen in all
    Thy life and death of woe !

2.   For ever on Thy burden'd heart
         A weight of sorrow hung;
      Yet no ungentle murmuring word
         Escap'd Thy silent tongue.

3.   Thy foes might hate, despite, revile,
         Thy friends unfaithful prove;
      Unwearied in forgiveness still,
         Thy heart could only love.

4.   Oh! give us hearts to love like Thee,—
         Like Thee, O Lord, to grieve
      Far more for other's sins, than all
         The wrongs that we receive.

5.   One with Thyself, may every eye
         In us, Thy brethren, see
      That gentleness and grace that spring
         From union, Lord with Thee.

———

80.   *John* xx. 28.

1.   J ESUS, Thy name I love,
            All other names above,
                  Jesus my Lord!
      Oh! Thou art all to me,
      Nothing to please I see,
      Nothing apart from Thee,
                  Jesus my Lord!

2. Thou, blessed Son of God,
   Hast bought me with Thy blood,
     Jesus my Lord !
   Oh ! how great is Thy love,
   All other loves above,
   Love that I daily prove,
     Jesus my Lord !

3. When unto Thee I flee,
   Thou wilt my refuge be,
     Jesus my Lord !
   What need I now to fear,
   What earthly grief or care,
   Since Thou art ever near ?
     Jesus my Lord !

4. Soon Thou wilt come again !
   I shall be happy then,
     Jesus my Lord !
   Then Thine own face I 'll see,
   Then I shall like Thee be,
   Then evermore with Thee,
     Jesus my Lord !

———

81.   *Revelations* ii. 28.

1. THERE is a morning star, my soul,
    There is a morning star ;
   10

' T will soon be near and bright, tho' now
  It seems so dim and far.
And when time's stars have come and gone,
And every mist of earth has flown,
That better star shall rise,
On this world's clouded skies,
              To shine for ever.

2.   The night is well nigh spent, my soul,
        The night is well nigh spent,
      And soon above our heads shall shine
        A glorious firmament,
      Unutterably pure and bright,—
      The Lamb once slain, its perfect light,—
      A light unchanging and divine,
      A star that shall unclouded shine,
                Descending never.

                              BONAR.

---

82.   1 *John* iv. 8.

1.   WE cannot always trace the way,
        Where Thou, our gracious Lord, dost
          move,
      But we can always surely say,
              That Thou art love.

2. When fear its gloomy cloud will fling
O'er earth,—our souls to heaven above
As to their sanctuary spring,
        For Thou art love.

3. When myst'ry shrouds our darken'd path,
We'll check our dread, our doubts reprove;
In this our soul sweet comfort hath,
        That Thou art love.

4. Yes! Thou art love; a truth like this
Can every gloomy thought remove,
And turn all tears, all woes to bliss;—
        Our God is love.

---

83.   *Psalm* civ. 34.

1. I JOURNEY through a desert drear and
   wild,
Yet is my heart by such sweet thoughts be-
   guiled,
Of Him on whom I lean, my strength, my
   stay,
I can forget the sorrows of the way.

2. Thoughts of His *love*,—the root of every
   grace,
Which finds in this poor heart a dwelling-
   place;

The sunshine of my soul, than day more
bright,
And my calm pillow of repose by night.

3. Thoughts of His *sojourn* in this vale of
tears;—
The tale of love unfolded in those years
Of sinless suffering and patient grace,
I love again, and yet again to trace.

4. Thoughts of His *death;*—upon the cross I
gaze,
And there behold its sad, yet healing rays;
Beacon of hope, which lifted up on high,
Illumes with heav'nly light the tear-dimm'd
eye.

5. Thoughts of His *coming;*—for that joyful
day
In patient hope I watch, and wait, and pray;
The day draws nigh, the midnight shadows
flee;
Oh! what a sun-rise will that advent be!

6. Thus, while I journey on my Lord to meet,
My thoughts and meditations are so sweet
Of Him on whom I lean, my strength, my
stay,
I can forget the sorrows of the way.

84.   *Exodus* xv. 2.

1. JEHOVAH is our strength,
        And He shall be our song;
    We shall o'ercome at length,
        Although our foes be strong:
    In vain doth Satan then oppose,
    The Lord is stronger than His foes.

2. The Lord our refuge is,
        And ever will remain;
    Since He hath made us His,
        He will our cause maintain;
    In vain our enemies oppose,
    For God is stronger than His foes.

3. The Lord our portion is,
        What can we wish for more?
    As long as we are His,
        We never can be poor:
    In vain do earth and hell oppose,
    For God is stronger than His foes.

4. The Lord our Shepherd is,
        He knows our every need;
    And since we now are His,
        His care our souls will feed:
    In vain do sin and death oppose,
    For God is stronger than His foes.

10*

5. Our God our Father is,
      Our names are on His heart;
    We ever shall be His,
      He ne'er from us will part:
    In vain the world and flesh oppose,
    For God is stronger than His foes.

———

85.   *John* xvii. 12.

1. O LAMB of God! still keep me
      Near to Thy wounded side;
    'T is only then in safety
      And peace I can abide.
    What foes and snares surround me!
      What doubts and fears within!
    The grace that sought and found me,
      Alone can keep me clean.

2. 'T is only in Thee hiding,
      I feel my life secure,—
    Only in Thee abiding,
      The conflict can endure:
    Thine arm the vict'ry gaineth
      O'er every hateful foe;
    Thy love my heart sustaineth
      In all its cares and woe.

3.   Soon shall my eyes behold Thee
      With rapture, face to face;
   One half hath not been told me
      Of all Thy power and grace;
   Thy beauty, Lord, and glory,
      The wonders of Thy love,
   Shall be the endless story
      Of all Thy saints above.

---

86.   *Canticles* ii. 16.

1.   LONG did I toil, and knew no earthly rest;
      Far did I rove, and found no certain
         home;
   At last I sought them in His sheltering breast,
      Who opes His arms and bids the weary
         come;
   In Christ I found a home, a rest divine,
   And I since then am His, and He is mine.

2.   Yes! He is mine! and nought of earthly
         things—
      Not all the charms of pleasure, wealth or
         power,
   The fame of heroes or the pomp of kings—
      Could tempt me to forego His love an hour;

" Go, worthless world," I cry, " with all that's
 thine ;
Go, I my Saviour's am, and He is mine."

3.   The good I have is from His stores supplied,
       The ill is only what He deems the best ;
     He for my Friend, I'm rich with naught be-
         side,
       And poor, without Him, though of all pos-
           sest ;
     Changes may come,—I take, or I resign,
     Content while I am His, and He is mine.

4.   Whate'er may change, in Him no change is
         seen,—
       A glorious sun that wanes not, nor declines ;
     Above the clouds and storms He walks un-
         seen,
       And sweetly on His people's darkness
           shines ;
     All may depart,—I fret not nor repine,
     While I my Saviour's am, and He is mine.

5.   While here, alas ! I know but half His love,
       But half discern Him, and but half adore ;
     But when I meet Him in the realms above,
       I hope to love Him better, praise **Him**
           more,

And feel and tell amid the choir divine,
How fully I am His, and He is mine.

---

87.   *Psalm* lvii. 1.

1. BE merciful to me, O God,
    Be merciful to me,
  For though I sink beneath Thy rod,
    Yet do I trust in Thee.

2. Thou art my refuge, and I know
    My burden Thou dost bear,
  And I would seek, where'er I go,
    To cast on Thee my care.

3. Thou knowest, Lord, my flesh how frail,
    Strong tho' my spirit be ;
  Oh ! then assist, when foes assail,
    The soul that clings to Thee.

4. And, gracious Lord, whate'er befal,
    A thankful heart be mine,—
  A heart that answers to Thy call,
    One that is wholly Thine.

5. And may I ne'er forget that Thou
    Wilt soon return again,
  And those who love Thy coming now,
    Shall shine in glory then.

88.   *Psalm cxlix. 1–4.*

1.   PRAISE ye Jehovah, praise the Lord most
          holy,
      Who cheers the contrite, girds with strength
          the weak ;
      Praise Him who will with glory crown the
          lowly,
      And with salvation beautify the meek.

2.   Praise ye the Lord for all His loving-kind-
          ness,
      And all the tender mercies He hath shewn ;
      Praise Him who pardons all our sin and
          blindness,
      And calls us sons, and takes us for His own.

3.   Praise ye Jehovah ! source of every bless-
          ing,—
      Before His gifts earth's richest boons are dim ;
      Resting in Him, His peace and joy possess-
          ing,
      All things are ours, for we have all in Him.

4.   Praise ye the Father ! God the Lord who
          gave us,
      With full and perfect love, His only Son ;

Praise ye the Son who died Himself to save
us !
Praise ye the Spirit !   Praise the Three in
One !

---

89.   *Psalm* xxxii. 7.

1.   THOU art my hiding-place, O Lord !
          In Thee I put my trust,
Encouraged by Thy holy word,
     A feeble child of dust :—
I have no argument beside,
     I urge no other plea,
And 't is enough my Saviour died,
     My Saviour died for me !

2.   When storms of fierce temptation beat,
          And furious foes assail,
My refuge is the mercy-seat,
     My hope within the veil.
From strife of tongues, and bitter words,
     My spirit flies to Thee ;
Joy to my heart the thought affords,
     My Saviour died for me !

3.   ' Mid trials heavy to be borne,
          When mortal strength is vain,—

A heart with grief and anguish torn,—
A body rack'd with pain,—
Ah ! what could give the sufferer rest,
Bid every murmur flee,
But this, the witness in my breast,
My Saviour died for me !

4. And when Thine awful voice commands
This body to decay,
And life, in its last lingering sands,
Is ebbing fast away,—
Then, though it be in accents weak,
And faint and tremblingly,
O give me strength in death to speak,
" My Saviour died for me !"

90.   *Colossians* iii. 11.

1. JESUS, my Saviour, look on me !
For I am weary and opprest ;
I come to cast my soul on Thee ;—
Thou art my rest.

2. Look down on me, for I am weak ;
I feel the toilsome journey's length ;
Thine aid omnipotent I seek ;—
Thou art my strength.

3. I am bewilder'd on my way ;
    Dark and tempestuous is the night :
    O shed Thou forth some cheering ray ;—
         Thou art my light.

4. I hear the storms around me rise,
    But when I dread th' impending shock,
    My spirit to her refuge flies ;—
         Thou art my rock.

5. When the accuser flings his darts,
    I look to Thee,—my terrors cease ;
    Thy cross a hiding-place imparts ;—
         Thou art my peace.

6. Standing alone on Jordan's brink,
    In that tremendous, latest strife,
    Thou wilt not suffer me to sink ;—
         Thou art my life.

7. Thou wilt my ev'ry want supply,
    E'en to the end, whate'er befall ;
    Through life, in death, eternally,
         Thou art my all.

                         MACDUFF.

91.   *Hebrews* iv. 15.

1.   JESUS, my sorrow lies too deep
          For human ministry ;
     It knows not how to tell itself
          To any but to Thee.

2.   Thou dost remember still, amid
          The glories of God's throne,
     The sorrows of mortality,
          For they were once Thine own.

3.   Yes ! for as if Thou would'st be God,
          E'en in Thy misery,
     There 's been no sorrow but Thine own
          Untouched by sympathy.

4.   Jesus, my fainting spirit brings
          Its fearfulness to Thee ;
     Thine eye at least can penetrate
          The clouded mystery.

5.   It is enough, my precious Lord,
          Thy tender sympathy !
     There is no sorrow e'er so deep,
          But I may bring to Thee.

92.   1 *Peter* i. 8.

1. JESUS, I love Thee, Thou dost know
         How true my love, how deep my woe,
              Almost too deep to bear !
    But Thou wilt guide me by Thy hand,
    Strong in Thy strength 1 yet may stand,
              Still resting in Thy care.

2. Thou wilt not leave the weakest one :
    Though every outward hope be gone,
              I know that Thou art nigh ;
    Man knows not what my sufferings are ;
    He cannot know ; he would not care ;
              But Thou art sympathy.

3. Thou wilt not let my footsteps fail,
    Nor let me, journeying through this vale,
              Bring on Thy Gospel shame ;
    Tho' nought is mine but sin and woe,
    Yet in Thy righteousness I go,
              And Triumph in Thy name.

4. And when the bitter cup is past,
    And when I sink in death at last,
              It is to be with Thee ;
    To come with Thee in clouds of heaven,
    Ransom'd, pure, holy, Thine, forgiven,
              Ever to reign with Thee.

93.   *Psalm* xxxix. 9.

1.   IT is Thy hand, my God !
          My sorrow comes from Thee ;
      I bow beneath Thy chastening rod ;
          'T is love that bruises me.

2.   I would not murmur, Lord,
          Before Thee I am dumb !—
      Lest I should breathe one murmuring word,
          To Thee for help I come.

3.   My God ! Thy name is love,
          A Father's hand is Thine ;
      With tearful eye I look above,
          And cry, " Thy will be mine."

4.   I know Thy will is right,
          Though it may seem severe ;
      Thy path is still unsullied light,
          Though dark it oft appear.

5.   Jesus for me hath died ;
          Thy Son Thou did'st not spare ;
      His pierced hands, His bleeding side,
          Thy love for me declare.

6.   Here my poor heart can rest,
          My God ! it cleaves to Thee ;

Thy will is love, Thine end is blest,
All work for good to me.

94.　　　　　*Isaiah* xlii. 16.

1.　I KNOW not the way I am going,
　　　But well do I know my guide;
With a child-like trust I give my hand
　　To the mighty Friend by my side.
The only thing that I say to Him,
　　As He takes it, is, " Hold it fast,
Suffer me not to lose my way,
　　And bring me home at last."

2.　As when some helpless wanderer,
　　　Alone in an unknown land,
Tells the guide his destined place of rest,
　　And leaves all else in his hand:
'T is home, 't is home, that we wish to reach;
　　He who guides us may choose the way;
Little we heed what path we take,
　　If nearer home each day.

95.　　　　　*Romans* xiii. 11.

1.　ONE sweetly solemn thought
　　　Comes to me o'er and o'er,—
　11*

I am nearer home to-day,
    Than I ever have been before.

2. Nearer my Father's house,
    Where the many mansions be;
Nearer the great white throne;
    Nearer the crystal sea.

3. Nearer the bound of life,
    Where we lay our burdens down;
Nearer leaving the cross;
    Nearer gaining the crown.

4. But lying darkly between,
    Winding down through the night,
Is the deep and unknown stream,
    To be cross'd ere we reach the light.

5. Jesus, perfect my trust,
    Strengthen the hand of my faith;
Let me feel Thee near when I stand
    On the edge of the shore of death:

6. Feel Thee near when my feet
    Are slipping over the brink;
For it may be I'm nearer home—
    Nearer now than I think.

                          CAREY.

96. 1 *Thessalonians* iv. 14.

1. A SLEP in Jesus! Blessed sleep!
    From which none ever wakes to weep;
    A calm and undisturbed repose,
    Unbroken by the last of foes!

2. Asleep in Jesus! Oh, how sweet
    To be for such a slumber meet!
    With holy confidence to sing,
    That Death has lost his venom'd sting!

3. Asleep in Jesus! Peaceful rest!
    Whose waking is supremely blest:
    No fear, no woe, shall dim that hour
    That manifests the Saviour's power.

4. Asleep in Jesus! Oh, for me
    May such a blissful refuge be!
    Securely shall my ashes lie
    Waiting the summons from on high.

5. Asleep in Jesus! Time nor space
    Debars this precious hiding-place;
    On Indian plains or Northern snows,
    Believers find the same repose.

6. Asleep in Jesus! Far from thee,
    Thy kindred and their graves may be;

But thine is still a blessed sleep,
From which none ever wakes to weep.

------

97.   *Hebrews* iv. 3.

1. JESUS, we rest in Thee!
        In Thee ourselves we hide;
    Laden with guilt and misery,
        Where could we rest beside?
    'T is on thy meek and lowly breast,
    Our weary souls alone can rest.

2. Thou holy One of God!
        The Father rests in Thee,
    And in the savour of that blood
        Once shed on Calvary.
    The curse is gone—through Thee we're blest;
    God rests in Thee—in Thee we rest.

3. The slaves of sin and fear,—
        Thy truth our bondage broke:
    Our happy spirits love to wear
        Thy light and easy yoke.
    The love which fills our grateful breast
    Makes duty joy, and labour rest.

4. Soon the bright glorious day,
    The rest of God shall come ;
Sorrow and sin shall pass away,
    And we shall reach our home ;
Then, of the promis'd land possess'd,
Our souls shall know eternal rest.

---

98.   1 *Thessalonians* iv. 13.

1. TAKE comfort, Christians, when your friends
    In Jesus fall asleep ;
Their better being never ends,—
    Why then dejected weep ?

2. Why inconsolable, as those
    To whom no hope is given !
Death is the messenger of peace,
    And calls the soul to heaven.

3. As Jesus died, and rose again,
    Victorious from the dead,
So His disciples rise, and reign
    With their triumphant Head.

4. The time draws nigh, when from the clouds
    Christ shall with shouts descend ;
And the last trumpet's awful voice
    The heavens and earth shall rend.

5. Then they who live shall changed be,
       And they who sleep shall wake;
    The graves shall yield their ancient charge,
       And earth's foundations shake.

6. The saints of God, from death set free,
       With joy shall mount on high;
    The heav'nly hosts with praises loud,
       Shall meet them in the sky.

7. Together to their Father's house,
       With joyful hearts they'll go,
    And dwell for ever with the Lord,
       Beyond the reach of woe.

8. A few short years of evil past,
       We reach the happy shore,
    Where death-divided friends at last
       Shall meet to part no more.

---

99.   *Acts* vii. 59.

1. MY soul, go boldly forth,
       Forsake this sinful earth;
    What hath it been to thee,
       But pain and sorrow?
    And think'st thou it will be
       Better to-morrow?

2. Why art thou for delay?
   Thou cam'st not here to stay;
   What tak'st thou for thy part,
       But heavenly pleasure?
   Where then should be thy heart,
       But where 's thy treasure?

3. Thy God, thy Head's above;
   There is the world of love;
   Mansions there purchased are
       By Christ's own merit,
   For these He doth prepare
       Thee by His Spirit.

4. Lord Jesus, take my spirit,
   I trust Thy love and merit:
   Take home thy wand'ring sheep,
       For thou hast sought it;
   My soul in safety keep,
       For thou hast bought it.

                            BAXTER.

---

100.   *2 Timothy* iv. 6.

1. THE hour of my departure 's come,
      I hear the voice that calls me home;
   At last, O Lord, let trouble cease,
   And let Thy servant die in peace.

2.   Not in mine innocence I trust ;
     I bow before Thee in the dust ;
     And through my Saviour's blood alone
     I look for mercy at Thy throne.

3.   I leave the world without a tear,
     Save for the friends I hold so dear ;
     To heal their sorrows, Lord, descend,
     And to the friendless prove a Friend.

4.   I come, I come, at Thy command,
     I give my spirit to Thy hand ;
     Stretch forth Thine everlasting arms,
     And shield me in the last alarms.

5.   The hour of my departure's come,
     I hear the voice that calls me home ;
     Now, O my God, let trouble cease,
     Now let Thy servant die in peace.

LOGAN.

101.   *Revelations* i. 5, 6, 7.

1.   A FEW more years shall roll,
        A few more seasons come ;
     And we shall lie with them that rest,
     Asleep within the tomb.

Then, O my Lord, prepare
  My soul for that great day ;
O wash me in Thy precious blood,
  And take my sins away.

2. A few more suns shall set
    O'er these dark hills of time ;
  And we shall be where suns are not,
    A far serener clime.
  Then, O my Lord, prepare
    My soul for that blest day ;
  O wash me in Thy precious blood,
    And take my sins away.

3. A few more storms shall beat
    On this wild rocky shore ;
  And we shall be where tempests cease,
    And surges swell no more.
  Then, O my Lord, prepare
    My soul for that calm day ;
  O wash me in Thy precious blood,
    And take my sins away.

4. A few more struggles here,
    A few more partings o'er,
  A few more toils, a few more tears,
    And we shall weep no more.

Then, O my Lord, prepare
  My soul for that blest day;
O wash me in Thy precious blood,
  And take my sins away.

5.   A few more sabbaths here
      Shall cheer us on our way;
    And we shall reach the endless rest,
      The eternal Sabbath-day.
    Then, O my Lord, prepare
      My soul for that sweet day;
    O wash me in Thy precious blood,
      And take my sins away.

6.   'T is but a little while,
      And He shall come again,
    Who died that we might live, who lives
      That we with Him may reign.
    Then, O my Lord, prepare
      My soul for that glad day;
    O wash me in Thy precious blood,
      And take my sins away.

                                   BONAR.

───────

102.   1 *Corinthians* xv. 58.

1.   GO labour on; spend, and be spent,—
        Thy joy to do the Father's will;

It is the way the Master went,
Should not the servant tread it still?

2. Go, labour on; 'tis not for nought;
Thy earthly loss is heavenly gain;
Men heed thee, love thee, praise thee not;
The Master praises;—what are men?

3. Go, labour on; your hands are weak,
Your knees are faint, your soul cast down;
Yet falter not; the prize you seek,
Is near,—a kingdom and a crown.

4. Go, labour on while it is day,
The world's dark night is hastening on;
Speed, speed thy work, cast sloth away;
It is not thus that souls are won.

5. Men die in darkness at your side,
Without a hope to cheer the tomb;
Take up the torch and wave it wide,
The torch that lights time's thickest gloom.

6. Toil on, faint not, keep watch and pray;
Be wise the erring soul to win;
Go forth into the world's highway,
Compel the wanderer to come in.

7. Toil on, and in thy toil rejoice;
   For toil comes rest, for exile home;
   Soon shalt thou hear the Bridegroom's voice,
   The midnight cry, " Behold I come."

BONAR.

---

103.   *Philippians* i. 21.

1. CHRIST, of all my hopes the ground,
      Christ, the spring of all my joy!
   Still in Thee let me be found,
      Still for Thee my powers employ.

2. Let Thy love my heart inflame;
    · Keep Thy fear before my sight;
   Be Thy praise my highest aim;
      Be Thy smile my chief delight.

3. Fountain of o'er-flowing grace,
      Freely from Thy fullness give;
   Till I close my earthly race,
      Be it " Christ, to me to live."

4. Firmly trusting in Thy blood,
      Nothing shall my heart confound;
   Safely I shall pass the flood,
      Safely reach Immanuel's ground.

5. When I touch the blessed shore,
   Back the closing waves shall roll ;
Death's dark stream shall never more
   Part from Thee my ravished soul.

6. Thus, oh ! thus an entrance give
   To the land of cloudless sky ;
Having known it " Christ to live,"
   Let me know it " gain to die."

---

104.   1 *Samuel* iii. 18.

1.   L ORD Jesus, as Thou wilt !
       Oh ! may Thy will be mine ;
Into Thy hand of love
   I would my all resign.
Thro' sorrow or thro' joy,
   Conduct me as Thine own,
And help me still to say,
   My Lord, Thy will be done !

2.   Lord Jesus, as Thou wilt !
   If needy here and poor,
Give me Thy people's bread,
   Their portion rich and sure.
The manna of Thy word
   Let my soul feed upon ;
     12*

And if all else should fail,—
My Lord, Thy will be done !

3. Lord Jesus, as Thou wilt !
    If among thorns I go,
Still sometimes here and there
    Let a few roses blow.
But Thou on earth along
    The thorny path hast gone ;
Then lead me after Thee,—
    My Lord, Thy will be done !

4. Lord Jesus, as Thou wilt !
    Though seen through many a tear,
Let not my star of hope
    Grow dim or disappear ;
Since Thou on earth hast wept
    And sorrowed oft alone,
If I must weep with Thee,
    My Lord, Thy will be done !

5. Lord Jesus, as Thou wilt !
    If lov'd ones must depart,
Suffer not sorrow's flood
    To overwhelm my heart :
For they are blest with Thee,
    Their race and conflict won,
Let me but follow them,—
    My Lord, Thy will be done !

6. Lord Jesus, as Thou wilt!
    When death itself draws nigh,
To Thy dear wounded side
    I would for refuge fly.
Leaning on Thee, to go
    Where Thou before hast gone;
The rest as Thou shalt please—
    My Lord, Thy will be done!

7. Lord Jesus, as Thou wilt!
    All shall be well for me,
Each changing future scene
    I gladly trust with Thee.
Straight to my home above
    I travel calmly on,
And sing in life or death—
    My Lord, Thy will be done!

B. SCHMOLK.

---

105.   *1 Peter* i. 3.

1. SING praise, the tomb is void,
    Where the Redeemer lay;
Sing of our bonds destroyed,
    Our darkness turned to day.

2. Weep for your dead no more,
    Friends, be of joyful cheer,

Our star moves on before,
   Our narrow path shines clear.

3. He, who so patiently
    The crown of thorns did wear,—
He hath gone up on high;
    Our hope is with Him there.

4. Now is His truth revealed,
    His majesty and might;
The grave has been unsealed,
    Christ is our life and light.

5. He, who for men did weep,
    Suffer, and bleed, and die,—
First fruits of them that sleep,—
    Christ hath gone up on high.

6. His victory hath destroyed
    The shafts that once could slay;
Sing praise! the tomb is void
    Where the Redeemer lay.

———

106.   *Matthew* v. 3.

1. LOWLY, my soul, be lowly,—
    Follow the paths of old:

The feather riseth lightly,
  But never so the gold !
The stream descending fast,
  Has gathered quietly, slowly,
A river rolls at last,—
  Therefore, my soul, be lowly.

2. Lowly, my eyes, be lowly;
    God, from His throne above,
Looks down upon the humble
  In kindness and in love.
Still as I rise I shall
  Have greater depths below me,
And haughty looks must fall,—
  Therefore, my eyes, be lowly.

3. Lowly, my hands, be lowly;
    Christ's poor around us dwell;
Stoop down, and kindly cherish
  The flock He loves so well.
Not toiling to secure ·
  This world's fame and glory,
Thy Saviour blessed the poor,
  Therefore, my hands, be lowly.

4. Lowly, my heart, be lowly,
    So God shall dwell with Thee;
It is the meek and patient
  Who shall exalted be.

Deep in the valley rest
   The Spirit's gifts most holy,
And they who seek are blest,—
   Therefore, my heart, be lowly.

5.   Lowly, I would be lowly !
     This frame, to earth allied,
  Must first to dust be humbled
     Ere it be glorified !
  My God, prepare me here
     For all that lies before me;
  I would in heaven appear,
     And so I would be lowly.

INGOLSTELLER.

———

107.   *Isaiah* vii. 4.

1.   BE still, my soul, let nothing stir
     Thee from the sweet repose
Of those who to their God refer
Their joys, their cares, their woes.

2.   Be quiet, why this anxious heed
About thy tangled ways ?
God knows them all, He giveth speed,
And He allows delays.

3.   What though He let thee not perform
    Some good and loved design ?
    Thou would'st not wish Him to conform
    His perfect will to thine !

4.   My God ! the hearing ear impart,
    To hear These tell Thy will,
    And then bestow the ready heart
    All meekly to fulfil.

                       E. W.

----

108.   *Hebrews* xi. 16.

1.   WE have no home but heaven ;—a pilgrim's
        garb we wear ;
  Our path is marked by changes, and strewed
    with many a care ;
  Surrounded with temptation ; by varied ills
    oppress'd ;
  Each day's experience warns us that this is
    not our rest.

2.   We have no home but heaven ;—then where-
    fore seek one here ?
  Why murmur at privation, or grieve when
    trouble 's near ?
  It is but for a season that we as strangers
    roam,
  And strangers must not look for the comforts
    of a home.

3. We have no home but heaven;—we want no
    home beside;
    O God, our Friend and Father, our footsteps
    thither guide,
    Unfold to us its glory, prepare us for its joy,
    Its pure and perfect friendship, its angel-like
    employ.

4. We have a home in heaven;—how cheering
    is the thought !
    How bright the expectations which God's
    own word has taught !
    With eager hearts we hasten the promised
    bliss to share;
    We have no home but heaven;—O would
    that we were there !

———

109. 1 *Corinthians* xi. 26. (SACRAMENTAL.)

1. NO gospel like this feast
        Spread for Thy Church by Thee
    Nor prophet, nor evangelist
        Preach the glad news so free.

2. All our redemption cost,
        All our redemption won;
    All it has won for us, the lost;
        All it cost Thee, the Son.

3. Thine was the bitter price,—
        Ours is the free gift, given;
    Thine was the blood of sacrifice,
        Ours is the wine of heaven.

4. Here we would rest midway,
        As on a sacred height,
    That darkest and that brightest day
        Meeting before our sight.

5. From that dark depth of woes
        Thy love for us has trod,
    Up to the heights of bless'd repose
        Thy love prepares with God;—

6. Till from self's chains released,
        One sight alone we see,
    Still at the cross, as at the feast,
        Behold Thee, only Thee.

------

110.   2 *Peter* i. 1.

1. FAITH is a very simple thing,
        Tho' little understood,
    It frees the soul from death's dread sting,
        By *resting* in the blood.

13

2. It looks not on the things around,
      Nor on the things *within*,
    It takes its flight to scenes above,
      Beyond the sphere of sin.

3. It sees upon the throne of God,
      A victim that was slain ;
    It rests its *all* on His shed blood,
      And says, " I 'm born again."

4. Faith is not what we *feel* or see,
      It is a simple *trust*
    In what the God of love has said
      Of Jesus, as " the just."

5. The perfect One that died for me,
      Upon His Father's throne,
    Presents our names before our God,
      And pleads Himself alone.

6. What Jesus is, and that alone,
      In faith's delightful plea ;
    It never deals with *sinful* self,
      Nor *rigtheous* self, in me.

7. It tells me I am counted " dead "
      By God in His own word,
    It tells me I am " born again "
      In Christ my risen Lord.

8. In that He died, He died to sin,
   In that He lives—to God;
   Then I am dead to nature's hopes,
   And justified thro' blood.

9. If He is free, then I am free
   From all unrighteousness;
   If He is just, then I am just,
   He is *my* righteousness.

10. What want I more to perfect bliss?
    A body like His own
    Will perfect me for greater joys,
    Than angels round the throne.

───────

111. *2 Corinthians* i. 11.

1. WHEN far from the hearts where our fond-
         est thoughts centre,
   Denied for a time their loved presence to
         share,
   In spirit we meet, when the closet we enter,
   And hold sweet communion together in
         prayer!

2. Oh! fondly I think, as night's curtains sur-
         round them,
   The Shepherd of Israel tenderly keeps,

The angels of light are encamping around
    them,
They are watched by the eye that ne'er slum-
    bers nor sleeps.

3. When the voice of the morning once more
    shall awake them,
And summon them forth to the calls of the
    day,
I will think of that God who will never for-
    sake them,
The Friend ever near though all else be away.

4. Then why should one thought of anxiety
    seize us,
Thou distance divide us from those whom we
    love ?
They rest in the covenant mercy of Jesus,
Their prayers meet with ours in the mansions
    above.

5. Oh ! sweet bond of friendship, whate'er may
    betide us,
Though on life's stormy billows our barks
    may be driven,
Though distance, or trial, or death may di-
    vide us,
Eternal re-union awaits us in heaven.

MACDUFF.

112.   *Psalm* lxiii. 5, 6.

(FOR A SICK ROOM.)

1. 'TIS not a lonely night watch
        Which by the couch I spend,
    Jesus is close beside us,
        Our Saviour and our Friend.

2. Often I strive all vainly,
        To ease thine aching head,
    Then, silently and gently,
        Himself He makes thy bed.

3. Do we not hear Him saying,
        " Your guilt on me was laid,"
    " Ye are my blood-bought jewels,"
        " Fear not, be not dismayed."

4. " I sit beside the furnace,"
        " The gold will soon be pure,"
    " And blessed are those servants,"
        " Who to the end endure."

5. Amen, O blessed Saviour,
        Dwell with us, in us here,
    Until we share Thy glory,
        When God shall wipe each tear.
                13*

113.   *John* xiv. 16.

1.   OH ! Holy Ghost, eternal God,
           Descending from above,
     Thou fill'st the soul thro' Jesus' blood,
           With faith, and hope, and love.

2.   Thou comfortest the heavy heart,
           By sin and grief oppressed ;
     Thou to the dead dost life impart,
           And to the weary rest.

3.   Thy sweet communion charms the soul,
           And gives true peace and joy,
     Which Satan's power can ne'er control,
           Nor all his wiles destroy.

4.   Let no false comfort lift us up
           To confidence that's vain ;
     Nor let their faith and courage droop,
           Who love the Lamb once slain.

5.   Breathe comfort where distress abounds,
           O make our conscience clean ;
     And heal with balm from Jesus' wounds,
           The festering sores of sin.

6.   Vanquish our lusts, our pride remove,
           Take out the heart of stone ;

Show us the Father's boundless love,
The merits of the Son.

7. The Father sent His Son to die;
The willing Son obeyed;
The Witness Thou, to ratify
The purchase Christ hath made.

---

114.   1 *Thessalonians* iv. 17.

1. " For ever with the Lord !"
Father, if 't is Thy will,
The promise of that faithful word
E'en here to me fulfill.

2. Be thou at my right hand,
Then can I never fail;
Uphold Thou me, and I shall stand,
Help, and I shall prevail.

3. So when my latest breath
Shall rend the vail in twain,
By death I shall escape from death,
And life eternal gain.

4. Knowing as I am known,
How shall I love that word,

And oft repeat before the throne,
" For ever with the Lord !"

5. Then though the soul enjoy
  Communion high and sweet,
While worms this body must destroy,
  Both shall in glory meet.

6. The trump of final doom
  Will speak the self-same word,
And heaven's voice thunder through the
    tomb,
  " For ever with the Lord !"

7. The tomb shall echo deep
  That death-awakening sound ;
The saints shall hear it in their sleep,
  And answer from the ground.

8. Then upward as they fly,
  That resurrection word
Shall be their shout of victory—
  " For ever with the Lord !"

9. That resurrection word,
  That shout of victory,
Once more—" For ever with the Lord!"
  Amen ! so let it be.

115.   *Luke* xiv. 22.

1. COME, sinner, to the Gospel feast,
    Oh ! come without delay ;
For there is room in Jesus' breast
    For all who will obey.

2. There 's room in God's eternal love
    To save thy precious soul ;
Room in the Spirit's grace above
    To heal and make thee whole.

3. There 's room within the Church, redeem'd
    With blood of Christ divine ;
Room in the white-robed throng convened,
    For that dear soul of thine.

4. There 's room in heaven among the choir,
    And harps, and crowns of gold ;
And glorious palms of victory there,
    And joys that ne'er were told.

5. There 's room around thy Father's board
    For thee and thousands more ;
Oh ! come and welcome to the Lord,
    Yea, come this very hour.

116.   *Colossians* iii. 1.

1. GO up, go up, my heart,
        Dwell with thy God above;
    For here thou canst not rest,
        Nor here give out thy love.

2. Go up, go up, my heart,
        Be not a trifler here;
    Ascend above these clouds,
        Dwell in a higher sphere.

3. Let not thy love flow out
        To things so soil'd and dim;
    Go up to heaven and God,
        Take up thy love to Him.

4. Waste not thy precious stores
        On creature-love below;
    To God that wealth belongs,
        On Him that wealth bestow.

5. Go up, reluctant heart,
        Take up thy rest above;
    Arise, earth-clinging thoughts;
        Ascend, my lingering love.

                                        BONAR.

117.   *Hebrews* vi. 18.

1.   J ESUS, I come to Thee,
        A sinner doom'd to die;
    My only refuge is Thy cross,
      Here at Thy feet I lie.

2.   Can mercy reach my case,
      And all my sins remove?
    Break, O my God, this heart of stone,
      And melt it by Thy love.

3.   Too long my soul has gone
      Far from my God astray;
    I've sported on the brink of hell,
      In sin's delusive way.

4.   But, Lord, my heart is fixed,
      I hope in Thee alone;
    Break off the chains of sin and death,
      And bind me to Thy throne.

5.   Thy blood can cleanse my heart,
      Thy hand can wipe my tears;
    Oh! send Thy blessed Spirit down
      To banish all my fears.

6.   Then shall my soul arise,
      From sin and Satan free;

Redeem'd from hell and every foe,
  I 'll trust alone in Thee.

---

118.   *Proverbs* xxvii. 1.

1.   TO-DAY mine, to-morrow thine !
        So we hear the slow bell ringing,
    When in God's acre to recline,
        We the dead are softly bringing :
    And the grave calls out, Resign !
    To-day mine, to-morrow thine !

2.   To-day life, to-morrow death !
        Life speeds its wings and tarries never ;
    Is not that a wisdom-breath ?--
        Think of life which stays for ever :
    Need of thinking each one hath :
    To-day life, to-morrow death !

3.   One follows another now
        As the ocean waves wind-driven ;
    For all with which hope can endow,
        What security is given ?
    Each in his sleeping-room must bow ;
    One follows another now !

4.   Oh, man ! it is the old law ; —
        How many years death counteth not.

Is thy health without one flaw ?
   Soon e'en thy name shall be forgot.
Earth to itself all earth will draw.
Oh, man ! it is the old law !

5. Oh ! to be wise as near my end !
   I wish to die before I'm dying :
That shall my soul from death defend,
   When death's last strength my soul is try-
      ing.
Prepare me thereto, God, my Friend !
Oh ! to be wise as near my end !

6. Blessed who in Christ shall die !
   Death is changed to life for ever ;
He has life when death is nigh,
   Life beyond, which endeth never !
Who hath it not, Undone, must cry !
Blessed who in Christ shall die !

                   B. SCHMOLK.

---

119.   *Psalm* cl. 6.

1. PRAISE the Lord, who died to save us ;
    Praise His name, for ever dear ;
Praise His blessed name, who gave us
   Eyes to see and ears to hear :
          Praise the Saviour,—
   Object of our love and fear.

14

2.   Grace it was, 't was grace abounding,
     Brought Him down to save the lost ;
Ye above, His throne surrounding,
     Praise Him, praise Him, all His host :
         Saints adore Him,—
Ye are they who owe Him most.

3.   Ye, of all His hand created,
     Objects are of grace alone,
Aliens once, but reinstated,
     Destined now to fill a throne :
         Sing with wonder,—
Sing of what our Lord hath done.

4.   Praise His name who died to save us,
     'T is by Him His people live :
And in Him the Father gave us
     All that boundless love could give :
         Life eternal,
In our Saviour we receive.

---

120.   *Hebrews* xiii. 8.

1.   THERE 'S nought on earth to rest upon,
     All things are changing here,
The smiles of joy we gaze upon,
     The friends we count most dear :

One Friend alone is changeless,
　　The One too oft forgot,
Whose love hath stood for ages past,—
　　Our Jesus changeth not.

2.　The sweetest flower on earth,
　　　That sheds its fragrance round,
E'er evening comes has withered,
　　And lies upon the ground :
The dark and dreary desert
　　Has only one green spot,
'T is found in living pastures,—
　　Our Jesus changeth not.

3.　Clouds soon o'ercast our summer sky,
　　　So beautiful, so bright,
And while we still admire it,
　　It darkens into night :
One sky alone is cloudless,
　　There darkness enters not,
'T is found alone with Jesus,—
　　And Jesus changeth not.

4.　E'en friendship's smile avails not
　　　To cheer us here below,
For smiles are all deceitful,
　　They quickly ebb and flow :

One smile alone can gladden,
　　Whate'er the pilgrim's lot,
It is the smile of Jesus,—
　　For Jesus changeth not.

5.　And thus our bark moves onward,
　　　O'er life's tempestuous sea,
While death's unerring hand
　　Is stamp'd on all we see:
But faith has found a living One,
　　Where hope deceiveth not,
Our life is hid with Jesus,—
　　And Jesus changeth not.

6.　There 's nought on earth to rest upon,
　·　All things are changing here,
The smiles of joy we gaze upon,
　　The friends we count most dear:
One Friend alone is changeless,—
　　The One too oft forgot,
Whose love has stood for ages past,—
　　Our Jesus changeth not.

　　　　　　　　　　　F. WHITFIELD.

———

121.　　　　1 *Timothy* vi. 12.

1.　FIGHTING the battle of life !—
　　　With a weary heart and head ;

For in the midst of the strife,
  The banners of joy are fled.

2. Fled and gone out of sight,
      When I thought they were so near,
    And the music of hope this night
      Is dying away on my ear.

3. Fighting the whole day long,
      With a very tired hand,—
    With only my armour strong—
      The shelter in which I stand.

4. There is nothing left of *me*,—
      If all *my* strength were shown,
    So small the amount would be,
      Its presence could scarce be known.

5. Fighting alone to-night,—
      With not e'en a stander by
    To cheer me in the fight,
      Or to hear me when I cry.

6. Only the Lord can hear,—
      Only the Lord can see
    The struggle within how dark and drear,
      Though quiet the outside be.

7. Fighting alone to-night !
    With what a sinking heart ;—
Lord Jesus, in the fight
    Oh ! stand not Thou apart !

8. Body and mind have tried
    To make the field my own :
But when the Lord is on my side,
    He doeth the work alone.

9. And when He hideth His face
    And the battle-clouds prevail,
It is only through His grace
    That I do not utterly fail.

10. The word of old was true,
    And its truth shall never cease,—
"The Lord shall fight for you,
    And ye shall hold your peace."

11. Lord, I would fain be still
    And quiet behind my shield ;
But make me to love Thy will,
    For fear I should ever yield.

12. Nothing but perfect trust,
    And love of thy perfect will,

Can raise me out of the dust,
    And bid my fears be still.

13. Lord, fix my eyes upon Thee,
    And fill my heart with Thy love;
  And keep my soul till the shadows flee,
    And the light breaks forth above.

---

122.   *Galatians* vi. 9.

1. "BE not weary," *toiling* Christian,
    Good the Master thou dost serve;
  Let no disappointment move thee,
    From thy service never swerve;
  Sow in hope, nor cease thy sowing;
    Lack not patience, faith, or prayer;
  Seed-time passeth,—harvest hasteneth,—
    Precious sheaves thou then shalt bear.

2. " Be not weary," *praying* Christian,
    Open is thy Father's ear
  To the fervent supplication,
    And the agonizing prayer;
  Prayer the Holy Ghost begetteth,
    Be it words, or groans, or tears,
  Is the prayer that's always answered;
    Banish then thy doubts and fears.

3. " Be not weary," *suffering* Christian,
     Scourg'd is each adopted child,
   Else would grow, in sad profusion,
     Nature's fruit, perverse and wild ;
   Chastening's needful for the spirit,
     Though, 't is painful for the flesh,
   God designs a blessing for thee ;—
     Let this thought thy soul refresh.

4. " Be not weary," *tempted* Christian,
     Sin can only lure on earth ;
   Faith is tried by sore temptation ;
     'Tis the furnace proves its worth ;
   Bounds are set unto the tempter,
     Which beyond he cannot go ;
   Battle on, on God relying,
     Faith will overcome the foe.

5. " Be not weary," *weeping* Christian,
     Tears endure but for the night,
   Joy, deep joy thy spirit greeting,
     Will return with morning 's light ;
   Every tear thou shedd'st is numbered
     Iu the register above,
   Heaven is tearless, sweet the prospect,—
     Sighless, tearless land of love !

6. " Be not weary," *hoping* Christian,
     Though the vision tarry long,

Hope will bring the blessing nearer;
 Change thy sorrow into song;
Nought shall press thy spirit downwards,
 If thy hopes all brightly shine,
Hold thy hope, whate'er thou losest,—
 Living, precious hopes are thine!

7. " Be not weary," *troubled* Christian,
 Rest remains for thee on high,
Dwell upon the untold glory,
 Of thy future home of joy;
There, nor sin, nor sorrow entereth;
 There thy soul attun'd to praise,
Shall, in strains of heavenly fullness,
 Songs of happy triumph raise.

8. " Be not weary," *loving* Christian,
 In this heavenly grace abound,
Jesus, well thou knowest, loved *thee*,
 Though in mad rebellion found;
Drink, drink deeply of His spirit;
 Jesus loves both great and small,
Nature loves but what is lovely;—
 Grace embraceth one and all.

9. Christian, thus in grace unwearied,
 Pass thy sojourn here below,
Spurn lukewarmness, let thy bosom
 Ever with true fervour glow!

Look to Christ, thy bright exemplar,
  Copy Him in all His ways,
Let thy life and conversation,
  Tell to thy Redeemer's praise.

A. M.

----

123.   *Isaiah* xxi. 11.

1. WHAT of the night, watchman, what of
           the night ?
    The wintry gale sweeps by,
    The thick shadows fall, and the night bird's
           call
    Sounds mournfully thro' the sky.

2. The night is dark, it is long and drear,
      But who, while others sleep,
    Is that little band, who together stand,
      And their patient vigils keep ?

3. All awake is the strained eye,
      And awake the listening ear ;
    For their Lord they wait, and watch at the
           gate
    His chariot wheels to hear.

4. Long have they waited—that little band,
      And ever and anon

To fancy's eye the dawn seem'd nigh,—
The night seem'd almost gone.

5. And often, through the midnight gale,
They thought they heard at last
The sound of His train, and they listened
again,—
And the sound died away on the blast.

6. Ages have rolled, and one by one,
Those watchers have passed away ;
They heard the call on their glad ear fall,
And they hastened to obey.

7. And in their place their children stand,
And still their vigils keep.
They watch and pray for the dawn of day,
For this is no time for sleep.

8. What of the night, watchman, what of the
night ?
Tho' the wintry gales sweep by,
When the darkest hour begins to lower
We know that the dawn is nigh.

9. Courage, ye servants of the Lord,
The night is almost o'er ;
Your Master will come and call you home,
To weep and to watch no more.

124.   *Psalm* lv. 17.

1. COME to the morning prayer,
        Come let us kneel and pray ;
    Prayer is the Christian pilgrim's staff
        To walk with God all day.

2. At noon beneath the Rock
        Of ages rest and pray ;
    Sweet is the shadow from the heat,
        When the sun smites by day.

3. At eve shut-to the door,
        Round the home-altar pray,
    And finding there " the house of God,"
        At " heaven's gate " close the day.

4. When midnight seals our eyes,
        Let each in spirit say,
    I sleep, but my heart waketh, Lord,
        With Thee to watch and pray.

———

125.   *Job* vii. 4.

1. THE weary day is tarrying ;
        Oh ! when will it pass away ?
    The head is sick, and the heart is faint ;
        Oh ! why do the hours delay ?

2. Like a deep dark gulf that lies between
   The traveller and his home,
   So a load of sorrow and care must pass
   Ere the hour of rest will come.

3. The long, long day is passing away,
   Though the hours are sad and slow ;
   But at length appears the blessed night
   Bringing rest to all below ;—

4. Bringing rest to the weary heart,
   And rest to the harass'd brain,
   A truce to the warfare of life,
   That the spirit of sleep may reign.

5. But the long night is tarrying
   In hours of restless pain,—
   We list to the toll of some distant clock,
   And the silence settles again.

6. The leaden hours—they linger long ;
   But still they pass away ;
   The night is done, and the blessed sun
   Breaks forth with a golden ray.

7. The Christian's life is a weary strife ;
   And often his heart would yield,
   But there's One to stand at his right hand,
   His wavering faith to shield.

15

8.   He feels, though his heart may fail,
     His Saviour's will is best ;
And at length the life and the struggle o'er,
     The soldier of Christ may rest.

---

126.   *Hebrews* xi. 16.

1.   KNOW ye that better land,
     Where care 's unknown ?
Know ye that blessed land
     Around the throne ?
There, there is happiness,
There streams of purest bliss ;
There, there are rest and peace—
     There, there alone.

2.   Yes, yes, we know that place,
     We know it well ;
Eye hath not seen His face,
     Tongue cannot tell ;
There are the angels bright,
There saints enrob'd in white,
All, all are cloth'd in light—
     There, there they dwell.

3.   Oh ! we are weary here,
     A little band,

Yet soon in glory there
　　　We hope to stand;
Then let us haste away,
Speed o'er this world's dark way,
Unto that land of day—
　　　That better land.

4. Come! hasten that sweet day,
　　　Let time begone,
Come! Lord, make no delay,
　　　On Thy white throne;
Thy face we wish to see
To dwell and reign with Thee,
And, Thine for ever be—
　　　Thine, Thine alone.

127. 　　　1 *Thessalonians* i. 8.

1. SOUND, sound the truth abroad,
　　Bear ye the word of God
　　　Through the wide world:
Tell what our Lord hath done,
Tell how the day is won,
And from his lofty throne
　　　Satan is hurl'd.

2. Far over sea and land,
'T is our own Lord's command,
　　　Bear ye His name;

Bear it to ev'ry shore,
Regions unknown explore,
Enter at every door:
Silence is shame.

3. Speed on the wings of love;
Jesus, who reigns above,
Bids us to fly:
They who His message bear,
Should neither doubt nor fear;
He will their friend appear,
He will be nigh.

4. When on the mighty deep,
He will their spirits keep,
Stay'd on His word:
When in a foreign land
No other friend at hand,
Jesus will by them stand,—
Jesus their Lord.

5. Ye, who forsaking all
At your lov'd Master's call,
Comforts resign;
Soon will the work be done,
Soon will the prize be won,
Brighter than yonder sun
Then shall ye shine.

128.   *Isaiah* li. 12.

1.   SWEET is the solace of Thy love,
      My heavenly Friend, to me,
  While through the hidden way of faith
    I journey home with Thee,
  Learning by quiet thankfulness
    As a dear child to be.

2.   Though from the shadow of thy peace
    My feet would often stray,
  Thy mercy follows every step
    And will not turn away;
  Yea, Thou wilt comfort me at last,
    As none beneath Thee may.

3.   Oft in a dark and lonely place,
    I hush my hasten'd breath,
  To hear the comfortable words
    Thy loving Spirit saith ;
  And feel my safety in Thy hand
    From every kind of death.

4.   Oh ! there is nothing in the world
    To weigh against Thy will;
  E'en the dark times I dread the most
    Thy covenant fulfil ;
  And when the glorious morning dawns
    I find Thee with me still.

15*

5. No other comforter I need,
        If Thou, Lord, be mine;—
    Thy rod will bring my spirit low,
        Thy fire my heart refine,
    And cause me pain that none can heal
        By other love than Thine.

6. Then in the secret of my soul,
        Though hosts my peace invade,
    Though through a waste and weary land
        My lonely way be made,
    Thou, even Thou, wilt comfort me—
        I need not be afraid.

7. Still in the solitary place
        I would a-while abide,
    Till with the solace of Thy love
        My heart is satisfied,
    And all my hopes of happiness
        Stay calmly at Thy side.

                                A. L. W.

                ———

129.   *Psalm* cxix. 65.

1. WHATEVER God does is well!
        His children find it so.
    Some He doth not with plenty bless,
    Yet loves them not the less,

But draws their hearts unto Himself away.—
Oh ! hearts obey.

2. Whatever God does is well,
   Whether he gives or takes !
   And what we from His hand receive
   Suffices us to live.
   He takes and gives, while yet He loves us
     still.—
   Then love His will.

3. Whatever God does is well !
   And what can our will do ?
   We cannot reap from what we sow
   But what His power makes grow.
   Sometimes He doth all other good destroy.
   To be Thy joy.

4. Whatever God does is well !
   And His will shall prevail.
   Doth He refuse thy hands to fill ?
   He knows Thy heart to still.
   A Christian from a very little gift
   Much joy can sift.

5. Whatever God does is well !
   Altho' the field look dark,
   Yet cheerful in His path we go ;
   And by our faith we know

That Christ for us hath heavenly riches
    bought.—
Can we lack aught?

6. Whatever God does is well!
    In patience let us wait:
    He doth Himself our burdens bear,
    He doth for us take care.
    And He, our God, knows all our weary
        days,—
    Come, give Him praise!

                                    N. SCHMOLK.

———

130.   *Psalm* cxix. 54.

1. WHILE travelling through this wilderness
        Weary and worn we roam,
    'T is sweet to cast a look above
        And think we're *going home :*—
    To know that there the trials
        Of our pilgrimage shall cease,
    And all the waves of earthly woe
        Be hushed to heavenly peace.
            Home, sweet home!
    Oh! for that land of rest above,
        Our own eternal home!

2. Here trees are not the trees that grow
      In beauty by the side
    Of that bright flood whose living streams
      Through sinless regions glide ;—
    We see not here th' immortal fruit,
      The fadeless flowers that bloom
    On hills of light and vales of peace,
      In our own bright Eden-home.
          Home, sweet home !
    Oh ! for that land of rest above,
      Our own eternal home ?

3. The tones we hear are not the tones
      Of music and of love,
    That breathe from thousand harps and songs
      Of endless joys above.
    We tread in haste along,
      With trembling and with fear,
    For this is not our home,
      We've no continuing here.
          Home, sweet home !
    Oh ! for that land of rest above,
      Our own eternal home !

4. Oh ! for the death of those that die
      Like daylight in the west—
    That sink in peace like the waves of eve,
      To calm untroubled rest.

They stand before their Father's face
　　Their tears and conflicts o'er;
Redeem'd and wash'd they stay at home,
　　And shall go out no more.
　　　　Home, sweet home!
Oh! for that land of rest above,
　　Our own eternal home!

———

131.　　　*Romans* viii. 33–35.

1.　SING Hallelujah! Christ doth live,
　　　And peace on earth restore;
Come, ransom'd souls, and glory give,
　　Sing, worship, and adore.
With grateful hearts to Him we pay
　　Our thanks in humble wise;
Who aught unto our charge shall lay?
　　'T is God that justifies.

2.　Who can condemn, since Christ has died,
　　And ever lives with God?
Now our whole debt is fully paid,
　　He saves us by His blood:
The ransom'd hosts in earth and heaven
　　Through countless choirs proclaim,
"He hath redeemed us, praise be given
　　To God and to the Lamb."

3. God raised Him up, when He for all
    Had freely tasted death,
And had redeem'd us from the fall;
    On this we ground our faith:
For God, well pleased, that sacrifice
    Declared, in sovereign grace,
And all-sufficient ransom-price
    For Adam's fallen race.

4. The God of peace to guilty man
    Doth pardoning grace afford,
Since from the dead He brought again
    Our Shepherd, Head, and Lord;—
That Shepherd who did freely bleed,
    Lost sinners to restore,
Who died, but now is risen indeed,
    And lives for evermore.

5. The God of mercies let us praise,
    Who saveth fallen men:
Who by His power, which Christ did raise,
    Begets His saints again
Unto a lively confidence,
    That they for Jesus' sake,
Shall of the blest inheritance
    Reserved for them partake.

6. His resurrection's power divine,
    By grace on us bestowed,

Renews us, that we, dead to sin,
   May live alone to God.
Thus we, supported by His might,
   From strength to strength proceed,
And walking in His truth and light;
   Praise Him in word and deed.

7.   In all we do constrain'd by love,
        We'll joy to Him afford,
   And to God's will obedient prove
        Through Jesus Christ our Lord.
   Sing Hallelujah, and adore
        On earth the Lamb once slain,
   Till we in heaven shall evermore
        Exalt His name.   Amen !

———

132.   *Ephesians* iii. 17.

1.   LORD, take my heart just as it is,
        Set up therein Thy throne ;
   So shall I love Thee above all,
        And live to Thee alone.

2.   I thank Thee, that in mercy Thou
        Hast waken'd me from death,
   Arous'd me out of sin's deep sleep,
        And call'd to walk by faith.

3.　Complete Thy work and crown Thy grace,
　　　That I may faithful prove,
　And listen to that still small voice,
　　　Which whispers only love.

4.　Which teaches me to know Thy will,
　　　And gives me power to do ;
　Which fills my heart with shame when I
　　　Do not that will pursue.

5.　This unction may I ever feel,
　　　This teaching of my Lord,
　And learn obedience to Thy voice,
　　　Thy soft reviving word.

———

133.　　　*Canticles* ii. 16.

1.　NOW I have found a Friend,
　　　Whose love shall never end,—
　　　　　Jesus is mine.
　Though earthly joys decrease,
　Though human friendships cease,
　Now I have lasting peace ;
　　　　　Jesus is mine.

2.　Though I grow poor and old,
　　He will my faith uphold,—
　　　　　Jesus is mine.

16

He shall my wants supply,
His precious blood is nigh,
Nought can my hope destroy,—
  Jesus is mine.

3. When earth shall pass away,
In the great judgment day,—
   Jesus is mine.
Oh ! what a glorious thing,
Then to behold my King,
On tuneful harps to sing,
   Jesus is mine.

4. Farewell mortality !
Welcome eternity !
   Jesus is mine.
He my redemption is,
Wisdom and righteousness,
Life, light, and holiness :
   Jesus is mine.

5. Father ! Thy name I bless,
Thine was the sovereign grace :
   Praise shall be Thine.
Spirit of holiness,
Sealing the Father's grace,
Thou mad'st my soul embrace
   Jesus as mine.

134.   _Psalm_ xlvi. 1, 2, 3.

1. WHEN the nations toss and roar,
        Like the billows on the shore,
    When their chains the people break,
    Leaders tremble, monarchs quake ;
    Midst the roaring of the sea,
    Christ, our hope is all in Thee !

2. When the nations are at peace,
    And the sounds of conflict cease ;
    When each port is choked with wares,
    And each field its harvest bears ;
    Mid the world's prosperity,
    Christ, our hope is all in Thee !

3. While the ages one by one
    Roll beneath the rolling sun ;—
    While the powers of death and life,
    Wage on earth a weary strife ;—
    Till the coming dawn we see,
    Christ, our hope is all in Thee !

---

135.   _Psalm_ xxxi. 15.

1. FATHER, I know that all my life
        Is portion'd out by Thee,

And the changes which are sure to come,
   I do not fear to see;
But I ask Thee for a present mind
   Intent on pleasing Thee.

2. I ask Thee for a thoughtful love,
   Through constant watching wise,
To meet the glad with joyful smiles,
   And to wipe the weeping eyes;
And a heart at leisure from itself,
   To soothe and sympathize.

3. I would not have the restless will
   That hurries to and fro,
Seeking for some great thing to do,
   Or secret thing to know;
I would be treated as a child,
   And guided where I go.

4. Wherever in the world I am,
   In whatso'er estate,
I have a fellowship with hearts,
   To keep and cultivate;
And a work of lowly love to do,
   For the Lord on whom I wait.

5. So I ask Thee for the daily strength
   To none that ask denied,

And a mind to blend with outward life
  While keeping at Thy side;
Content to fill a little space,
  If Thou be glorified.

6. And if some things I do not ask
      In my cup of blessing be,
    I would have my spirit fill'd the more
      With grateful love to Thee ;
    More careful not to serve Thee *much*,
      But to please Thee perfectly.

7. There are briars besetting every path,
      That call for patient care,
    There is a cross in every lot,
      And an earnest need for prayer;
    But a lowly heart that leans on Thee,
      Is happy anywhere.

8. In a service which Thy will appoints,
      There are no bonds for me,
    For my inmost heart is taught " the truth,"
      That makes Thy children " free ;"
    And a life of self-renouncing love
      Is a life of liberty.

                                    A. L. W.

  16*

136.   *Ecclesiastes* xi. 1.

1. UPON the stormy waters
        The bread of life we cast,
    With cheerful trust believing
        It shall be found at last.
    We see it but a moment,
        Far drifting o'er the main,
    But deathless, undecaying,
        It shall be found again.

2. One eye shall ever watch it,
        The eye of Him who sees
    Each tiny seedling scatter'd
        By summer's passing breeze;
    That eye which sees the coral,
        As year by year it grows,
    And counts the myriad crystals
        Of Himalayan snows.

3. Sometimes with bitter weeping
        The seed of life is sown,
    With well-nigh hopeless pleadings,
        To Jesus only known.
    With hope deferr'd, the mother
        Oft looks upon her child,
    No plant of heaven is springing,
        Though weeds grow rank and wild.

4. The shades of evening gather
       Upon the Sabbath sky,
    From pastors and from teachers
       The prayer ascends on high.
    Once more their hands have broken
       The true and heavenly bread ;—
    Let them believe not vainly
       The table hath been spread !

5. Yes ! on the stormy waters
       We cast the bread of life,
    Vain are the surging waters,
       Vain is the tempest's strife.
    His never failing promise
       Jehovah will fulfill,
    And the seed be found in glory,
       When those proud waves are still.

---

137.   *Hebrews* iv. 1.

1. OH ! where shall rest be found,
       Rest for the weary soul ?
    'T were vain the ocean depths to sound,
       Or pierce to either pole ;
    The world can never give
       The bliss for which we sigh ;
    'T is not the *whole* of life to live ;
       Nor *all* of death to die.

2. Beyond this vale of tears
       There is a life above,
    Unmeasur'd by the flight of years;
       And all that life is love :—
    There is a death, whose pang
       Outlasts the fleeting breath.
    Oh ! what eternal horrors hang
       Around " the eternal death."

3. Lord God of truth and grace,
       Teach us that death to shun,
    Lest we be banish'd from Thy face
       And evermore undone ;
    Here would we end our quest ;
       Alone are found in Thee,
    The life of perfect love,--the rest
       Of immortality.

                              MONTGOMERY.

————

138.   *Luke* xxii. 19.

(SACRAMENTAL.)

1. HERE, O my Lord, I see Thee face to face ;
       Here would I touch and handle things
          unseen ;
    Here grasp with firmer hand th' eternal grace,
    And all my weariness upon Thee lean.

2. Here would I feed upon the bread of God;
Here drink with Thee the royal wine of
heaven;
Here would I lay aside each earthly load,
Here taste afresh the calm of sin forgiven.

3. I have no help but Thine; nor do I need
Another arm save Thine to lean upon;
It is enough, my Lord, enough indeed;
My strength is in Thy might, Thy might
alone.

4. I have no wisdom save in Him, who is
My wisdom and my teacher both in one;
No wisdom can I lack while Thou art wise,
No teaching do I crave, save Thine alone.

5. Mine is the sin, but Thine the righteousness;
Mine is the guilt, but Thine the cleansing
blood.
This is my robe, my refuge, and my peace—
Thy blood, Thy righteousness, O Lord my
God.

6. Too soon we rise; the symbols disappear;
The feast, but not the love, is pass'd and
gone;

The bread and wine remove, but Thou art
    here—
Nearer than ever—still my shield and sun.

7.   Feast after feast thus comes and passes by ;
    Yet passing, points to the great feast above ;
    Giving sweet foretastes of the festal joy,
    The Lamb's great bridal feast of bliss and
       love.

BONAR.

---

139.   *Canticles* i. 3.

1.   THERE is a name I love to hear,
      I love to speak its worth ;
    It sounds like music in mine ear,
      The sweetest name on earth.

2.   It tells me of a Saviour's love
      Who died to set me free ;
    It tells me of His precious blood,
      The sinner's perfect plea.

3.   It tells me of a Father's smile,
      Beaming upon His child ;
    It cheers me through this " little while,"
      Through desert, waste, and wild.

4. It tells me what my Father hath
     In store for ev'ry day,
   And, though I tread a darksome path,
     Yields sunshine all the way.

5. It tells of One whose loving heart
     Can feel my deepest woe,
   Who in my sorrow bears a part
     That none can bear below.

6. It bids my trembling heart rejoice,
     It dries each rising tear,
   It tells me in " a still small voice "
     To trust and never fear.

7. Jesus ! the name I love so well,
     The name I love to hear !
   No saint on earth its worth can tell,
     No heart conceive how dear.

8. This name shall shed its fragrance still
     Along this thorny road,
   Shall sweetly smooth the rugged hill
     That leads me up to God.

9. And there with all the blood-bought throng,
     From sin and sorrow free,

I 'll sing the new eternal song
  Of Jesus' love to me.

F. WHITFIELD.

---

140.   *Psalm* xciv. 12.

1. THE more the cross the nearer heaven ;—
      Where is no cross there God is not ;
    The world's turmoil doth hide His face,
    Hell, sense, and self, make Him forgot.
    Oh ! where God draws a blessed lot,
    His mercy some dark lines doth trace.

2. The more the cross, the better Christian ;—
    God lays the touchstone to each soul ;
    How many a garden must lie waste
    Did not a tear-storm o'er it roll !
    Refining grief, a living coal,
    Upon the Christian's heart is placed.

3. The more the cross, the more believing ;—
    In desert lands the palm trees grow ;
    And when the grape is strongly press'd,
    Then doth its sweetness overflow ;
    And strength lies hid in every woe,
    As pearls do in the salt wave rest.

4. The more the cross, the more the praying ;—
    The bruised plant yields sweetest balm ;

Man doth not seek to find the pole
In quiet seas and steady calms;
And how should we have David's psalms
Had he not had a troubled soul?

5. The more the cross, the more the longing;—
Out of the vale man upward goes;
Whose pathway through the desert lies,
He craves the land where Jordan flows.
When here the dove finds no repose,
Straight to the ark with joy she flies.

6. The more the cross, the sweeter death;—
For man rejoices then to die;
When as his body is laid down
Much pain and sorrow are laid by;
His cross there on his grave doth lie—
See man doth wear the victor's crown!

7. Oh! Jesus, Lord, the crucified!
Now let the cross more welcome be;
Nor let my soul complaining toss,
But plant Thou such a heart in me,
As patiently shall look to Thee
For gain up yonder, for my loss.

SCHMOLK.

141.   *Revelation* v. 9.

1. COME let us join to sing of Jesus' love ;
   Sing how for us He left His throne above,
   Came down on earth, a man by birth,
   Then died upon the tree,
   And brought salvation, endless, rich, and free.

2. Sing how He burst the barriers of the grave,
   And rise in triumph, guilty men to save,
   Ascended high, no more to die,
   But seated on His throne,
   'Mid angel choirs our worthless names to own.

3. Sing how before His Father's throne He
        pleads,
   For all mankind in mercy intercedes,
   Pities their woes, subdues their foes,
   Their every want supplies,
   And bids their souls in triumph to Him rise.

4. Sing how He pour'd His Spirit from on high
   To give His people life no more to die,
   And by His word, His Spirit's sword,
   Subdues the heart of stone,
   While angels sing another vict'ry won.

5. Sing of His grace which all our hearts re-
   new'd,
   Cleansed us from sin in His atoning blood,
     Removed our guilt, and gave relief
   From Satan's galling chain,
   And soon will raise our souls with Him to
     reign.

6. In higher worlds we'll join His grace to
     praise,
   Where heavenly choirs will add their highest
     lays;
     Worthy the Lamb, prais'd be His name,
   Who saved us by His blood,
   And rais'd our souls to dwell in light with
     God.

---

142.   *Revelation* xxi. 4.

1. MY heavenly home is bright and fair,
     Nor pain, nor death can enter there;
   Its glittering towers the sun outshine,
   That heavenly mansion shall be mine.
        I'm going home, I'm going home,
        I'm going home, to die no more.

2. My Father's house is built on high,
   Far, far above the starry sky:

When from this earthly prison free,
That heavenly mansion mine shall be.
   I'm going home, etc.

3.   While here a stranger far from home,
   Affliction's waves may round me foam;
   And though like Lazarus sick and poor,
   My heavenly mansion is secure.
      I'm going home, etc.

4.   Let others seek a home below,
   Which flames devour or waves o'erflow;
   Be mine the happier lot to own
   A heavenly mansion near the throne.
      I'm going home, etc.

5.   Then fail this earth, let stars decline,
   And sun and moon refuse to shine,
   All nature sink and cease to be,
   This heavenly mansion stands for me.
      I'm going home, etc.

---

143.   *Deuteronomy* xxxiii. 25.

1.   WAIT my soul upon the Lord,
      To His gracious promise flee,
   Laying hold upon His word,
      " As thy days, thy strength shall be."

2. If the sorrows of thy case
    Seem peculiar still to thee,
  God has promised needful grace,
    " As thy days, thy strength shall be."

3. Days of trial, days of grief,
    In succession thou may'st see,
  This is still thy sweet relief,—
    " As thy days, thy strength shall be."

4. Rock of ages ! I 'm secure,
    With thy promise full and free,
  Faithful, positive, and sure—
    " As thy days, thy strength shall be."

---

144.   *Job* iii. 17.

1. REST, from anxious thought,
        From pressing, hurrying care !
  Rest here so vainly sought,
  So richly furnish'd *there.*
  Oh, Saviour dear ! how sweet 't will be
  To rest my weary head on Thee.

2. Peace, peace, a calm repose,
  No shadows hov'ring still
        17*

Around, of coming woes,
Peace shall each bosom fill.
Oh, Saviour dear ! how sweet 't will be
To be at peace because with Thee.

3.　Vigour and strength shall there
In mind and spirit reign,
No conflict then shall wear
Me with unceasing pain.
Oh, Saviour dear ! how sweet 't will be
With perfect pow'rs to worship Thee.

————

145.　　　　　*John* xiv. 14.

1.　MY prayer to the promise shall cling—
I will not give heed to a doubt ;
For I ask for the one needful thing,
Which I cannot be happy without.

2.　A spirit of lowly repose
In the love of the Lamb that was slain,
A heart to be touch'd with his woes,
And a care not to grieve Him again.

3.　The peace that my Saviour has bought,
The cheerfulness nothing can dim,
The love that can bring every thought
Into perfect obedience to Him.

4. The wisdom His mercy to own
　　In the way He directs me to take,—
　To glory in Jesus alone,
　　And to love, and do good for His sake.

5. All this Thou hast offer'd to me
　　In the promise whereon I will rest ;
　For faith, oh, my Saviour, in Thee !
　　Is the substance of all my request.

6. Thy word has commanded my prayer,
　　Thy Spirit has taught me to pray,
　And all my unholy despair
　　Is ready to vanish away.

7. Thou wilt not be weary of me,
　　Thy promise my faith will sustain,
　And soon, very soon I shall see
　　That I have not been asking in vain.

A. L. W.

_____

146.　　　　　*Matthew* xvi. 26.

1. WHAT is the thing of greatest price
　　　The whole creation round ?
　That which was lost in paradise,
　　That which in Christ is found.

2. The soul of man—Jehovah's breath !
      That keeps two worlds at strife ;
    Hell moves beneath to work its death,
      Heaven stoops to give it life.

3. God to reclaim it did not spare
      His well beloved Son ;
    Jesus, to save it, deign'd to bear
      The sins of all in one.

4. The Holy Spirit seal'd the plan,
      And pledged the blood divine
    To ransom every soul of man ;
      That blood was shed for mine.

5. And is this treasure borne below
      In earthly vessels frail ?
    Can none its utmost value know
      Till flesh and spirit fail ?

6. Then let us gather round the cross,
      This knowledge to obtain,
    Not by the soul's eternal loss,
      But everlasting gain.

                            MONTGOMERY.

147. *Hebrews* iv. 8.

1. OH ! for the calm beyond the storms
     In the presence of the Lord,
       Where with angels bright,
       Both day and night,
     We shall hear His sacred word !

2. Oh ! for the body free from pain,
     The spirit free from sin,
       Which He will give
       To the souls that live,
     Who shall dwell His courts within.

3. Oh! for the joy no eye hath seen,
     No human heart hath known ;
       For faint and low
       Fall the echoes below
     Of the songs around His throne.

4. But oh ! for grace to serve Him here,
     To rest upon His love,
       To walk with God
       On our earthly road,
     And to anchor our joys above !

5. Oh ! for a faith to see the Lord
     Through darkness and through tears,
       To hear His voice,
       And still to rejoice,
     And watch till the day appears !

148.   2 *Corinthians* ix. 15.

1.   BLESSED be God, our God !
        Who gave for us His well-beloved Son,
      The gift of gifts, all other gifts in one.
     Blessed be God, our God !

2.   What will He not bestow ?
        Who freely gave this mighty gift, unbought.
      Unmerited, unheeded, and unsought,
     What will He not bestow ?

3.   He spared not His Son !
        ' T is this that silences each rising fear,
        ' T is this that bids the hard thought disap-
           pear—
     He spared not His Son !

4.   Who shall condemn us now ?
        Since Christ has died, and ris'n, and gone
           above
      For us to plead at the right hand of love,
     Who shall condemn us now ?

5.   ' T is God that justifies !
        Who shall recall His pardon or His grace ?
      Or who the broken chain of guilt replace ?
     ' T is God that justifies !—

6. The victory is ours !
   For us in might came forth the mighty One,
   For us He fought the fight, the triumph won:
   The victory is ours.

BONAR.

---

149.   *Proverbs* xviii. 24.

1. L ORD ! no guardian to defend me
       In the world I have like Thee,
   None so willing to befriend me ;
       Thou art all in all to me.

2. Oh ! may life be one great mission,
       Christ to follow, serve, and please,
   Copying His meek submission,
       Sacrificing self and ease.

3. Zealous in each sacred duty,
       May I be more Saviour-like ;
   May each plant of Christian beauty
       In my soul its fibres strike ;—

4. Bearing fruit, whose holy savour
       Sheds its fragrance round my path,
   Seeking nothing but His favour,
       Dreading nothing but His wrath.

5.   What is life? a scene of troubles,
     Following swiftly one by one;
Phantom visions—airy bubbles,   .
     Which appear, and then—are gone!

6.   What at best the world's vain fashion?
     Quickly it must past away;
Vexing care and whirlwind passion,
     Surging like the angry spray.

7.   One brief moment, Lord, may sever
     All that earth can friendship call;
But *Thy* friendship is for ever,
     It outlives the wreck of all.

                        MACDUFF.

---

150.   1 *Corinthians* v. 17.

1.   HALLELUJAH!   I believe!
     Now the giddy world stands fast,
Now my soul has found an anchor
     Till the night of storm is past.
All the gloomy mists are rising,
     But a clue is in my hand,
Thro' earth's labyrinth to guide me
     To a bright and heavenly land.

2. Hallelujah ! I believe !
    Sorrow's bitterness is o'er,
And affliction's heavy burden
    Weighs my spirits down no more.
On the cross the mystic writing
    Now reveal'd before me lies
And I read the words of comfort,
    "As a father, I chastise."

3. Hallelujah ! I believe !
    Now no longer on my soul
All the debt of sin is lying,—
    One great Friend has paid the whole !
Icebound fields of legal labour
    I have left with all their toil ;
While the fruits of love are growing
    From a new and genial soil.

4. Hallelujah ! I believe !
    Now life's mystery is gone,
Gladly thro' its fleeting shadows,
    To the end I journey on.
Thro' the tempest, or the sunshine,
    Over flowers or ruins led,
Still the path is *homeward* hasting,
    Where all sorrow shall have fled.

5. Hallelujah ! I believe !
    Now, oh ! love, I know thy power,

18

Thine no false or fragile fetters,
　　Not the rose-wreaths of an hour !
Christian bonds of holy union
　　Death itself does not destroy ;
Yes ! to live, and love for ever,
　　Is our heritage of joy.

MÖWES.

────────

151.　　　　*Hebrews* xii. 2.

1.　I LOOK to Jesus, and the cloud
　　　　Of my transgressions melts away,
　　E'en as the blackest midnight shroud
　　　　Gives place to the returning day.

2.　I look to Jesus, and the stains
　　　　Of my life's guilt, tho' dark and deep,
　　Are wash'd, till not a spot remains,
　　　　And I can safely wake and sleep.

3.　I look to Jesus, and the face
　　　　Of God is turn'd on me in love,
　　I feel a Father's fond embrace,
　　　　And all my doubts and fears remove.

4.　I look to Jesus, and behold !
　　　　My heart is lighten'd of its cares,
　　My love for earthly things grows cold,
　　　　And pleasure vainly spreads her snares.

5. I look to Jesus, when my foes
      With violence my peace assail ;
    On His dear breast I find repose,
      And all their hateful efforts fail.

6. I look to Jesus, and the sight
      Of all that He endured for me,
    Makes e'en my greatest suff'rings light,
      Compared with His deep agony.

7. I look to Jesus, when my zeal,
      And faith, and love, grow dead and cold ;
    Then doth He Calvary reveal,
      And makes me in His service bold.

8. I look to Jesus, when the waves
      Of dark corruptions rage within,
    And He from their dominion saves,
      From their pollution makes me clean.

9. I look to Jesus, and I see
      Heaven's golden portals opening wide,
    With ready welcome e'en to me,
      Tho' vile, to enter and abide.

10. Thus let me, Lord, while life doth last,
      In faith look ever up to Thee,
    And when life's sinful days are past,
      I shall Thy face in glory see.

                                    C. T. ASTLEY.

152.   *Hebrews* xiii. 14.

1.   I 'M but a stranger here ;
     Earth is a desert drear,
       Heaven is my home.
Danger and sorrow stand
Round me on every hand,
Heaven is my father-land,
       Heaven is my home.

2.   What though the tempests rage,
Short is my pilgrimage,
       Heaven is my home.
And time's wild wintry blast
Soon will be overpast,
I shall reach home at last.
       Heaven is my home.

3.   There at my Saviour's side,
I shall be glorified,
       Heaven is my home,
There with the good and blest
Those I loved most and best,
I shall for ever rest ;
       Heaven is my home.

4.   Therefore I 'll murmur not,
Whate'er my earthly lot,
       Heaven is my home.

For I shall surely stand
There at my Lord's right hand ;—
Heaven is my father-land,
    Heaven is my home.

———

153.   1 *Timothy* i. 17.

1.   GLORY to God the Father be,
     Glory to God the Son,
Glory to God the Holy Ghost,
     Glory to God alone !

2.   My soul doth magnify the Lord,
     My spirit doth rejoice
In God, my Saviour and my God ;
     I hear His joyful voice.

3.   I need not go abroad for joy
     Who have a feast at home ;
My sighs are turned into songs,
     The Comforter is come.

4.   Down from on high the blessed Dove
     Is come into my breast,
To witness God's eternal love ;—
     This is my heavenly feast.

18*

5. This makes me, Abba, Father, cry,
　　With confidence of soul ;
　It makes me cry, my Lord, my God,
　　And that without control.

6. Eye hath not seen, nor ear hath heard,
　　From fancy 't is conceal'd,
　What Thou, Lord, hast laid up for Thine,
　　And hast to me reveal'd.

7. I see Thy face, I hear Thy voice,
　　I taste Thy sweetest love,
　My soul doth leap, but, oh ! for wings,
　　The wings of Noah's dove.

8. Then should I flee far hence away,
　　Leaving this world of sin ;
　Then should my Lord put forth His hand
　　And kindly take me in.

9. Then should my soul with angels feast,
　　On joys that always last ;
　Bless'd be my God, the God of joy,
　　Who gives me here a taste !

154.　　　　　*Matthew* x. 29.

1. MIGHTY God ! on whom the cares
　　Of all creation lie ;

And whose ample bosom bears
The load so easily.
Midst the worlds that lean on Thee
Thou hast loving thoughts of me.

2.   Ever quickly Thou dost hear
     Thy children's feeble cry,
     And dost keep them everywhere
     Beneath Thy watchful eye.
     But 'midst the worlds that lean on Thee
     Thou hast faithful thoughts of me.

3.   Anxious cares and heavy woes
     Oft agitate my breast ;
     And no balm on earth that grows
     Can give my spirit rest.
     But midst worlds that lean on Thee
     Thou hast gentle thoughts of me.

---

155.   *Numbers* xxi. 4.

1.   PILGRIM of earth, who art journeying to
              heaven !
     Heir of eternal life ! child of the day !
     Cared for, watch'd over, beloved and forgiven,
     Art thou discouraged because of the way ?

2. *Cared for, watch'd over*, tho' often thou
        seemest
   Justly forsaken, nor counted a child —
   Loved and forgiven, tho' rightly thou deemest
   Thyself all unlovely, impure, and defiled.

3. Weary and thirsty, no water-brook near thee,
   Press on, nor faint at the length of the way ;
   The God of thy life will assuredly hear thee ;
   He will provide thee with strength for the
        day.

4. Break through the brambles and briars that
        obstruct thee ;
   Dread not the gloom and the blackness of
        night ;
   Lean on the hand that will safely conduct
        thee ;
   Trust to *His* eye to whom darkness is light !

5. Be trustful, be steadfast, whatever betide
        thee,
   Only one thing do thou ask of the Lord—
   Grace to go forward wherever He guide thee,
   Simply believing the truth of His word.

6. Still on thy spirit deep anguish is pressing—
   Not for the yoke that His wisdom bestows,

A heavier burden thy soul is distressing,
A heart that is slow in His love to repose ;—

7. Earthliness, coldness, unthankful behaviour ;
   Oh ! thou may'st sorrow, but do not despair :
   Even this grief thou may'st bring to thy
        Saviour ;
   Cast upon Him e'en this burden and care !

8. Bring all thy hardness ; His pow'r can sub-
        due it :
   How full is the promise ! the blessing how
        free !
   " Whatsoever ye ask in my name, I will do
        it."
   " Abide in my love, and be joyful in me."

---

156 *Matthew* vi. 6.

1. GO when the morning shineth—
      Go when the noon is bright—
   Go when the eve declineth—
      Go in the hush of night :
   Go with pure mind and feeling,
      Fling earthly thoughts away,
   And in thy chamber kneeling,
      Do thou in secret pray.

2. Remember all who love thee,
      All who are loved by thee,
    Pray too for those who hate thee,
      If any such there be.
    Then for thyself in meekness,
      A blessing humbly claim,
    And link with each petition,
      Thy great Redeemer's name.

3. Or if 't is here denied thee
      In solitude to pray,
    Should holy thoughts come o'er thee
      When friends are round thy way;
    E'en then the silent breathing
      Of thy spirit raised above,
    Will reach His throne of glory,
      Who is mercy, truth, and love.

4. Oh ! not a joy or blessing
      With this can we compare,
    The power that He has given us,
      To pour our souls in prayer !
    Whene'er thou pin'st in sadness,
      Before His footstool fall,
    And remember in thy gladness
      His grace who gave thee all.

157.   *Psalm cxix. 105.*

1. L AMP of our feet, whereby we trace
      Our path, as here we stray ;
    Stream from the fount of heav'nly grace—
      Brook by the traveller's way.

2. Bread of our souls ! whereon we feed,
      Our manna from on high ;
    Our guide, our chart, wherein we read
      Of realms beyond the sky.

3. Pillar of fire ! through watches dark ;
      Or radiant cloud by day !
    When waves would whelm our tossing bark
      Our anchor and our stay.

4. Pole star on life's tempestuous deep !
      Beacon when doubts surround ;
    Compass ! by which our course we keep ;
      Our plummet-line to sound !

5. Our shield and buckler in the fight !
      In victory's hour the palm !
    Comfort in grief ! in weakness—might !
      In sickness—Gilead's balm.

6. Childhood's instructor, manhood's trust,
      Old age's firm ally,

Our hope, when we go down to dust,
    Of immortality.

7. Word of the living God !
        Will of His glorious Son !
    Without Thee, how could earth be trod,
        Or heaven itself be won ?

———

158.   *Psalm* lxxxiv. 14.

1. O LORD ! I look to Thee :
        To Thee lift up my heart,
    In heaven I would Thy glory see,
        Now, therefore, grace impart.

2. Grace to prevent my sin,
        My passions to subdue,
    My heart to change, my soul to win,
        My spirit to renew.

3. Grace every hour to bend
        My stubborn will to Thine.
    Till I in mind and heart ascend
        To where the angels shine.

4. Grace that I ever may
    ·   Walk humbly with my God,

And choose the self-renouncing way
    The lowly Jesus trod.

5. Grace to each stroke to bow,
    Gladly each cross to bear,
That, suff'ring with the Saviour now,
    I soon His joy may share.

6. Grace to be kind to all ;
    All to forbear in love ;
Gently to deal with those that fall,
    Like Him who reigns above.

7. Grace, even to my foes,
    In tenderness to speak,
And, tho' they wrong me and oppose,
    To be like Jesus—meek.

8. Grace, onward still to go,
    Forward each day to press,
Till Thou the blood-bought prize bestow,
    Christ's crown of righteousness.

9. Lord ! give me this rich grace !
    Oh, give Thyself to me,
That I may dwell before Thy face,
    And all Thy glory see.

C. T. ASTLEY.

19

159.　　　　　*Acts* xx. 38.

1.　FRIEND after friend departs,—
　　　Who hath not lost a friend?
　There is no union here of hearts
　　　That finds not here an end:
　Were this frail world our final rest,
　Living or dying none were blest.

2.　Beyond the flight of time,
　　　Beyond this vale of death,
　There surely is some blessed clime
　　　Where life is not a breath,
　Nor life's affections transient fire,
　Whose sparks fly upward and expire!

3.　There is a world above,
　　　Where parting is unknown,
　A whole eternity of love,
　　　Form'd for the saints alone:
　And faith beholds the dying here
　Translated to that happier sphere.

4.　Thus star by star declines,
　　　Till all are pass'd away;
　As morning high and higher shines
　　　To pure and perfect day:

Nor sink these stars in empty night—
They hide themselves in Christ's own light.

MONTGOMERY.

---

160. *Psalm* xxxix. 12.

1. I AM wandering down life's shady path,
    Slowly, slowly, wandering down ;
I am wandering down life's rugged path,
    Slowly, slowly, wandering down.

2. Morn, with its store of buds and dew,
    Lies far behind me now ;
Morn, with its wealth of song and light,
    Lies far behind me now.

3. The pleasant heights of breezy life,
    The pleasant heights are past ;
The sunny slopes of buoyant life,
    The sunny slopes are past.

4. I shall rest in yon low valley soon,
    There to sleep my toil away ;
I shall rest in yon sweet valley soon,
    There to sleep my tears away.

5. Laid side by side with those I love,
    How calm that rest shall be !

Laid side by side with those I love,
　How soft that sleep shall be !

6.　I shall rise and put on glory,
　　When the great morn shall dawn ;
　I shall rise and put on beauty
　　When the glad morn shall dawn.

7.　I shall mount to yon fair city,
　　The dwelling of the blest ;
　I shall enter yon bright city,
　　The palace of the blest.

8.　I shall meet the many parted ones,
　　In that our home of joy :
　Lost love for ever found again,
　　In that dear home of joy.

9.　We have shared our earthly sorrows,
　　Each with the other here ;
　We shall share our earthly gladness,
　　Each with the other there.

10.　We have mingled tears together,
　　We shall mingle smiles and song :
　We have mingled sighs together,
　　We shall mingle smiles and song.

BONAR

161. *John* i. 29.

1. MY faith looks up to Thee,
   Thou Lamb of Calvary,
      Saviour divine ;
   Now hear me while I pray,
   Take all my guilt away :
   O let me from this day
      Be wholly Thine.

2. May Thy rich grace impart
   Strength to my fainting heart,
      My zeal inspire :
   As Thou hast died for me,
   Oh may my love to Thee,
   Pure, warm, and changeless be,
      A living fire.

3. When life's dark maze I tread,
   And griefs around me spread,
      Be Thou my guide ;
   Bid darkness turn to day,
   Wipe sorrow's tears away,
   Nor let me ever stray
      From Thee aside.

4. When ends life's transient dream,
   When death's cold sullen stream
      Shall o'er me roll,

Blest Saviour, then in love,
Fear and distrust remove,
Oh ! bear me safe above,
    A ransom'd soul.

---

162.   *Romans* xiv. 8.

1.   " WE are the Lord's." His all sufficient
             merit,
Seal'd on the cross, to us this grace accords ;
" We are the Lord's," and all things shall
             inherit ;
Whether we live or die, " We are the Lord's."

2.   " We are the Lord's." Then let us gladly
             tender
Our souls to Him in deeds, not empty words ;
Let heart, and tongue, and life, combine to
             render
No doubtful witness that " We are the
             Lord's."

3.   " We are the Lord's." No darkness brooding
             o'er us
Can make us tremble, while this star affords
A steady light along the path before us—
Faith's full assurance that " We are the
             Lord's."

4. " We are the Lord's." No evil can befall us
   In the dread hour of life's fast loosening
           cords ;
  No pangs of death shall even then appal us ;
  'Death we shall vanquish, for " We are the
         Lord's."

C. T. ASTLEY.

---

163.   *Acts* xxi. 14.

1.   A S Thou wilt, my God ! I ever say ;
         What Thou wilt is ever best for me ;
  What have I to do with earthly care,
    Since to-morrow I may leave with Thee ?
  Lord, Thou knowest I am not my own,
  All my hope and help depend on Thee alone.

2.   As Thou wilt ! still I can believe,
    Never did the word of promise fail ;
  Faith can hold it fast, and feel it sure,
    Tho' temptations cloud, and fears assail.
  Why art thou disquieted, my soul,
  When thy Father knows and rules the whole ?

3.   As Thou wilt ! still I can endure
    Patiently my daily cross to bear ;
  Why should I complain, a pardon'd child,
    If the children's portion here I share ?

As Thou wilt ! my Father and my God !
I can drink the cup, and bless the rod.

4. As Thou wilt ! still I can hope on.
      Sunshine may return, when storms have
          pass'd ;
    Thine all-seeing eye of sleepless love
      Watches o'er my path from first to last.
    When Thou wilt ! upon the desert plain
    Springs may rise anew, and rivers flow again.

5. As Thou wilt ! all life's journey through,
      To Thy will my own I would resign ;
    If on earth I have but little store,
      Be it so ! all heaven shall be mine :
    Or if but Thyself, my God, art given,
    Nothing more I need or ask in earth or
          heaven.

6. As Thou wilt ! when Thine hour is come,
      Let Thy servant, Lord, in peace depart ;
    Good it is to love and serve Thee here,
      Better to be with Thee where Thou art.
    When, or where, or how the call may be,
    It will not come too early or too late for me.

7. As Thou wilt ! oh, Lord ! I ask no more.
      With the promise, faith pursues her way ;

Patience can endure through sorrow's night,
  Hope can look beyond to heaven's own
    day.
Love can wait, and trust, and labour still ;—
Life and death shall be according to Thy
    will !

NEUMEISTER.

164.　　　　　*Psalm* iv. 1.

1.　WHEN morn awakes our hearts
      To form the early prayer ;
  When toil-worn day departs,
      And gives a pause to care ;
  When those our soul loves best,
      Kneel with us in Thy fear,
  To ask Thy peace and rest,
      Our God, our Father, hear !

2.　When worldly snares without,
      And evil thoughts within,
  Of grace would raise a doubt,
      Or lure us back to sin ;—
  When human strength proves frail,
      And will but half sincere,
  When faith begins to fail,
      Our God, our Father, hear !

3.   When in our cup of mirth
         The drop of trembling falls,
      And the frail props of earth
         Are crumbling round our walls ;
      When back we gaze with grief,
         And forward glance with fear,
      When faileth man's relief,
         Our God, our Father, hear !

4.   And when death's awful hand
         Unbars the gates of time,
      Eternity's dim land
         Disclosing, dread, sublime :
      When flesh and spirit quake
         Before Thee to appear—
      Oh ! then for Jesus' sake,
         Our God, our Father, hear !

---

165.   *1 Samuel* vii. 12.

1. THUS far the Lord has led us, in darkness
              and in day,
      Thro' all the varied stages of the narrow
              homeward way ;
      Long since He took that journey, He trod
              that path alone,
      Its trials and its dangers full well Himself
              hath known.

2. Thus far the Lord hath led us; the promise
       has not fail'd,
    The enemy encounter'd oft has never quite
       prevail'd;
    The shield of faith has turn'd aside, or
       quench'd each fiery dart,
    The Spirit's sword in weakest hands has
       forced him to depart.

3. Thus far the Lord hath led us; the waters
       have been high,
    But yet in passing thro' them, we felt that He
       was nigh.
    A very present helper in troubles we have
       found,
    His comforts most abounded when our sor-
       rows did abound.

4. Thus far the Lord hath led us; our need hath
       been supplied,
    And mercy has encompass'd us about on
       every side,
    Still falls the daily manna, the pure rock-
       fountains flow,
    And many flowers of love and hope along
       the wayside grow.

5. Thus far the Lord hath led us; and will He
   now forsake
   The feeble ones whom for His own it pleased
   Him to take ?
   Oh, never, never ! earthly friends may cold
   and faithless prove,
   But His is changeless pity and everlasting
   love.

6. Calmly we look behind us, on joys and sorrows past,
   We know that all is mercy now, and shall be
   well at last ;
   Calmly we look before us,—we fear no future
   ill,
   Enough for safety and for peace, if *Thou* art
   with us still.

7. Yes, " they that know Thy name, Lord, shall
   put their trust in Thee,"
   While nothing in themselves but sin and
   helplessness they see.
   The race Thou hast appointed us, with pa-
   tience we can run,
   Thou wilt perform unto the end, the work
   Thou hast begun.

166.   *Revelation* v. 9.

1. I GIVE Thee thanks unfeigned,
      O Jesus, Friend in need,
    For what Thy soul sustained
      When Thou for me didst bleed.
    Grant to lean unshaken
      Upon Thy faithfulness,
    Until I hence am taken,
      To see Thee face to face.

2. I'll here with Thee continue,
      (Though poor, despise me not,)
    I'm one of Thy retinue:
      As were I on the spot,
    When, earning my election,
      Thy heart-strings broke in death,
    With shame and love's affection
      I'll watch Thy latest breath.

3. What heavenly consolation
      Doth in my heart take place,
    When I Thy toil and passion
      Can in some measure trace.
    Ah! should I, while thus musing
      On my Redeemer's cross,
    E'en life itself be losing,
      Great gain would be that loss.

20

4.   Own me, Lord, my Preserver,
       My Shepherd, me receive ;
     I know Thy love's strong fervour
       By all Thy pain and grief ;
     Thou richly didst supply me
       With soul-sustaining food,
     Nor does Thy love deny me .
       Thy holy flesh and blood.

5.   Lord, at my dissolution
       Do not from me depart ;
     Support at the conclusion
       Of life, my fainting heart ;
     And when I pine and languish,
       Seiz'd with death's agony,
     O by Thy pain and anguish
       Set me at liberty !

6.   Lord, grant me Thy protection ;
       Remind me of Thy death
     And glorious resurrection,
       When I resign my breath ;
     Ah ! then, though I be dying,
       Midst sickness, grief and pain,
     I shall, on Thee relying,
       Eternal life obtain.

167.   *Canticles* viii. 5.

1.   L EANING on Thee, my Guide and Friend,
       My gracious Saviour! I am blest;
     Tho' weary, Thou dost condescend
          To be my rest.

2.   Leaning on Thee, with child-like faith,
       To Thee the future I confide;
     Each step of life's untrodden path
          Thy love will guide.

3.   Leaning on Thee, I breathe no moan,
       Though faint with languor, parch'd with
       heat;
     Thy will has now become my own—
          That will is sweet.

4.   Leaning on Thee, midst torturing pain
       With patience Thou my soul dost fill;
     Thou whisperest " What did I sustain ? "
          Then I am still.

5   Leaning on Thee, I do not dread
       The havoc that disease may make;
     Thou who for me Thy blood hast shed
          Wilt ne'er forsake.

6. Leaning on Thee, though faint and weak,
    Too weak another voice to hear,
  Thy heavenly accents comfort speak,
            "Be of good cheer."

7. Leaning on Thee, no fear alarms;
    Calmly I stand on death's dark brink;
  I feel "the everlasting arms,"
            I cannot sink.

---

168.   *Exodus* xxv. 22.

1. WHEN to my closet I repair,
    To breathe my soul's desires in prayer,
  And bending low at Jesus' feet,
  I look towards the mercy-seat,
  This promise, Lord, shall be my plea—
  There, sinner, I will meet with Thee.

2. When Holy Scripture I peruse,
  And o'er its sacred pages muse,
  Oh! then this precious word fulfil;
  And while I seek to learn Thy will,
  Draw near, in answer to my prayer,
  And, gracious Saviour, meet me *there*.

3. When in Thy temple courts I stand,
  Amid Thy little chosen band,

Assist me then my soul to raise
In earnest prayer and cheerful praise ;
There let me Thy salvation see,
And, gracious Saviour, meet with me.

4. Or should it be Thy wise decree
To lay Thy chastening hand on me,
And make the couch of suffering mine,
Yet would Thy servant not repine,
If only this my portion be,
My Saviour ! *there* to meet with Thee.

5. When sorrow's gloomy path I tread,
And threatening clouds meet o'er my head,
I'll onward go without a fear,
If only Jesus' voice I hear :
E'en then the darkness light shall be,
If *there* my Saviour meet with me.

6. And when my closing hour draws nigh—
That solemn hour when I shall die—
When Jordan's banks I shall descend,
Leaving behind each earthly friend,
To Canaan's shores my spirit bear,
And, gracious Saviour ! meet me *there*.

169.   *Ecclesiastes* ix. 10.

1. MAKE haste, O man, to live,
       For thou so soon must die;
    Time hurries past thee like the breeze,
       How swift its moments fly !
       Make haste, O man, to live !

2. To breathe, and wake, and sleep,
       To smile, to sigh, to grieve ;
    To move in idleness through earth,
       This, this is not to live !
       Make haste, O man, to live !

3. Make haste, O man, to do
       Whatever must be done ;
    Thou hast no time to lose in sloth,
       Thy day will soon be gone.
       Make haste, O man, to live !

4. Up then with speed, and work,
       Fling ease and self away ;
    This is no time for thee to sleep,
       Up, watch, and work, and pray !
       Make haste, O man, to live !

5. The useful, not the great,
       The thing that never dies ;

The silent toil that is not lost,—
Set these before thine eyes.
    Make haste, O man, to live !

6. The seed whose leaf and flower,
      Tho' poor in human sight,
    Brings forth at last eternal fruit,
      Sow thou both day and night.
        Make haste, O man, to live !

7. Make haste, O man, to live,
      Thy time is almost o'er ;
    O sleep not, dream not, but arise,
      The Judge is at the door.
        Make haste, O man, to live !

                                    BONAR.

---

170.   *Isaiah* xliii. 2.

1. BE steady, be steady, oh ! my soul,
      For the sea is come and the billows roll ;
    With the help of God and none beside,
    We shall safely pass the raging tide.

2. Jesus, Jehovah, be our stay
    Over the dark and troublous way ;
    Embark'd in Thee, we shall feel no fear,
    Though the storm, the trial of life, be near.

3. Forget Him not, oh! my soul, remove
    All thoughts that breathe not of Jesus' love—
    His perfect love—who so freely gave
    His innocent life, thy life to save.

4. Oh! let the sweet remembrance be
    Laid up in thine inmost treasury,
    There it shall brighten more and more,
    The most precious pearl of that secret store.

———

171.   *Psalm* cxxxv. 6.

1. WHAT God decrees, child of His love,
        Take patiently, tho' it may prove
    The storm thy wrecks thy treasure here;
    Be comforted! thou need'st not fear
            What pleases God.

2. The wisest will is God's own will;
    Rest on this anchor and be still;
    For peace around thy path shall flow,
    When only wishing here below
            What pleases God.

3. The truest heart is God's own heart,
    Which bids thy grief and fear depart,

Protecting, guiding, day and night,
The soul that welcomes here aright
    What pleases God.

4.   Oh ! could I sing as I desire,
My grateful heart should never tire,
To tell the wondrous love and power,
Thus working out from hour to hour
    What pleases God.

5.   The King of kings, He rules the earth,
He sends us sorrow here or mirth,
He bears the ocean in His hand ;
And thus we meet, on sea or land,
    What pleases God.

6.   His church on earth He dearly loves,
Altho' He oft its sin reproves,
The rod itself His love can speak,
He smites till we return to seek
    What pleases God.

7.   Then let the crowd around thee seize
The joys that for a season please,
But willingly their path forsake,
And for thy blessed portion take
    What pleases God.

8. Art thou despised by all around?
    Do tribulations here abound?
    Jesus will give the victory,
    Because His eye can see in thee
                What pleases God.

9. Thy heritage is safe in heaven;
    There shall the crown of joy be given;
    There shalt thou hear and see and know,
    As thou could'st never here below,
                What pleases God.

                                GERHARDT.

---

172.   *Isaiah* 1. 10.

1. THE way seems dark about me, overhead
        The clouds have long since met in gloomy
                spread;
    And when I look'd to see the day break
            through,
    Cloud after cloud came up with volume new.

2. And in that shadow I have pass'd along,
    Feeling myself grow weak as it grew strong,
    Walking in doubt and searching for the way,
    And often at a stand, as now to-day.

3. Lord ! I am not sufficient for these things ;
   Give me the light that Thy sweet presence
       brings ;
   Give me Thy grace, give me Thy constant
       strength—
   Lord ! for my comfort now appear at length.

4. It may be that my way doth seem confused,
   Because my heart of Thy way is afraid ;
   Because my eyes have constantly refused
   To see the only opening Thou hast made.

5. Because my will would cross some flowery
       plain,
   Where Thou hast thrown a hedge from side
       to side ;
   And turneth from the stony path of pain,
   Its trouble, or its ease, not even tried.

6. If thus I try to force my way along,
   · The smoothest road encumber'd is to me ;
   For were I as an angel swift or strong,
   I could not go unless allow'd by Thee.

7. And now I pray Thee, Lord, to lead Thy
       child,
   Poor wretched, wanderer from Thy grace and
       love—

Whatever way Thou pleasest through the
      wild,
So it but take me to my home above.

---

173.   *Luke* ii. 14.

1. G LORY to God on high !
         Peace upon earth and joy !
        Good will to man.
    Ye, who the blessing prove,
    Join with the hosts above ;
    Sing ye a Saviour's love,—
        Too vast to scan.

2.   Mercy and truth unite ;
    This is a joyful sight !
        All sights above.
    Jesus the curse sustains ;
    Bitter the cup He drains ;
    Nothing for us remains,
        Nothing but love.

3.   Love, that no tongue can teach,
    Love, that no thought can reach,
        No love like His !
    Heaven is its blessed source,
    Death could not stop its course,

Nothing can check its force,
Matchless it is.

4.   Join then this love to sing,
Join to exalt our King,
    Sinners forgiven.
To the great One in Three,
Honour and majesty,
Now and for ever be,
    Here and in heaven.

---

174.   *Isaiah* lii. 7.

1.   HOW sweet the Gospel trumpet sounds !
    Its notes are grace and love ;
Its echo through the world resounds
From Jesus' throne above.

    CHORUS.   It is the sound, the joyful sound,
    Of mercy rich and free ;
    Pardon it offers, peace proclaims,
    Sinner ! it speaks to thee.

2.   It tells the weary soul of rest,
The poor of heavenly wealth,
Of joy to heal the mourning breast ;
It brings the sin-sick health.
    It is the sound, &c.

21

3. Its words announce a heavenly feast
        Of water, milk, and wine,
    And manna in the wilderness,
        Provisions all divine.
            It is the sound, &c.

4. It speaks of boundless grace by which
        The vilest are forgiven ;
    To Christians it proclaims a rich
        Inheritance in heaven.
            It is the sound, &c.

5. To men in every clime, degree,
        Its message is address'd ;
    The Jew and Gentile, bond and free,
        Are with its blessings bless'd.
            It is the sound, &c.

---

175.   *John* x. 11.

1. JESUS is our Shepherd, wiping every tear ;
        Folded in His bosom, what have we to
            fear ?
    Only let us follow whither He doth lead,
    To the thirsty desert or the dewy mead.

2. Jesus is our Shepherd ;—well we know His
        voice ;

How the gentlest whisper makes our heart
    rejoice!
Even when it chideth tender in its tone;
None but He shall guide us; we are His alone.

3.   Jesus is our Shepherd;—for the sheep He
      bled,
   Every lamb is sprinkled with the blood He
      shed;
   Then on each He setteth His own secret
      sign,—
   " They that have My Spirit, these," saith He,
      " are mine."

4.   Jesus is our Shepherd;—guarded by His arm,
   Though the wolves may raven, none can do
      us harm;
   When we tread death's valley, dark with
      fearful gloom,
   We will fear no evil, victors o'er the tomb.

5.   Jesus is our Shepherd;—with His goodness
      now
   And His tender mercy, He doth us endow!
   Let us sing His praises with a gladsome heart,
   Till in heaven we meet Him, never more to
      part.

176. *Psalm* xxxi. 3.

1. GENTLY, Lord, O gently lead us
        Thro' this gloomy vale of tears,
    Thro' the changes Thou 'st decreed us,
        Till our last great change appears.
    Oh ! refresh us with Thy blessing,
        Oh ! refresh us with Thy grace,
    May Thy mercies never ceasing,
        Fit us for Thy dwelling place.

2. When temptation's darts assail us,
        When in devious paths we stray,
    Let Thy goodness never fail us,
        Lead us in Thy perfect way.
    Oh ! refresh us with Thy blessing, &c.

3. In the hour of pain and anguish,
        In the hour when death draws near,
    Suffer not our hearts to languish,
        Suffer not our souls to fear.
    Oh ! refresh us with Thy blessing, &c.

4. When this mortal life is ended,
        Bid us in Thine arms to rest,
    Till by angel hands attended,
        We awake among the blest.
    Oh ! refresh us with Thy blessing, &c.

5. Then O͡ crown us with Thy blessing,
    Thro' the triumphs of Thy grace,
Then shall praises never ceasing,
    Echo thro' Thy dwelling place.
Oh ! refresh us with Thy blessing, &c.

---

177.   *Job* iii. 18.

1. LIE down, frail body, here,
    Earth has no fairer bed,
No gentler pillow to afford,—
    Come, rest thy home-sick head.

2. Lie down, with all thy aches,
    There is no aching here;
How soon shall all thy life-long ills
    For ever disappear !

3. Thro' these well-guarded gates
    No foe can entrance gain;
No sickness wastes, nor once intrudes
    The memory of pain.

4. Foot-sore and worn thou art,
    Breathless with toil and fight;
How welcome now the long-sought rest
    Of this all-tranquil night !

        21*

5.   Rest for the toiling hand,
        Rest for the thought-worn brow,
     Rest for the weary, way-sore feet,
        Rest from all labour now.

6.   Rest for the fever'd brain,
        Rest for the throbbing eye ;
     Thro' these parch'd lips of thine no more
        Shall pass the moan or sigh.

7.   Soon shall the trump of God
        Give out the welcome sound,
     That shakes thy silent chamber walls,
        And breaks the turf-seal'd ground.

8.   Ye dwellers in the dust,
        Awake, come forth, and sing ;
     Sharp has your frost of winter been,
        But bright shall be your spring.

9.   'T was sown in weakness here ;
        'T will then be raised in power.
     That which was sown an earthly seed,
        Shall rise a heavenly flower.

                                        BONAR.

178.   *Isaiah* xliii. 1.

1.   YE trembling souls, dismiss your fears,
        Be mercy all your theme,—
Mercy, which like a river flows
     In one continual stream.

2.   Fear not the powers of earth or hell;
        God will these powers restrain,
His mighty arm their rage repel
     And make their efforts vain.

3.   Fear not the want of outward good;
        He will for His provide,
Grant them supplies of daily food,
     And all they need beside.

4.   Fear not that He will e'er forsake,
        Or leave His work undone;
He 's faithful to His promises,
     And faithful to His Son.

5.   Fear not the terrors of the grave,
        Or death's tremendous sting;
He will from endless wrath preserve,
     To endless glory bring.

6.   You, in His wisdom, power, and grace,
        May confidently trust;

His wisdom guides, His power protects,
His grace rewards the just.

BEDDOME.

---

179.   *Hebrews* xii. 2.

1. J ESUS in thy memory keep,
        Would'st thou be God's child and friend;
    Jesus in thy heart shrin'd deep,
        Still thy gaze on Jesus bend.
    In thy toiling, in thy resting,
    Look to Him with every breath,
    Look to Jesus' life and death.

2. Look to Jesus, till reviving
        Faith and love thy life-springs swell;
    Strength for all things good deriving
        From Him who did all things well:
    Work, as He did, in thy season,
    Works which shall not fade away,
    Work while it is call'd to-day.

3. Look to Jesus, prayerful, waking,
        When thy feet on roses tread;
    Follow, worldly pomp forsaking,
        With thy cross where He hath led
    Look to Jesus in temptations,

Baffled shall the tempter flee,
And God's angels come to Thee.

4. Look to Jesus, when distressed,
       See what He, the Holy bore ;
    Is thy heart with conflict pressed ?
       Is thy soul still harass'd sore ?
    See His sweat of blood, His conflict,
    Watch His agony increase,
    Hear His prayer and feel His peace.

5. By want's fretting cares surrounded,
       Does long pain press forth thy sighs ?
    By ingratitude deep wounded,
       Does a scornful world despise ?
    Friends forsake thee or deny thee ?
    See what Jesus did endure,
    He who as the light was pure.

6. Look to Jesus still to shield thee,
       When no longer thou may'st live :
    In that last need He will yield thee
       Peace the world can never give.
    Look to Him, thy head low bending ;
    He who finish'd all for thee,
    Takes thee, then with Him to be.

                                        FRANZEN.

180.   *Ephesians* iv. 8.

1. SOUND the high praises of Jesus our King,
      He came and He conquer'd—His victory
    sing;
    Sing, for the power of the tyrant is broken,
      The triumph's complete over death and the
        grave:
    Vain is their boasting, Jehovah hath spoken:
      And Jesus proclaim'd Himself mighty to
        save.
    Sound the high praises of Jesus our King,
    He came and He conquered—His victory sing.

2. Praise to the Conqueror, praise to the Lord,
    The enemy quail'd at the might of His word;
    In heaven He ascends and unfolds the glad
        story,
      The host of the blessed exult in His fame;
    In love He looks down from the throne of
        His glory,
      And rescues the ruin'd who trust in His
        name.
    Sound the high praises of Jesus our King,
    He came and He conquer'd—His victory sing.

181.   *Psalm* lxii. 5.

1. OH ! foolish heart, be still,
    And vex thyself no more,
Wait thou for God until
    He opens pleasure's door.
Thou know'st not what is good for thee,
    But God doth know,—
Let Him thy strong reliance be,
    And rest thee so.

2. He counted all my days,
    And ev'ry joy and tear,
'Ere I knew how to praise,
    Or e'en had learn'd to fear.
Before I Him, my Father, knew,
    He call'd me, child :
His help has guarded me all through
    This weary wild.

3. The least of all my cares
    Is not to Him unknown ;
He sees, and He prepares
    The pathway for His own :
And what His hand assigns to me,
    That serves my peace,—
The greatest burden it might be,
    Yet joy's increase.

4. I live no more on earth,
        Nor seek my full joy here;
    The world seems little worth,
        When heaven is shining clear;
    Yet joyfully I go my way,
        So free, so blest !
    Sweetening my toil from day to day
        With thoughts of rest.

5. Give me, my Lord, whate'er
        Will bind my heart to Thee ;
    For that I make my prayer,
        And know Thou hearest me !
    But all that might keep back my soul,
        Make Thee forgot—
    Tho' of earth-good it were the whole,
        Oh ! give it not.

6. When sickness-pains, distress,
        And want doth follow fear,
    And men their hate express,
        My sky shall still be clear.
    Then wait I, Lord, and wait for Thee;
        And I am still—
    Tho' *mine* should unaccomplish'd be,
        Do Thou *Thy* will !

7. Thou art the strength and stay
        Of ev'ry weary soul ;

Thy wisdom rules the way;
  Thy pity does control.
What ill can happen unto me
  When thou art near ?
Thou wilt, oh ! God, my keeper be,
  I will not fear.

C. F. GELBERT.

---

182.   *Isaiah* xxxviii. 14.

1. I AM oppressed ; my gracious God !
      I cry beneath Thy chastening rod ;
              Lord, undertake for me !

2. I am oppressed ; I look around
      And see Thy judgment's heavy cloud ;
              Oh ! undertake for me !

3. I am oppressed ; I weep with those
      Who sorrow 'neath a Christian's woes ;
              Then undertake for me !

4. I am oppressed ; I bear within
      A heart that's fill'd with shame and sin,
              Yet undertake for me !

5. I am oppressed ; at my right hand
      The tempter of my soul doth stand ;
              Lord, undertake for me !

6. I am oppressed ; behold my tears,
   Receive my prayer, remove my fears ;
         Still undertake for me !

7. I am oppressed ; O ! Saviour say
   That Thou wilt wipe my tears away,
         And undertake for me !

———

183.   *Psalm lxv. 8–13.*

1. THE God of harvest praise,
     In loud thanksgiving raise
       Hand, heart and voice ;
   The valleys laugh and sing,
   Forests and mountains ring,
   The plains their tribute bring,
       The streams rejoice.

2. Garden and orchard ground
   Autumnal fruits have crown'd,
       The vintage glows ;
   Here plenty pours her horn,
   There the full tide of corn,
   Sway'd by the breath of morn,
       The land o'erflows.

3. The wind, the rain, the sun,
   Their genial work have done ;—
        Would'st thou be fed ?
   Man to thy labour bow,
   Thrust in the sickle now,
   Reap where thou once did'st plough—
        God sends thee bread.

4. Thy few seeds scatter'd wide,
   His hand hath multiplied ;—
        Here thou may'st find
   Christ's miracles renew'd,
   With self-producing food
   He feeds a multitude—
        He feeds mankind.

6. The God of harvest praise ;
   Hands, hearts and voices raise
        With one accord.
   From field to garner throng,
   Bearing your sheaves along ;
   And in your harvest song,
        Bless ye the Lord.

7. Yea, bless His holy name,
   And your soul's thanks proclaim
        Through all the earth.

To glory in your lot
Is comely; but be not
His benefits forgot,
      Amidst your mirth.

MONTGOMERY.

---

184.   *Psalm* xxix. 10.

1. HE sitteth o'er the waterfloods,
     And He is strong to save;
He sitteth o'er the waterfloods,
     And guides each drifting wave.

2. Though loud around the vessel's prow
     The waves may toss and break,
Yet at His word they sink to rest
     As on a tranquil lake.

3. He sitteth o'er the waterfloods,
     When waves of sorrow rise;
And while He holds the bitter cup
     He wipes the tearful eyes.

4. He knows how long the wilful heart
     Requires the chast'ning grief;
And soon as sorrow's work is done,
     'T is He who sends relief.

5. He sitteth o'er the waterfloods,
        As in the days of old ;
    When o'er the Saviour's sinless head
        The waves and billows roll'd.

6. Yes, all the billows pass'd o'er Him ;
        Our sins—they bore Him down ;
    For us He met the crushing storm—
        He met th' Almighty's frown.

7. He sitteth o'er the waterfloods ;—
        Then doubt and fear no more,
    For He who pass'd through *all* the storms
        Has reach'd the heavenly shore.

8. And ev'ry tempest-driven bark
        With Jesus for its guide,
    Will soon be moor'd in harbour calm,
        In glory to abide.

---

185.   *Psalm* lxv. 2.

1. O THOU who hearest prayer,
        The God of power and might,
    To seek Thy face be all our care,
        Our whole delight.

22*

O God of grace and love,
  Regard us from Thy throne;
Send down to us the heavenly Dove,
  Seal us Thine own.

2. We have no other trust,
      But Thy dear sacrifice;
    Our hope, Thou holy One and just,
      Do not despise:
    Sinful, we plead Thy blood,
      Weak, we implore Thy power;
    Saviour, remember us for good
      In danger's hour.

3. Come with Thy saving strength,
      With healing virtue come,
    And let Thy guiding hand at length
      Conduct us home:
    Till saved from all annoy
      Of earthly fear and strife,
    We enter into endless joy,
      And heavenly life.

---

186.   *Ecclesiastes* ix. 10.

1. 'TIS not for man to trifle! Time is short,
      And sin is here.

Our life is but the falling of a leaf.
   A dropping tear.
We have no time to sport away the hours,
   All must be earnest in a world like ours.

2.   Not *many* lives, but only *one* have we,—
      One, only one ;—
   How sacred should that one life ever be !—
      That narrow span !—
   Day after day fill'd up with blessed toil,
   Hour after hour still bringing in new spoil.

3.   Our sorrows are no phantom of the night,
      No idle tale ;
   No cloud that floats along a sky of light,
      On summer gale.
   They are the true realities of earth,
   Friends and companions even from our birth.

4.   O life below,—how brief, and poor, and sad !
      One heavy sigh.
   O life above,—how long, how fair, and glad ;
      An endless joy.
   Oh, to be done with daily dying here !
   Oh, to begin the the living in yon sphere !

5.   O day of time, how dark ! O sky and earth,
      How dull your hue !

O day of Christ, how bright! O sky and earth,
  Each fair and new !
Come, better Eden, with thy fresher green ;
Come, brighter Salem, gladden all the scene !

                                        BONAR.

------

187.   *Isaiah* lv. 3.

1. SINNER, hear thy Saviour's call,
      He now is passing by ;
    He has seen thy grievous thrall,
      And heard thy mournful cry.
    He has pardon to impart,
      Grace to save thee from thy fears ;
    See the love that fills His heart,
      And wipe away thy tears.

2. Why art thou afraid to come
      And tell Him all thy case ?
    He will not pronounce thy doom,
      Nor frown thee from His face.
    Wilt thou fear Immanuel ?
      Wilt thou dread the Son of God,
    Who to save thy soul from hell,
      Has shed His precious blood ?

3. Think how on the cross He hung,
      Pierced with a thousands wounds,

Hark ! from each, as from a tongue,
　The voice of pardon sounds.
See from all His open'd veins
　Blood of wondrous virtue flow,
Shed to wash away thy stains.
　And ransom thee from woe.

4.　Though His majesty be great,
　　His mercy is no less,
Though He thy transgression hate,
　　He feels for thy distress.
By Himself the Lord has sworn,
　　He delights not in thy death,
But invites thee to return,
　　That thou may'st live by death.

5.　Raise thy downcast eyes and see
　　What throngs His throne surround ;
These, tho' sinners once like thee,
　　Have full salvation found.
Yield not then to unbelief,
　　While He says " There yet is room,"
Tho' of sinners thou art chief,
　　Since Jesus calls thee, *come.*

188.   *John* xix. 30.

1. CHRIST'S grave is vacant now,
        Left for the throne above,
    His cross asserts God's right to bless,
        In His own boundless love.

2. 'T was there blood was shed,
        'T was there the life was pour'd,
    There mercy gain'd her diadem,
        While justice sheath'd her sword.

3. And thence the child of faith
        Sees judgment all gone by,
    Perceives the sentence fully met,
        " The soul that sins shall die ;"—

4. Learns how that God in love
        Gave Christ the sins to bear
    Of all who own His Lordship now,
        That they His place might share ;—

5. And cries with wondering joy,
        " As He is so am I,"
    Pure, holy, loved as Christ Himself
        Who shall my peace destroy ?

6. Reach my blest Saviour first,
        Take Him from God's esteem,

Proves Jesus bears one spot of sin,
Then tell me I 'm unclean.

7. Nay ! for He purged my guilt
By His own precious blood,
And such its virtue, not a stain
E'er meets the eye of God.

---

189. *Psalm* lxxiii. 24.

1. FATHER ! whose hand hath led me so
securely,
Father ! whose ear hath listen'd to my prayer,
Father ! whose eye hath watch'd o'er me so
surely,
Whose heart hath lov'd me with a love so
rare ;
Vouchsafe, O heavenly Father, to instruct me
In the straight way wherein I ought to go,
To life eternal and to heaven conduct me,
Through health and sickness and through
weal and woe.

2. O my Redeemer ! who hast my redemption
Purchas'd and paid for by Thy precious blood,
Thereby procuring an entire exemption
From the dread wrath and punishment of
God ;

Thou who hast saved my soul from condemn-
    ation,
Redeem it also from the power of sin ;
Be Thou the Captain still of my salvation,
Through whom alone I can the victory win.

3. O Holy Ghost ! who from the Father flowest
    And from the Son, O teach me how to pray ;
    Thou, who the love and peace of God be-
      stowest,
    With faith and hope inspire and cheer my
      way ;
    Direct, control, and sanctify each motion
    Within my soul, and make it thus to be
    Prayerful, and still, and full of deep devotion,
    A holy temple worthy, Lord, of Thee.

                    FROM LYRA DOMESTICA.

---

190.   *Revelations* v. 11, 12.

1. SING, sing His lofty praise,
    Whom angels cannot raise,
      But whom they sing ;
  Jesus, who reigns above,
  Object of angels' love,
  Jesus, whose grace we prove,
      Jesus, our King.

2 Jesus the curse sustain'd,
 Bitter the cup He drain'd,
   Happy for us ;
 Angels were fill'd with awe,
 When their own King they saw
 Honour His holy law,
   Honour it thus.

3 Rich is the grace we sing,
 Poor is the praise we bring,
   Not as we ought ;
 But when we see His face,
 In yonder glorious place,
 Then we shall sing His grace,
   Sing without fault.

4. Yet we will sing of Him,—
 Jesus, our lofty theme,
   Jesus we 'll sing ;
 Glory and power are His,
 His too the kingdom is,
 Triumph, ye saints, in this,
   Jesus is King.

---

191.   *Exodus* xiv. 15.

1. " FORWARD let the people go "
     Israel's God will have it so ;

Though the path be through the sea,
Israel, what is that to thee ?
He who bids thee pass the waters,
Will be with His sons and daughters.

2. Israel, art thou sorely tried ?
Art thou press'd on ev'ry side ?
Does it seem as if no power
Could relieve thee in this hour ?
Wherefore art thou thus dishearten'd ?
Is the arm that saves thee shorten'd ?

3. Stand thou still this day, and see
Wonders wrought, and wrought for thee ;
Safe thyself on yonder shore,
Thou shalt see thy foes no more,
Thine to see the Saviour's glory,   ·
Thine to tell the wondrous story.

4. Yes ! thy God shall yet be known,
Far and wide as God alone ;
At His feet shall idols fall,
For thy God is Lord of all ;
His is strength and His salvation—
He shall reign o'er ev'ry nation.

192. *Psalm* ix. 1.

1. WITH my whole heart to Thee I'll raise,
   Eternal Lord, a song of praise,
   And Thy great works declare :
   I'll glory and rejoice in Thee,
   Thou high exalted Trinity !
   On Thee I'll cast my care.

2. Seated upon Thy glorious throne,
   Thou art the Lord, and Thou alone,
   Worlds, times, events arranging ;
   And when the worlds shall pass away,
   Thou shalt endure, nor know decay,
   In midst of change unchanging.

3. Mankind, awaking from the dust,
   Shall hear with awe Thy judgments just
   Pronounce their final doom ;
   And all who here reject Thy grace,
   For ever banished from Thy face,
   Shall go to endless gloom.

4. But to the saints who know Thy name,
   Who whilst on earth Thy power proclaim,
   And celebrate Thy love,
   To all the humble and the meek,
   As a dear Father Thou wilt speak,
   And they shall reign above.

5.　Lord! make me meek and humble **now**,
　　Let me with joy my faith avow,
　　　And Jesus' name confess;
　　Increase my love, increase my zeal,
　　And let me not the light conceal,
　　　With which Thou deign'st to bless.

C. T. ASTLEY.

193.　　　　　*Luke* xxiv. 29.

1.　" A BIDE with me," Thou gracious Guide
　　　　My lamp by night, my sun by day;
　　Thy gracious presence at my side
　　Bids ev'ry anxious fear away.

2.　" Abide with me " when lips beloved
　　Shall lisp on earth their sad farewell;
　　The best of friends is not removed,
　　If Thou within my bosom dwell.

3.　" Abide with me " when sleepless laid
　　On sick bed—weary—lone—distressed;
　　Bless'd Saviour! let my throbbing head
　　Lie pillow'd on Thy peaceful breast.

4.　" Abide with me " when death is near,
　　To calm the waves of ebbing life;
　　Be nigh to wipe earth's closing tear,
　　And bear me from its ended strife.

5. " Abide with me " on that great day,
   When sea and earth shall yield their dead ;
   Oh ! may I *rise* without dismay,
   Exulting in my risen Head !

6. " Abide with me " through endless bliss ;
   Jesus, be Thou my " All in all ;"
   Thy presence makes the happiness
   Of heaven's eternal festival.

MACDUFF.

———

194.   *Psalm* xxv. 10.

1. GOD of my life, how good, how wise,
       Thy judgments to my soul have been !
   They were but mercies in disguise—
       The painful remedies of sin :
   How different now Thy ways appear—
   Most merciful when most severe !

2. Since first the maze of life I trod,
       Hast thou not hedged about my way--
   My worldly vain designs withstood,
       And robb'd my passions of their prey—
   Withheld the fuel from the fire,
   And cross'd my ev'ry fond desire ?

23*

3. Thou would'st not let Thy captive go,
      Or leave me to my carnal will;
    Thy love forbade my rest below—
      Thy patient love pursued me still,
    And forced me from my sin to part,
    And tore the idol from my heart.

4. But can I now the loss lament,
      Or murmur at Thy friendly blow?
    Thy friendly blow my soul hath rent
      From ev'ry *seeming* good below:
    Thrice happy loss! which makes me see
    My happiness is all in Thee.

5. How shall I bless Thy thwarting love,
      So near in my temptation's hour!
    It flew my ruin to remove—
      It snatch'd me from my nature's power—
    Broke off my grasp of creature-good,
    And plunged me in th' atoning blood.

6. See then, at last, I all resign—
      I yield me up Thy lawful prey:
    Take this poor long-sought soul of mine,
      And bear me in Thine arms away,
    Whence I may never more remove—
    Secure in Thy eternal love.

                                    C. WESLEY.

195. 2 *Corinthians* v. 4.

1. OFT' have I sat in secret sighs
      To feel my flesh decay,
    Then mourn'd aloud with weeping eyes,
      To view the tott'ring clay.

2. But I forbid my sorrows now,
      Nor dares the flesh complain ;
    Diseases bring their profit too,
      The joy o'ercomes the pain.

3. My cheerful soul now all the day
      Sits waiting here and sings,
    Looks thro' the ruins of her clay,
      And practises her wings.

4. Faith almost changes into sight,
      While from afar she spies
    Her fair inheritance in light
      Above created skies.

5. Had but the prison walls been strong,
      Without a flaw therein,
    In darkness she had dwelt too long,
      And less of glory seen.

6. But now the everlasting hills
      Through ev'ry chink appear,

And something of the joy she feels,
    While she 's a prisoner here.

7.   Oh ! may these walls stand tott'ring still,
    The breaches never close,
If I must here in darkness dwell,
    And all this glory lose.

8.   Oh ! rather let this flesh decay,
    The ruins wider grow,
Till glad to see th' enlarged way,
    I stretch my pinions through.

                           WATTS.

---

196.   *Matthew* viii. 20.

1.   BIRDS have their quiet nest,
    Foxes their holes, and man his peaceful
      bed,
All creatures have their rest,
But Jesus had not where to lay His head.

2.   Winds have their hour of calm,
And waves to slumber on the voiceless deep,
    Eve hath its breath of balm
To hush all senses and all sounds to sleep.

3   The wild deer hath its lair,   .
The homeward flocks the shelter of their
        shed,
    All have their rest from care—
But Jesus had not where to lay His head.

4. And yet He came to give
The weary and the heavy laden rest,
    To bid the sinner live,
And soothe our griefs to slumber on His
        breast!

5. What then am I, my God,
Permitted thus the paths of peace to tread?
    Peace purchased by the blood
Of Him who had not where to lay His nead.

6. Oh! why should I have peace?
Why? but for that unchanged, undying love,
    Which would not, could not cease,
Until it made me heir of joys above.

7. Yes,—but for pardoning grace,
I feel, I never should in glory see
    The brightness of that face,
That once was pale and agonized for me.

8. Let the birds seek their rest,
Foxes their holes, and man his peaceful bed,

Come, Saviour, in my breast
Deign to repose Thine oft rejected head.

9. Come, give me rest, and take
The only rest on earth Thou lov'st, within
    A heart, that for Thy sake,
Lies bleeding, broken, penitent for sin.

---

197.   *Revelations* ii. 9.

1. GATE of my heart, fly open wide,
    Shrine of my heart, spread forth ;
The treasure will in thee abide,
    Greater than heaven and earth.
Away with all this poor world's treasures,
And all this vain world's tasteless pleasures,
    My treasure is in heaven ;
For I have found true riches now,
My treasure, Christ, my Lord, art Thou,
    Thy blood so freely given !

2. This treasure ever I employ,
    This ever aid shall yield me,
In sorrow it shall be my joy,
    In conflict it shall shield me.
In joy the music of my feast ;
And when all else has lost its zest

This manna still shall feed me ;
In thirst my drink, in want my food,
My company in solitude,
　To comfort and to lead me !

3.　Death's poison cannot harm me now,
　　　Thy blood new life bestowing ;
　My shadow from the heat art Thou,
　　　When the noon-tide is glowing.
　And when by inward grief opprest,
　My aching heart in Thee shall rest,
　　　As a tired head on the pillow.
　Should storms of persecution toss,
　Firm anchor'd by Thy saving cross,
　　　My bark rests on the billow !

4.　And when at last Thou leadest me
　　　Into Thy joy and light,
　Thy blood shall clothe me royally,
　　　Making my garments white,
　Thou 'lt place upon my head the crown,
　And lead me to the Father's throne,
　　　And raiment fit provide me ;
　Till I by Him to Thee betrothed,
　By Thee in bridal costume clothed,
　　　Stand as a bride beside Thee !

P. GERHARDT.

198.   *Psalm* lxxiv. 22.

1. COME, Thou Almighty King,
 Help us Thy name to sing,
  Help us to praise !
Father all glorious,
O'er all victorious,
Come and reign over us,
  Ancient of days.

2. Jesus, our Lord, arise,
Scatter our enemies,
  And make them fall ;
Let Thine Almighty aid
Our sure defence be made,
Our souls in Thee be stayed ;
  Lord, hear our call.

3. Come, Thou incarnate Word,
Gird on Thy mighty sword,
  Our prayer attend !
Come, and Thy people bless,
And give Thy word success.
Spirit of holiness,
  On us descend.

4. Come, holy Comforter,
Thy sacred witness bear
  In this glad hour !

Thou, who Almighty art,
Now rule in ev'ry heart,
And ne'er from us depart,
  Spirit of power.

5. To Thee, great One in Three,
Eternal praises be,
   Hence, evermore :
Thy sovereign majesty
May we in glory see,
And to eternity
   Love and adore.

----

199.   *Psalm* lxxiv. 21.

1. I NEED Thee, precious Jesus ! for I am full
   of sin ;
My soul is dark and guilty, my heart is dead
   within ;
I need the cleansing fountain, where I can
   always flee,—
The blood of Christ most precious, the sinner's perfect plea.

2. I need Thee, precious Jesus ! for I am very
   poor,
A stranger and a pilgrim, I have no earthly
   store ;

24

I need the love of Jesus to cheer me on my
way,
To guide my doubting footsteps, to be my
strength and stay.

3. I need Thee, precious Jesus! I need a friend
like Thee,
A friend to soothe and sympathize, a friend
to care for me,
I need the heart of Jesus to feel each anxious
care,
To tell my every want, and all my sorrow
share.

4. I need Thee, precious Jesus! for I am very
blind,
A weak and foolish wanderer, with a dark
and evil mind;
I need the light of Jesus to tread the thorny
road,
To guide me safe to glory where I shall see
my God.

5. I need Thee, precious Jesus! I need Thee
day by day,
To fill me with Thy fullness, to lead me on
my way;

1 need Thy Holy Spirit to teach me what I
am,
To show me more of Jesus, to point me to
the Lamb.

6. I need Thee, precious Jesus! and hope to see
Thee soon,
Encircled with the rainbow and seated on
Thy throne;
There with Thy blood-bought children my
joy shall ever be
To sing Thy praises, Jesus!—to gaze, my
Lord, on Thee.

---

200. 2 *Corinthians* iv. 17.

1. IS it a long way off?
Oh, no! a few more years,
A few more bitter tears,—
We shall be there.
Sometimes the way seems long,
Our comforters all go,
Woe follows after woe,
Care after care.

2. Oh! brethren dear how weak,
How faint and weak we are!

Yet Jesus leads us far
  Through tangled ways
Into the very heart
Of this dark wilderness,
Where dangers thickest press,
  And Satan strays.

3. But He is strong and wise,
    And we, His children blind,
    Must trust His thoughtful mind
      And tender care.
    So gentle is His love,
    We may be sure that sight
    Would show us all is right,
      And answer'd prayer.

4. 'T is no uncertain way
    We tread, for Jesus still
    Leads with unerring skill
      Where'er we roam ;
    And from the desert wild
    Soon shall our path emerge,
    And land us on the verge
      Of our dear home.

                              E. W.

201   *Psalm* xxv. 4.

1.   T HY way, not *mine*, O Lord,
      However dark it be!
  Lead me by Thine own hand,
      Choose but the path for me.

2.   Smooth let it be or rough,
      It will be still the best :
  Winding or straight it matters not,
      It leads me to Thy rest.

3.   I dare not choose my lot,
      I would not, if I might ;
  Choose Thou for me, my God,
      So shall I walk aright.

4.   The kingdom that I seek
      Is Thine, so let the way
  That leads to it be Thine,
      Else surely I shall stray.

5   Take Thou my cup, and it
      With joy or sorrow fill ;
  As best to Thee may seem,
      Choose Thou my good and ill.

6.   Choose Thou for me my friends,
      My sickness or my health ;

24*

Choose Thou my cares for me,
    My poverty or wealth.

7.   Not mine, not mine the choice,
        In things, or great, or small ;
     Be Thou my Guide, my Strength,
        My Wisdom, and my All.

BONAR.

---

202.   *Isaiah* xlv. 22.

1.   BY faith I see my Saviour dying
                On the tree ;
     To ev'ry sinner He is crying,
                Look to me.
     He bids the guilty soul draw near,
     Come, come to me, dismiss your fear,
     Hark, hark, these precious words I hear,
                Look to me.

2.   Did Christ, while I was sin pursuing,
                Pity me ?
     And did He save my soul from ruin ?
                Can it be ?
     Oh, yes ! He did salvation bring,
     He is the Saviour, Priest, and King,
     And now my happy soul can sing,
                Mercy 's free.

3. How sweet the truth—ye sinners hear it—
　　　　　Mercy 's free.
Ye saints of God to all declare it—
　　　　　Mercy 's free.
Visit the heathen's dark abode,
Proclaim to all the love of God,
And spread the joyous news abroad—
　　　　　Mercy 's free.

4. Long as I'm here, I'll still be telling,
　　　　　Mercy 's free.
And ever on His love be dwelling ;—
　　　　　Mercy 's free.
And when the vale of tears I've past,
When lodged above the stormy blast,
His praise I'll sing while ages last,
　　　　　Whose mercy 's free.

203.　　　　　*Isaiah* li. 11.

1. WILL that not joyful be,
　　　When we walk by faith no more ?
When the Lord we loved before,
　　　As brother-man we see,
When He welcomes us above,
When we share His smile of love,
　　　Will that not joyful be ?

2.   Will that not joyful be,
     When to meet us rise and come
     All our buried treasures home,
        A gladsome company ?
     When our arms embrace again
     Those we mourned so long in vain,
        Will that not joyful be !

3.   Will that not joyful be,
     When the foes we dread to meet,
     Every one beneath our feet
        We tread triumphantly ?
     When we never more can know
     Slightest touch of pain or woe,
        Will that not joyful be ?

4.   Will that not joyful be,
     When we hear what none can tell,
     And the ringing chorus swell
        Of angel's melody ?
     When we join their songs of praise,
     Hallelujahs with them raise,
        Will that not joyful be ?

5.   Yes ! that will joyful be !
     Let the world her gifts recall,
     There is bitterness in all ;
        Her joys are vanity.

Courage, dear ones of my heart !
Tho' it grieves us here to part,
  There we will joyful be !

VON SCHWEINTZ.

---

204.   *Revelations* vi. 10.

1. HOW long, O Lord our Saviour,
      Wilt thou remain away ?
    Our hearts are growing weary
      Of Thy so long delay :
    Oh ! when shall come the moment,
      When, brighter far than morn,
    The sunshine of Thy glory
      Shall on Thy people dawn ?

2. How long, O gracious Master,
      Wilt Thou Thy household leave ?
    So long hast Thou now tarried,
      Few Thy return believe :
    Immersed in sloth and folly,
      Thy servants, Lord, we see ;
    And few of them stand ready
      With joy to welcome Thee.

3. How long, O Heavenly Bridegroom,
      How long wilt Thou delay ?

And yet how few are grieving
   That Thou dost absent stay;
Thy very bride her portion
   And calling hath forgot,
And seeks for ease and glory,
   Where Thou, her Lord, art not.

4. Oh! wake Thy slumbering virgins;
   Send forth the solemn cry,
Let all Thy saints repeat it,
   "The Bridegroom draweth nigh!"
May all our lamps be burning,
   Our loins all girded be,
Each longing heart preparing
   With joy Thy face to see!

---

205.   *Psalm* lxiii. 6.

1. IN the still silence of the voiceless night,
   When, chased by airy dreams, the slumbers flee,
Whom in the darkness doth my spirit seek,
        O God, but Thee?

2. And if there be a weight upon my breast,
   Some vague impression of the day foregone,
Scarce knowing what it is, I fly to Thee,
        And lay it down.

3. Or if it be the heaviness that comes
   In token of anticipated ill,
   My bosom takes no heed of what it is,
                  Since 't is Thy will.

4. Often in spite of present care,
   Or anything beside, how joyfully
   Passed that almost solitary hour,
                  My God, with Thee !

5. For what is there on earth that I desire,
   Of all that it can give or take from me,
   Or whom in heaven doth my spirit seek,
                  O God, but Thee ?

---

206.   *Psalm lxix. 18.*

1. COME nearer, nearer still,
        Let not Thy light depart;
   Bend, break this stubborn will,
        Dissolve this iron heart.

2. Less wayward let me be,
        More pliable and mild ;
   In glad simplicity,
        More like a truthful child.

3. Less, less of self each day,
        And more, my God of Thee ;—

O keep me in the way,
   However rough it be.

4. Less of the flesh each day,
     Less of the world and sin;
More of Thy Son, I pray,
     More of Thyself within.

5. Riper and riper now,
     Each hour let me become,
Less fond of things below,
     More fit for such a home.

6. More moulded to Thy will,
     Lord, let thy servant be,
Higher and higher still,
     Liker and liker Thee.

7. Leave nought that is unmeet;
     Of all that is mine own,
Strip me; and so complete
     My training for Thy throne.

BONAR.

———

207.   *Psalm* cxlviii. 2.

1. YE angels, who stand round the throne,
     And view my Immanuel's face,

In rapturous songs make Him known,
    Tune, tune your soft harps to His praise.
He formed you, the spirits ye are,
    So happy, so noble, so good ;
When others sunk down to despair,
    Confirmed by His power ye stood.

2. Ye saints, who stand nearer than they,
    And cast your bright crowns at His feet,
His grace and His glory display ;
    Oh ! tell of His love as is meet.
He saved you from hell and the grave—
    He ransomed from death and despair,
For you He was mighty to save,
    Almighty to bring you safe there.

3. Oh ! when will the period appear,
    When I shall unite in your song ?
I 'm weary of lingering here ;
    And I to your Saviour belong.
I 'm fettered and chained up in clay,
    I struggle and pant to be free ;
I long to be soaring away,
    My God and my Saviour to see !

4. I want to put on my attire,
    Wash'd white in the blood of the Lamb ;

26

I want to be one of your choir,
　　And tune my sweet harp to His name.
I want, oh ! I want to be there,
　　Where sorrow and sin bid adieu,
Your joy and your friendship to share,
　　To wonder and worship with you.

———

208.　　　　1 *John* iii. 2.

1.　WHAT shall we be, and whither shall we go,
　　　　When the last conflict of our life is o'er,
　　And we return from wandering to and fro,
　　　　To our dear home thro' heaven's eternal
　　　　　door ?
　　When we shake off the last dust from our
　　　　feet,
　　　　When we wipe off the last drop from our
　　　　　brow,
　　And our departed friends once more shall
　　　　greet,—
　　　　The hope which cheers and comforts us
　　　　　below !

2.　What shall we be, when we ourselves shall
　　　　see
　　　Bathed in the flood of everlasting light,

And from all guilt and sin entirely free,
   Stand pure and blameless in our Maker's
      sight ?
No longer from His holy presence driven,
   Conscious of guilt and stung with inward
      pain,
But friends of God and citizens of heaven,
   To join the ranks of His celestial train !

3.   What shall we be, when we drink in the
      sound
   Of heavenly music from the spheres above,
When golden harps to listening hosts around
   Declare the wonders of redeeming love ?
When far and wide thro' the resounding air
   Loud Hallelujahs from the ransomed rise,
And holy incense, sweet with praise and
      prayer,
   Is wafted to the Highest thro' the skies !

4.   What shall we be, when the freed soul shall
      rise
   With unrestrain'd and bold aspiring flight
To Him, who by His wondrous sacrifice
   Hath open'd heaven and scatter'd sin's dark
      night ?

When from the eye of faith the thin veil
drops,
    Like wreaths of mist before the morning's
rays,
And we behold the end of all our hopes,
    The Son of God in full refulgent blaze!

5. What shall we be, when we shall hear Him
say,
    " Come, O ye blessed,"—when we see Him
stand,
Robed in the light of everlasting day,
    Before the throne of God at His right hand ?
When we behold the eyes from which once
flowed
    Tears o'er the sin and misery of man,
And the deep wounds from which the precious blood,
    That made atonement for the world, once
ran !

6. What shall we be, when hand in hand we go
    With blessed spirits risen from the tomb,
Where streams of living waters softly flow,
    And trees still flourish in primeval bloom ?
Where in perpetual youth no cheek looks old
    By the sharp touch of cruel time imprest,

Where no bright eye is dimm'd, no heart
    grows cold,
  No grief, no pain, no death invades the
    blest !

7. What shall we be, when every glance we cast
    At the dark valley underneath our feet,
  And every retrospect of troubles past
    Makes heaven brighter and its joys more
      sweet ?
  When the remembrance of our former woe,
    Gives a new relish to our present peace,
  And draws our heart to Him, to whom we
      owe
    Our past deliverance and our present bliss !

8. What shall we be, who have in Christ be-
    lieved ?
    What thro' His grace shall be our sweet
      reward ?
  Eye hath not seen, ear heard, or heart con-
    ceived,
    What God for those who love Him hath
      prepared.
  Let us the steep ascent boldly climb,
    Our toil and labour will be well repaid ;
    26*

Let us haste onward, till in God's good time
We reap the fruit—a crown that doth not
fade.

FROM LYRA DOMESTICA.

---

209. *Hebrews* x. 37.

1. " A LITTLE while of mingled joy and
sorrow,
A few more years to wander here below,
To wait the dawning of that golden morrow,
When night shall break above our night
of woe.

2. A few more thorns about our pathway grow-
ing,
Ere yet our hands may cull the heavenly
flowers—
The morn of joy, but first the tearful sowing,
Ere we may rest these weary souls of ours.

3. A few more hours of weariness and sighing,
Of mourning o'er the power of inner sin;
A little while of daily crucifying
Unto this world the evil heart within.

4. A little longer in this vale of weeping,
Of yearning for the sinless home above;

A little while of watching, and of keeping,
  Our garments, by the power of Him we
    love.

5. " A little while " for winning souls to Jesus,
      Ere yet we see His beauty face to face ;
    A little while for healing soul-diseases,
      By telling others of a Saviour's grace.

6. " A little while " to tell the joyful story
      Of Him who made our guilt and curse His
        own ;
    A little while ere we behold the glory,
      To gain fresh jewels for our heavenly crown.

7. " A little while,"—and we shall dwell for ever
      Within our bright, our everlasting Home,
    Where time, or space, or death no more can
        sever
      Our grief-wrung hearts ;—and pain can
        never come.

8. 'T is but " a *little* while ;"—the way is dreary,
      The night is dark—but we are nearing land ;
    Oh ! for the rest of heaven, for we are weary,
      And long to mingle with the deathless
        band !

210.   *Hebrews* xi. 10.

1. THERE is a city of the saints,
    Where we ere long shall stand,
When we shall strike these desert tents,
    And quit the desert-sand.

2. Fair vision ! how thy distant gleam,
    Brightens time's saddest hue ;
Far fairer than the fairest dream,
    And yet so strangely true !

3. Fair vision ! how thou liftest up
    Our drooping brow and eye ;
With the calm joy of thy sure hope,
    Fixing our souls on high.

4. Thy light makes now the darkest page
    In memory's scroll grow fair :
Blanching the lines which time and age
    Had only deepen'd there.

5. With thee in view, the rugged slope
    Becomes a level way,
Smooth'd by the magic of thy hope,
    And gladden'd by thy ray.

6. With thee in view, how poor appear
    The world's most winning smiles ;

Vain is the tempter's subtlest snare,
And vain hell's varied wiles.

7. Now welcome toil, and care, and pain !
And welcome sorrow too !
All toil is rest, all grief is gain,
With such a prize in view.

8. Come crown and throne, come robe and
palm !
Burst forth glad streams of peace !
Come, holy city of the Lamb !
Rise, Sun of righteousness !

9. When shall the clouds that veil thy rays
For ever be withdrawn ?
Why dost thou tarry, day of days ?
When shall thy brightness dawn ?

BONAR.

---

211. *Revelations* xxii. 17.

1. COME to the blood-stained tree ;
The victim bleeding lies ;
God sets the sinner free,
Since Christ a ransom dies.
The Spirit will apply
His blood to cleanse thy stain :

O burdened soul, draw nigh,
   For none can come in vain.

2.   Dark though thy guilt appear,
     And deep its crimson dye,
There 's boundless mercy here,
     And Jesus bids thee try.
Oh ! do not doubt His word,
     There 's pardon full and free,
For justice smote the Lord,
     And sheathes her sword for thee.

3.   Look not within for peace,
     Within there 's nought to cheer;
Look up and find release
     From sin, and self, and fear.
If gloom thy soul enshroud,
     If tears faith's eye bedim,
If doubts around thee crowd,
     Come tell thou all to Him.

4.   Rest to the weary soul
     And aching breast is given,
Grace makes the wounded whole,
     Love fills the heart with heaven.
For thee, my soul, for thee,
     These priceless joys were bought,
Accept the mercy free
     That Christ to earth has brought.

5. Come, with the ransomed train,
       The Saviour's praises sing,
    Rejoice! The Lamb was slain,
       Adore! He reigns a King.
    And soon before His face,
       We'll praise in heaven above,
    Triumphant through His grace,
       Enraptured with His love.

-----

212.   *John* xv. 4.

1. O ABIDE, abide in Jesus,
       Who for us bare griefs untold,
    And Himself, from pain to ease us,
       Suffer'd pangs a thousand fold:
    'Bide with Him, who still abideth
       When all else shall pass away,
    And, as Judge supreme, presideth
       In that dread and awful day.

2. All is dying: hearts are breaking,
       Which to ours were once fast bound,
    And the lips have ceased from speaking,
       Which once utter'd such sweet sound,
    And the arms are powerless lying,
       Which were our support and stay,
    And the eyes are dim and dying,
       Which once watched us night and day.

3. Everything we love and cherish,
       Hastens onward to the grave,
    Earthly joys and pleasures perish,
       And whate'er the world e'er gave;
    All is fading, all is fleeing,
       Earthly **flames** must cease to glow,
    Earthly beings cease from being,
       Earthly blossoms cease to blow.

4. Yet unchanged, while all decayeth,
       Jesus stands upon the dust;
    " Lean on me alone," He sayeth,
       " Hope, and love, and firmly trust."
    O abide, abide in Jesus,
       Who Himself for ever lives,
    Who from death eternal frees us,
       Yea, who life eternal gives.

                         FROM LYRA DOMESTICA.

213.   *Canticles* ii. 16.

1. MINE! what rays of glory bright,
       Now upon the promise shine!
    I have found the Lord my light;
    I am His, and He is mine.

2. *Mine*, the promise often read,
       Now in living truth impress'd,

Once acknowledg'd in the head,
Now a fire in the breast.

3. *Mine no more* the crimson stains,
    Here I see them blotted out;
    Mine no more the bonds and chains,
    Mine no more the fear and doubt.

4. Mine, acceptance at the throne,
    Mine, the Father's owning smile,
    Mine, the Father's love unknown,—
    What shall from that love beguile?

5. Mine the yoke that's lined with love,
    Mine th' imputed righteousness,
    Mine, the armour for the fight,
    Mine, the way of holiness.

6. Mine, the mighty Paraclete,
    Mine, His comfort and His grace,
    Mine, the hope surpassing sweet,—
    Jesus! I shall see Thy face.

7. Mine,—unto a worm like me,
    Such a weight of glory 's given;
    Yea—to know the mystery
    Here in part—the whole in heaven.

27

8. Mine, the promise cannot change,
   Mine, though oft my eyes are dim ;—
   Nought can from His love estrange
   Those who once are bought by Him.

9. Mine ! tho' oft my hand may fail,
   He is strong, and holds me fast ;
   His dear blood shall still prevail,
   He shall lead me home at last.

10. Mine ! when death the bars shall break,
    'Mid those glories all divine,
    " Satisfied," I shall awake,
    Clasp His feet, and call *Him mine.*

                                        E. Z. B.

---

214.   *Psalm* xxx. 7.

1. I THOUGHT that I was strong, Lord,
       And did not need Thine arm ;
   Tho' troubles thronged around me,
       My heart felt no alarm.

2. I thought that I was rich, Lord,
       That all good things were mine,
   And earth and all its pleasures
       Did my vain heart entwine.

3. But Thou hast broke the spell, Lord,
    And roused me from my dream ;
The light has waked Lord, my soul,
    With bright unerring beam.

4. I know that I am weak, Lord,
    That nothing is my own ;
But Thou wilt make me strong, Lord,
    Leaning on Thee alone.

5. I know that I was blind, Lord,
    I did not see Thy light ;
But now my eyes are open'd,
    For Thou hast given me sight.

6. Yes ! Thou hast given me sight, Lord,
    And I can see within ;
I see my heart defiled, Lord,
    With deepest stain of sin.

7. But with this bitter grief, comes
    A rush of joy untold,
Like sunrise on the mountains,
    Flooding their heights with gold.

8. For I know Thy blood has cleansed me,
    And I know that I 'm forgiven ;

And all the roughest paths here,
    Will surely end in heaven.

9. For I know that I am Thine, Lord,
        And that none can pluck away
    The feeblest sheep that ever
        Did make Thine arm its stay.

10. My soul in death was sleeping,
        But Thou hast given it life;
    And strengthened by thy Spirit,
        I'm ready for the strife:

11. Ready for pain and sickness,
        Ready for care and grief,
    For I know I have in Thee, Lord,
        An ever sure relief;

12. Ready to work and suffer,
        To love, and hope, and pray;
    Ready to go to Thee, Lord,
        When Thou shalt call away.

---

215.   *Psalm* xxvii. 9.

1.   OH! Jesus, leave not me;—
        Tho' full of sin I be,
    Love, love me yet.

Oh ! take me to Thy breast,
For there I 'll find true rest,
And with Thy love possessed,
  All else forget.

2. When I 'm with Thee above,
    I 'll thank Thee for Thy love,
      That sends this pain.
    Tho' dark my way appear,
    And washed with many a tear,
    The prospect yet will clear,
      When heaven I gain.

3. Oh, guide me, Saviour ! now ;
    Submissive, may I bow
      Unto Thy will.
    If trials be my lot,
    My home a far-off spot—
    Yet, Saviour, leave me not !
      Be near me still !

------

216.   1 *Chronicles* xiii. 14.

1. OH, happy house ! O home supremely blest,
      Where Thou, Lord Jesus Christ, art
        entertained,
          27*

As the most welcome and beloved guest,
With true devotion and with love unfeign'd;
Where all hearts beat in unison with Thine,
Where eyes grow brighter as they look on
          Thee,
Where all are ready at the slightest sign,
To do Thy will, and do it heartily.

2.   Oh, happy house! where man and wife are
          one,
Thro' love of Thee, in spirit, heart, and mind;
Together joined by holy bands, which none,
Not death itself, can sever or unbind;
Where both on Thee unfailingly depend,
In weal and woe, in good and evil days,
And hope with Thee eternity to spend,
In sweet communion and eternal praise.

3.   Oh, happy house! where with the hands of
          prayer
Parents commit their children to the Friend,
Who, with a more than mother's tender care,
Will watch and keep them safely to the end;
Where they are taught to sit at Jesus' feet,
And listen to the words of life and truth,
And learn to lisp His praise in accents sweet,
From early childhood to advancing youth.

4. Oh, happy house ! where man and maid pur-
        sue
  Their daily labours as unto the Lord,
  Desiring only that whate'er they do,
  May be according to His will and word ;—
  As servants, yet as friends and brethren too,
  Their love with deep humility combined,
  No less in little than in great things true,
  They serve Him gladly with a willing mind

5. Oh, happy house ! where Thou dost share the
        weal,
  Where none forget Thee whatsoe'er befall ;
  Oh, happy house ! where Thou the wounds
        dost heal,
  The Healer and the Comforter of all ;
  Till every one his stated task hath done,
  And all at length shall peacefully depart
  To the bright realms where Thou Thyself art
        gone,—
  The Father's house where Thou already art.

                FROM LYRA DOMESTICA.

217. *Romans* xiii. 11.

(FOR A NEW YEAR.)

1. REJOICE, my fellow-pilgrim, for another
     stage is o'er,
   Of the weary homeward journey, to be trav-
     ell'd thro' no more:
   No more *these* clouds and shadows shall
     darken all our sky;
   No more *these* snares and stumbling-blocks
     across our path shall lie.

2. Rejoice, my fellow-soldier, for another long
     campaign
   Is ended, and its dangers have not been met
     in vain;
   Some enemies are driven back, some ramparts
     overthrown;
   Some earnests given that victory at length
     shall be our own.

3. Rejoice, my fellow-servant, for another year
     is past;
   The heat and burden of the day will not for
     ever last;
   And yet the work is pleasant now, and sweet
     the Master's smile;
   And well may we be diligent, thro' all our
     "little while."

4. Rejoice, my Christian brother, for the race is
nearly run,
And *home* is drawing nearer with each revolving sun ;
And if some ties are breaking here, of earthly
hope and love,
More sweet are the attractions of the better
land above.

5. The Light that shone thro' all the past will
still our steps attend ;
The Guide who led us hitherto will lead us
to the end ;
The distant view is brightening, with fewer
clouds between ;
The golden streets are gleaming now, the
pearly gates are seen.

6. Oh ! for the joyous greetings *there*, to meet
and part no more ;
For ever with the Lord and all His lov'd ones
gone before !
New mercies from our Father's hand with
each new year may come,
But that will be the best of all,—a blissful
welcome home.

FROM THOUGHTS FOR THOUGHTFUL HOURS.

218.   *Psalm* xxxvi. 9.

1. SOURCE of my life's refreshing springs,
     Whose presence in my heart sustains me,
Thy love appoints me pleasant things,
Thy mercy orders all that pains me.

2. If loving hearts were never lonely,
If all they wish might always be,
Accepting what they look for only,
They might be glad, but not in Thee.

3. Well may Thy own belov'd, who see
In all their lot their Father's pleasure,
Bear loss of all they love, save Thee—
Their living, everlasting treasure.

4. Well may Thy happy children cease
From restless wishes, prone to sin,
And in Thine own exceeding peace,
Yield to Thy daily discipline.

5. We need as much the cross to bear,
As air to breathe —as light to see—
It draws us to Thy side in prayer,
It binds us to our strength in Thee.

219.   2 *Timothy* iv. 8.

1. COME Lord, and tarry not:
       Bring the long-looked for day ;
   O why these years of waiting here,
       These ages of delay ?

2. Come, for Thy saints still wait ;
       Daily ascends their sigh :
   The Spirit and the bride say, Come,—
       Dost Thou not hear the cry ?

3. Come, for Thy Israel pines
       An exile from Thy fold ;
   O call to mind Thy faithful word,
       And bless them, as of old !

4. Come, for the good are few ;
       They lift their voice in vain ;
   Faith waxes fainter on the earth,
       And love is on the wane.

5. Come, for the corn is ripe ;
       Put in Thy sickle now,
   Reap the great harvest of the earth,
       Sower and reaper Thou !

6. Come, in Thy glorious might,
       Come, with the iron rod,

Scattering Thy foes before Thy face,
Most mighty Son of God.

7. Come, and make all things new,
      Build up this ruin'd earth,
Restore our faded Paradise,
      Creation's second birth.

8. Come, and begin Thy reign
      Of everlasting peace,
Come, take the kingdom to Thyself,
      Great King of righteousness.

BONAR.

---

220.   *Luke* xxiv. 30, 31.

(S A C R A M E N T A L.)

1. SHEPHERD of souls, refresh and bless
      Thy chosen pilgrim flock,
With manna from the wilderness,
      With water from the rock.

2. Hungry and thirsty, faint and weak,
      (As Thou when here below,)
Our souls the joys celestial seek,
      That from Thy sorrows flow.

3.   He would not live by bread alone,
  But by Thy word of grace,
 In strength of which we travel on
  To our abiding place.

4.   Be known to us in breaking bread,
  But do not then depart,—
 Saviour, abide with us, and spread
  Thy table in our heart.

5.   Then sup with us in love divine ;
  Thy body and Thy blood,
 That living bread and heavenly wine,
  Be our immortal food.

———

221.   *Canticles* 1, 2.

1.   STILL on thy loving heart let me repose,
  Jesus, sweet Author of my joy and rest ;
 Oh ! let me pour my sorrows, cares, and woes
  Into Thy true and sympathising breast.
 Thy love grows never cold, but its pure flame
  Seems every day more strong and bright to
   glow ;
 Thy truth remains eternally the same,
  Pure and unsullied as the mountain snow.

2.   Oh! what is other love compared with Thine,
   Of such high value, and eternal worth?
  What is man's love compared with love
    divine,
   Which never changes in this changing
    earth;
  Love, which in this cold world grows never
    cold,
   Love, which decays not with the world's
    decay,
  Love, which is young when all things else
    grow old,
   Which lives when heaven and earth shall
    pass away?

3.   How little love unchangeable and fixed
   In this dark valley doth to man remain,
  With what unworthy motives is it mixed,
   How full of grief, uncertainty and pain;
  Love is the object which attracts all eyes,
   We win it, and already fear to part,
  A thousand rivals watch to seize the prize,
   And tear the precious idol from our heart.

4.   But Thou (in spite of our offences past,
   And those alas! which still in us are found)
  Hast loved us, Jesus, with a love so vast,
   No span can reach it, and no plummet
    sound.

Tho' the poor love we give Thee in return
　Should wane and flicker, Thine is ever true,
Its sacred fires eternally doth burn,
　Tho' everlasting, always fresh and new.

5.　Thou, who art ever ready to embrace
　　All those, who truly after Thee inquire,
　Thou, who hast promised in Thy heart a place
　　To all who love Thee and a place desire ;
　Oh ! Lord, when I am anxious and oppressed,
　　And dim with tears mine eyes can hardly
　　　see,
　Oh ! let me lean upon Thy faithful breast,
　　Rejoicing that e'en I am loved by Thee.

FROM LYRA DOMESTICA.

222.　　　*John* xxi. 15-17.

1.　" THOU knowest," Lord, the weariness and
　　　　　sorrow
　Of the sad heart that comes to Thee for rest,
　Cares of to-day and burdens of to-morrow,
　　Blessings implored and sins to be confes-
　　　sed,—
　I come before Thee at Thy gracious word,
　　And lay them at Thy feet—Thou knowest
　　　Lord !

2. " Thou knowest" all the past, how long and
   blindly,
     On the dark mountains the lost wanderer
     strayed,
   How the good Shepherd follow'd, and how
   kindly
       He bore it home upon his shoulders laid,
   And healed the bleeding wounds and soothed
     the pain,
   And brought back life, and hope, and strength
     again.

3. " Thou knowest" all the present, each temp-
       tation,
     Each toilsome duty, each forebodying fear ;
   All to myself assign'd of tribulation,
     Or to beloved ones, than self more dear !
   All pensive memories as I journey on,
   Longings for vanished smiles and voices gone.

4. " Thou knowest" all the future gleams of
       gladness,
     By stormy clouds too quickly overcast,—
   Hopes of sweet fellowship and parting sadness,
     And the dark river to be cross'd at last,—
   Oh ! what could confidence and hope afford
   To tread that path but this, " Thou knowest
     Lord ?"

5. " Thou knowest," not alone as God all
  knowing,
  As man, our mortal weakness Thou hast
   proved
On earth, with purest sympathies o'erflowing,
  O Saviour, Thou hast wept, and Thou hast
   loved !
And love and sorrow still to Thee may come,
And fine a hiding-place, a rest, a home.

6. Therefore I come, Thy gentle call obeying,
  And lay my sins and sorrows at Thy feet,
On everlasting strength my weakness staying,
  Cloth'd in Thy robe of righteousness com-
   plete.
Then rising and refreshed, I leave thy throne,
And follow on to know as I am known.

---

223.   *Galatians* ii. 20.

1 WHILE others pray for grace to die,
  O Lord, I pray for grace to live,
For every hour a fresh supply,
O see my need and freely give.

2. I do not dread the hour of death,
 If I am Thine, no fears remain ;
  28*

I know that with my parting breath
I yield for ever mortal pain.

3. E'en if the darkness should appear
Too deep for faith as well as sight,
If I am Thine Thou wilt be near,
And take me to Thy heavenly light.

4. But Oh! my Lord, in life's highway
I crave the sunshine of Thy face;
And every moment of the day
I need Thy strong supporting grace.

5. I dare not—will not—Lord, deny,
That heart and feet both go astray;
Therefore the more to Thee I cry
To keep me in the chosen way.

6. The more my sin and unbelief
Keep me from walking near to Thee,
The more, Lord Jesus, is my grief—
The more I long Thy face to see.

---

224.   1 *Peter* v. 7.

1. YES! for me, for me He careth,
With a brother's tender care;

Yes ! with me, with me He shareth
Ev'ry burden, ev'ry fear.

2. Yes ! o'er me, o'er me He watcheth,
Ceaseless watcheth, night and day ;
Yes ! even me, even me He snatcheth
From the perils of the way.

3. Yes ! for me He standeth pleading,
At the mercy-seat above ;
Ever for me interceding,
Constant in untiring love.

4. Yes ! in me, in me He dwelleth ;—
I in Him, and He in me !
And my empty soul He filleth.
Here and through eternity.

5. Thus I wait for His returning,
Singing all the way to heaven ;
Such the joyful song of morning,
Such the tranquil song of even.

BONAR.

———

225. *Hebrews* xii. 2.

1. LOOK up, my soul, to Christ thy joy,
With a believing mind ;

With all the ills which thee annoy,
   The way to Jesus find :
Here in this world thou hast no home,
Nor lasting joy ;—to Jesus come ;—
He is the pearl of greatest price,
    Who all thy wants supplies.

2. Steadfast in faith to Jesus cleave,
   His faithfulness review,
And ev'ry burden with Him leave,
  Whose love is daily new :
His ways with thee are just and right,
He puts thy enemies to flight,
However threatening they appear,—
   Take courage, He is near.

3. Thy closet enter, pray and sigh,
   To Jesus tell thy grief,
His ear is open to thy cry,
  His hand to give relief ;
Tho' men forsake thee, hate, and grieve,
Thy Saviour thee will never leave,
His word is pass'd, he 'll aid afford,—
   Rely upon the Lord.

4. Lift up thy heart to Him on high,
   And leave this sordid earth ;
Behold, with a believing eye.
  Christ's excellence and worth :

Devote thy life, thy all, to Him,
Who did thy soul from death redeem,
In love to thee the cross endured,
    And life for thee procured.

5. Arise, and see the things above;
    Let heaven be all thine aim,
Where Jesus dwells in bliss and love,
    And earth and sin disclaim:
The world and all its empty joy
His potent breath will soon destroy;
Abiding rest and peace of mind,
    In Christ alone we find.

---

226.   *John* xiv. 6.

1. AMID life's wild commotion,
    Where nought the heart can cheer,
Who points beyond its ocean
    To heaven's brighter sphere?
Our feeble footsteps guiding,
    When from the path we stray,
Who leads to bliss abiding?—
    Christ is our only *Way.*

2. When doubts and fears distress us,
    And all around is gloom,

And shame and fear oppress us,
    Who can our souls illume?
Heaven's rays are round us gleaming,
    And making all things bright,
The sun of *Truth* is beaming,
    In glory on our sight.

3.   Who fills our hearts with gladness
        That none can take away?
Who shows us 'midst our sadness,
    The distant realms of day?
'Mid fears of death assailing,
    Who stills the heart's wild strife?
'T is Christ! our aid unfailing,
    The *Way*, the *Truth*, the *Life!*

ARNDT.

---

227.   *Psalm* lxvi. 16.

1.   COME and rejoice with me!
        For once my heart was poor,
And I have found a treasury
    Of love, a boundless store.

2.   Come and rejoice with me!
        I, once so sick at heart,
Have met with One who knows my case,
    And knows the healing art.

3.   Come and rejoice with me !
     For I was wearied sore,
  And I have found a mighty arm
     Which holds me evermore.

4.   Come and rejoice with me !
     My feet so wide did roam,
  And One has sought me from afar,
     And beareth me safe home.

5.   Come and rejoice with me !
     For I have found a Friend,
  Who knows my heart's most secret depths,
     Yet loves me without end.

6.   I knew not of His love :
     Yet He had loved me long,
  With love so faithful and so deep,
     So tender and so strong.

7.   And now I know it all,
     Have heard and known His voice,
  And hear it still from day to day ;—
     Can I enough rejoice ?

228.   1 *Peter* ii. 7.

1. PRECIOUS is the name of Jesus!
       Who can half its worth unfold?
   Far beyond angelic praises,
       Sweetly sung to harps of gold.

2. Precious as the Mediator,
       By the Father raised on high,
   Precious when He took our nature,
       Laid His awful glory by.

3. Precious—when to Calvary groaning
       He sustain'd the cursed tree;
   Precious—when His death atoning
       Made an end of sin for thee.

4. Precious—in His death victorious,
       He the host of hell o'erthrows;
   In His resurrection glorious,
       Victor crown'd o'er all His foes.

5. Precious, Lord, beyond expressing,
       Are Thy beauties all divine;
   Glory, honour, power and blessing,
       Be henceforth for ever Thine!

229.   *Hebrews* vi. 19.

1. MY bark is on a troubled sea ;
        The winds and waves may adverse be ;
    But hope, my anchor's firmly cast
    Within the vail, for ever fast.

2. How oft, when tempest-tossed at night,
    I watch in vain for dawning light,
    Yet think, when terrors would prevail,
    My anchor is within the vail.

3. Within the vail,—where Jesus stands,
    And shows to God His blood-stained hands ;
    Within the vail,—He went to bear
    My name upon the breast-plate there.

4. My hope must have His righteousness,
    For it can rest on nothing less ;
    Within the vail,—is still my prayer,
    Oh ! may my anchor enter there.

5. Altho' the billows round me roll,
    They never can o'erwhelm my soul ;
    Within the vail my anchor's cast,
    Unshaken by the stormy blast.

6. Whene'er I quit this changing scene,
    May I depart in hope serene ;

29

And find, when heart and flesh shall fail,
My anchor cast within the vail.

———

230.   1 *Peter* ii. 21.

1.   HOW shall I follow Him I serve ?
          How shall I copy Him I love ?
      Nor from those blessed footsteps swerve,
      Which lead me to His seat above ?

2.   Privations, sorrows, bitter scorn,
      The life of toil, the mean abode,
      The faithless kiss, the crown of thorn,—
      Are these the consecrated road ?

8.   'T was thus He suffered, though a Son,
      Foreknowing, choosing, feeling all,
      Until the perfect work was done,—
      And drank the bitter cup of gall.

4.   Lord, should my path thro' suffering lie,
      Forbid it I should e'er repine ;
      Still let me turn to Calvary,
      Nor heed my griefs, remembering Thine.

5.   O let me think how Thou didst leave
      Untasted every pure delight,

To fast, to faint, to watch, to grieve,
The toilsome day, the homeless night ;

6. To faint, to grieve, to die for me ;
Thou camest not Thyself to please ;
And dear as earthly comforts be,
Shall I not love *Thee* more than these ?

---

231.   1 *Chronicles* xxix. 15.

1. HEAVENWARD our path still goes,
Sojourners on earth we wander,
Till we reach our blest repose,
In the land of promise yonder :
Here we stay a pilgrim band,
There must be our fatherland.

2. Heavenward ! My soul arise,
For thou art a heavenly being,
Thou should'st seek no earthly prize,
When from this world thou art fleeing ;
Hearts with heavenly wisdom blest
Can in heaven alone find rest.

3. Heavenward ! Death's mighty hand
Guides me there to joy and gladness—
There, within that blessed land,
Victor over pain and sadness,

Christ Himself has gone before—
Can *I* dread an unknown shore ?

4. Heavenward ! oh, heavenward !
   There shall be my lot and treasure—
   Let me strive my heart to guard
   From each vain and worldly pleasure :
   Heavenward my thoughts must tend,
   Till in heaven my cares shall end.

SCHMOLCK.

----

232.   *Hebrews* xii. 2.

1. OH, eyes that are weary,
    And hearts that are sore,
  Look off unto Jesus,
  And sorrow no more.
  The light of His countenance
  Shineth so bright,
  That on earth, as in heaven,
  There need be no night.

2. Looking off unto Jesus,
  My eyes cannot see
  The troubles and dangers
  That throng around me :

They cannot be blinded
With sorrowful tears,
They cannot be shadow'd
With unbelief-fears.

3. Looking off unto Jesus,
My spirit is blest,—
In the world I have turmoil,
In Him I have rest.
The sea of my life
All about me may roar, —
When I look unto Jesus
I hear it no more.

4. Looking off unto Jesus,
I go not astray ;
My eyes are on Him,
And He shows me the way.
The path may seem dark
As He leads me along,
But following Jesus
I cannot go wrong.

5 Looking off unto Jesus,
My heart cannot fear ;
Its trembling is still
When I see Jesus near:

I know that His power
My safe-guard will be,
For " why are ye troubled ?"
He saith unto me.

6. Looking off unto Jesus
Oh ! may I be found,
When the waters of Jordan
Encompass me round !
Let them bear me away,
In His presence to be :
'T is but seeing Him nearer
Whom always I see.

7. Then, then shall I know
The full beauty and grace
Of Jesus, my Lord,
When I stand face to face :
I shall know how His love
Went before me each day,
And wonder that ever
My eyes turned away.

---

233. *Psalm* xxv. 5.

1. COME to me, Lord, when first I wake,
As the faint lights of morning break ;

Bid purest thoughts within me rise,
Like fragrant incense to the skies.

2. Come to me in the sultry noon,
    Or earth's low communing will soon
    Of Thy dear face eclipse the light,
    And change my fairest day to night.

3. Come to me in the evening shade,
    And if my heart from Thee hath strayed,
    Oh ! bring it back,—and from afar
    Shine on me like the evening star.

4. Come to me in the midnight hour,
    When sleep withdraws its balmy power,
    Let my lone spirit find its rest,
    Like John, upon my Saviour's breast.

5. Come to me through life's changing way ;
    And when its pulses cease to play,
    Then, Saviour, bid me come to Thee,
    That where Thou art I too may be.

---

234.   *Acts* xxi. 14.

1. MY will would like a life of ease,
        And power to do, and time to rest,

And wealth and health my will would please,
    But, Lord, I know Thy will is best.

2. If I have strength to do Thy will,
    That should be power enough for me ;
  Whether to walk or to sit still,
    Th' appointment of the day may be.

3. And if by sickness I may grow
    More patient, holy, and resigned,
  Strong health I need not wish to know,
    And greater ease I cannot find.

4. And rest—I need not seek it here—
    For perfect rest remaineth still ;
  When in Thy presence we appear
    Rest shall be given by Thy will.

5. Lord, I have given my life to Thee,
    And every day and hour is Thine,
  What Thou appointest, let them be,
    Thy will is better, Lord, than mine.

---

235.   *Revelation* xix. 1.

1. SING hallelujah ! praise the Lord !
    Sing with a cheerful voice ;

Exalt our God with one accord,
And in His name rejoice.
Ne'er cease to sing, thou ransom'd host;
Praise Father, Son, and Holy Ghost,
Until in realms of endless light,
Your praises shall unite.

2. There we to all eternity
Shall join th' angelic lays;
And sing in perfect harmony,
To God our Saviour's praise :—
" He hath redeem'd us by His blood,
And made us kings and priests to God ;"
For us—for us the Lamb was slain,
Praise ye the Lord.   Amen !

---

236.   *Isaiah* **xlv. 22.**

1. THERE is life for a look at the crucified
        One ;
    There is life at this moment for thee,
Then look, sinner, look unto Him and be
        saved,
    Unto Him who was nailed to the tree.

2. Oh ! why was He there as the bearer of sin,
    If on Him all thy sins were not laid ?

Oh! why from His side flowed the sin-cleans-
ing blood,
If His dying thy debt hath not paid?

3. It is not thy tears of repentance or prayers,
But the *blood* that atones for the soul;
On Him, then, who shed it, thou mayest at
once
Thy weight of iniquities roll.

4. His anguish of soul on the cross hast thou
seen?
His cry of distress hast thou heard?
Then why, if the terrors of wrath He en-
dured,
Should pardon to thee be deferred?

5. Thou art healed by His stripes, (would'st
thou add to the word?)
And He is thy righteousness made;
The best robe of heaven He bids thee put on;
Say, could'st thou be better arrayed?

6. Then doubt not thy pardon, since God has
declared,
There remaineth no more to be done,
That once in the end of the world He ap-
peared,
And completed the work He begun.

7. But take with rejoicing from Jesus at once
    The life everlasting He gives,
And know with assurance thou never canst
    die,
    Since Jesus thy righteousness lives.

8. There is life for a look at the crucified One,
    There is life at this moment for thee;
Then look, sinner, look unto Him and be
    saved,
    And know thyself spotless as He.

---

237.   1 *Peter* ii. 11.

1. A PILGRIM here I wander,
    On earth have no abode;
My fatherland is yonder,
    My home is with my God.
For here I journey to and fro,
    There, in eternal rest,
Will God His gracious gift bestow
    On all the toil-oppress'd.

2. For what hath life been giving,
    From youth up till this day,
But constant toil and striving,
    Far back as thought can stray?

How many a day of toil and care,
  How many a night of tears,
Hath pass'd in grief that none could share,
  In lonely anxious fears !

3. How many a storm hath lighten'd
      And thunder'd round my path !
    And winds and rains have frighten'd
      My heart with fiercest wrath ;
    And cruel envy, hatred, scorn,
      Have darken'd oft my lot ;
    And patiently reproach I 've borne,
      Though I deserved it not.

4. Then through this life of dangers
      I 'll onward take my way,
    For in this land of strangers
      I do not think to stay.
    Still forward on the road I fare
      That leads me to my home :
    My Father's comfort waits me there,
      When I have overcome.

5. Ah, yes ! my home is yonder,
      Where all the angelic bands
    Praise Him with awe and wonder,
      In whose Almighty hands

All things that are and shall be, lie,
  By Him upholden still,
Who casteth down and lifts on high
  At His most holy will.

6. That home have I desired;
  'T is there I would be gone;
Till I am well-nigh tir'd,
  O'er earth I've journey'd on;
The longer here I roam, I find
  The less of real joy,
That e'er could please or fill my mind,—
  For all hath some alloy.

7. Where now my spirit stayeth
  Is not her true abode;
This earthly house decayeth,
  And she will drop its load.
When comes the hour to leave beneath
  What now I use and have,
And when I've yielded up my breath,
  Earth gives me but a grave.

8. But Thou, my joy and gladness,
  Jesus, my life and light,
Will raise me from this sadness,
  This long tempestuous night,

Into the perfect gladsome day.
　　Where, bathed in joy divine,
Among Thy saints, and bright as they,
　　I too shall ever shine.

9.　　There shall I dwell for ever,
　　Not as a guest alone,
With those who cease there never
　　To worship at Thy throne;
There in my heritage, I'll rest,
　　From baser things set free,
And join the chorus of the blest
　　For ever, Lord, to Thee!

FROM LYRA GERMANICA.

238.　　　　　*John* xvi. 18.

1.　OH! for the peace which floweth as a river,
　　　Making life's desert places bloom and
　　　smile!
　　Oh! for the faith to grasp heaven's bright
　　　" for ever,"
　　Amid the shadows of that "little while!"

2.　" A little while" for patient vigil-keeping,
　　　To face the storm, to wrestle with the
　　　strong;

" A little while " to sow the seed with weep-
    ing,
    Then bind the sheaves and sing the harvest
    song.

3. " A little while " to wear the robe of sadness,
    And toil with weary step through miry
    ways;
    Then to pour forth the fragrant oil of glad-
    ness,
    And clasp the girdle round the robe of
    praise.

4. " A little while," midst shadow and illusion,
    To strive, by faith, love's mysteries to spell;
    Then read each dark enigma's bright solution,
    And hail sight's verdict, " He doth all
    things well."

5. " A little while " the earthen pitcher taking
    To wayside brooks, from far-off fountains
    fed;
    Then the cool lip its thirst for ever slaking,
    Beside the fulness of the fountain-head.

6. " A little while " to keep the oil from failing,
    " A little while " faith's flickering lamp to
    trim;

And then the Bridegroom's coming footsteps
    hailing,
    To haste to meet Him with the bridal
      hymn.

7.   Thus He who is Himself the gift and giver,
    The future glory, and the present smile,
    With the bright promise of the glad " for
      ever,"
    Can light the shadows of the " little while."

---

239.   *Philippians* iv. 11.

1.   M Y Lord hath taught me how to want
      A place wherein to put my head ;
    While He is mine, I 'll be content
    To beg or lack my daily bread.

2.   Heaven is my roof, earth is my floor,
    Thy love can keep me dry and warm ;
    Christ and Thy bounty are my store,
    Thy angels guard me from all harm.

3.   Must I forsake the soil and air,
    Where first I drew my vital breath ?
    That way may be as near and fair ;
    Thence I may come to Thee by death.

4. All countries are my Father's lands—
Thy sun, Thy love, doth shine on all ;
We may in all lift up pure hands,
And with acceptance on Thee call.

5. What, if in prison I must dwell,—
May I not there converse with Thee ?
Save me from sin, Thy wrath, and hell,
Call me Thy child, and I am free.

6. No walls or bars can keep Thee' out ;
None can confine a holy soul ;
The streets of heaven it walks about,
None can its liberty control.

RICHARD BAXTER.

---

240.   *Isaiah* liii. 5.

1. THY works, not mine, O Christ !
      Speak gladness to this heart ;
They tell me all is done ;
      They bid my fear depart.
            To whom, save Thee,
            Who can alone
            For sin atone,
            Lord, shall I flee ?

30*

2. Thy pains, not mine, O Christ!
      Upon the shameful tree,
    Have paid the law's full price,
      And purchased peace for me.
                To whom, save Thee, etc.

3. Thy wounds, not mine, O Christ!
      Can heal my bruised soul,
    Thy stripes, not mine, contain
      The balm that makes me whole.
          .   To whom, save Thee, etc.

4. Thy cross, not mine, O Christ!
      Has borne the awful load
    Of sins, that none in heaven
      Or earth could bear, but God.
                To whom, save Thee. etc.

5. Thy death, not mine, O Christ!
      Has paid the ransom due;
    Ten thousand deaths like mine,
      Would have been all too few.
                To whom, save Thee, etc.

6. Thy righteousness, O Christ!
      Alone can cover me;
    No righteousness avails,
      Save that which is of Thee.
                To whom, save Thee, etc.

7.   Thy righteousness alone
        Can clothe and beautify :
     I wrap it round my soul ;—
        In this I'll live and die.
                To whom, save Thee, etc.

                                    BONAR.

———

241.   2 *Corinthians* ix. 15.

1.   COME, worship at Emmanuel's feet ;
        Behold in Him what wonders meet !
     Words are too feeble to express
     His worth, His glory, or His grace.

2.   He is the Head—each member lives,
     And owns the vital power He gives,
     The saints below, and saints above,
     Joined by His Spirit and His love.

3.   He is the Vine—His heavenly root
     Supplies each branch with life and fruit ;
     Oh ! may a lasting union join
     My soul to Christ, the living Vine.

4.   He is the Rock—how firm He proves !
     The Rock of ages never moves ;
     But the sweet streams that from Him flow,
     Attend us all the journey through.

5.   He is the Sun of righteousness,
     Diffusing light, and joy, and peace ;
     What healing in His beams appears,
     To chase our clouds and dry our tears !

6.   Yet faintly to us mortals here,
     His glory, grace, and worth appear ;
     His beauties we shall clearly trace,
     When we behold Him face to face.

---

242.   *2 Kings* xx. 19.

1.   WHATE'ER my God ordains is right !
         His will is ever just ;
     Howe'er He orders now my cause,
         I will be still and trust.
             He is my God,
             Though dark my road ;
     He holds me that I shall not fall,
     Wherefore to Him I leave it all.

2   Whate'er my God ordains is right !
         He never will deceive ;
     He leads me by the proper path,
         And so to Him I cleave,

And take content
What He hath sent ;—
His hand can turn my griefs away,
And patiently I wait His day.

3.   Whate'er my God ordains is right !
He taketh thought for me ;
The cup that my Physician gives
No poison'd draught can be,
But medicine due ;
For God is true,
And on that changeless truth I build,
And all my heart with hope is fill'd.

4.   Whate'er my God ordains is right !
Though I the cup must drink,
That bitter seems to my faint heart,
I will not fear nor shrink ;
Tears pass away
With dawn of day ;
Sweet comfort yet shall fill my heart.
And pain and sorrow all depart.

5.   Whate'er my God ordains is right !
My Light, my Life is He,
Who cannot will me aught but good,
I trust Him utterly ;

For well I know,
In joy or woe,
We soon shall see as sunlight clear,
How faithful was our Guardian here.

6. Whate'er my God ordains is right!
   Here will I take my stand,
Though sorrow, need, or death make earth
   For me a desert land.
      My Father's care
      Is round me there;
He holds me that I shall not fall,
And so to Him I leave it all.

                    FROM LYRA GERMANICA.

---

243.   *Hebrews* xiii. 14.

1. I AM a stranger here;
      No home, no rest I see;
   Not all earth counts most dear
      Can win a sigh from me.
            I'm going home.

2. Jesus, Thy home is mine,
      And I Thy Father's child;

With hopes and joys divine,
  The world 's a dreary wild.
          I 'm going home.

3. Home! oh! how soft and sweet,
      It thrills upon the heart!
    Home! where the brethren meet
      And never, never part.
          I 'm going home.

4. Home! where the Bridegroom takes
      The purchase of His love:
    Home! where the Father waits
      To welcome saints above.
          I 'm going home.

5. Yes! when the world looks cold,
      Which did my Lord revile,
    A lamb within the fold,
      I can look up and smile.
          I 'm going home.

6. When earth's delusive charms
      Would snare my pilgrim feet,
    I fly to Jesus' arms,
      And yet again repeat,
          I 'm going home.

7. When breaks each mortal tie
   That holds me from the goal,
This, this can satisfy
   The cravings of my soul,—
      I 'm going home.

8. Ah ! gently, gently lead,
   Along the painful way,
Bid every word and deed,
   And every look to say,
      I 'm going home.

——

244.   *Philippians* iv. 6.

1. HAST Thou within a care so deep,
   It chases from thine eyelids sleep?
To thy Redeemer take that care,
And change anxiety to prayer.

2. Hast Thou a hope with which thy heart
Would almost feel it death to part?
Entreat thy God that hope to crown,
Or give thee strength to lay it down.

3. Hast thou a friend whose image dear,
May prove an idol worshipped here?
Implore the Lord that nought may be,
A shadow between heaven and thee.

4. Whate'er the care which breaks thy rest—
Whate'er the wish that swells thy breast—
Spread before God that wish, that care,
And change anxiety to prayer.

---

245. *Psalm* xlii. 5.

1. WHY restless, why so weary,
    My soul, why so cast down?
Is all around thee dreary?
    And hath the cross no crown?

2. Where is the God that found thee,
    Who once could make thee glad?
His arms are still around thee;
    Then wherefore art thou sad?

8. O trust the Lord who bought thee;
    O trust the sinner's Friend;
The wondrous love that sought thee
    Will keep thee to the end;—

4. 'T will give a glorious morrow
    To this thy night of pain,
And make thy dews of sorrow
    Like shining after rain.

31

246.   *Revelation* xxii. 5.

1.   NO shadows yonder !—
     All light and song !—
Each day I wonder,
And say, How long
Shall time me sunder
From that dear throng ?

2.   No weeping yonder,—
All fled away !
While here I wander
Each weary day,
And sigh as I ponder
My long, long stay.

3.   No partings yonder !—
Time and space never
Again shall sunder,—
Hearts cannot sever,—
Dearer and fonder
Hands clasp for ever.

4.   None wanting yonder !—
Bought by the Lamb,
All gathered under
The evergreen palm,
Loud as night's thunder
Ascends the glad psalm.

                            BONAR.

247.   *Galatins* vi. 14.

1. NEVER further than Thy cross !
    Never higher than thy feet !
    Here earth's precious things seem dross ;
    Here earth's bitter things seem sweet.

2. Gazing thus our sin we see,
    Learn Thy love whilst gazing thus ;—
    Sin which laid the cross on Thee,
    Love which bore the cross for us.

3. Here from pomp and pride retired,
    Nothing we would seem and be ;
    Dust, yet with Thy life inspir'd,
    Nothing, but beloved by Thee.

4. Symbols of our liberty
    And our service here unite,
    Captives by Thy cross made free,
    Soldiers of Thy cross we fight.

5. Pressing onwards as we can,
    Still to this our life shall tend ;
    Where faith's earliest steps began,
    May life's latest moments end !

6. 'Till amid the hosts of light,
    We in Thee redeem'd, complete,
    Through Thy cross made pure and white,
    Cast our crowns before Thy feet.

248.   *Genesis* xxxii. 26.

1.   I WILL not let Thee go, Thou Help in time
        of need !
    Heap ill on ill,
    I trust Thee still,
   E'en when it seems as Thou would'st slay
        indeed !
    Do as Thou wilt with me,
    I yet will cling to Thee ;
   Hide Thou Thy face,—yet, Help in time of
        need,
    I will not let Thee go !

2.   I will not let Thee go.—Should I forsake my
        bliss ?
    No, Lord, Thou 'rt mine,
    And I am Thine,
   Thee will I hold when all things else I miss.
    Though dark and sad the night,
    Joy cometh with the light ;
   O Thou my Sun, should I forsake my bliss ?
    I will not let Thee go !

3.   I will not let Thee go, my God, my life, my
        Lord !
    Not death can tear
    Me from His care,
   Who for my sake His soul in death outpour'd.

Thou diedst for love to me ;
I say, in love to Thee,
E'en when my heart shall break, my God, my
Life, my Lord,
I will not let Thee go !

FROM LYRA GERMANICA.

---

249. *Matthew* vi. 34.

1. "TAKE no thought for the morrow," its
trials, or dangers,
Why burden thy spirit with deepening gloom ?
Ah ! to-day hath enough to distress and per-
plex thee,
It needeth no shadow of dark things to come.

2. " Take no thought for the morrow'" no sorrow shall touch thee,
But that which thy God in His love hath
decreed ;
Go to Christ with thy grief—as it daily
ariseth,
And seek for His strength in the *moment* of
need.

31*

3. " Take no thought for the morrow," rich mercy
        abounding,
    Has marked ev'ry step of thy path-way till
        now ;
    Put thy trust, then, in God, for the still dis-
        tant future,
    Effacing those dark lines of care from thy
        brow.

4. " Take no thought for the morrow," its dawn-
        ing may find thee
    A spirit at rest 'neath the altar of God,
    With the *last* battle fought, and the *last* trial
        ended,
    The victory won through Emmanuel's blood.

------

250.   *Genesis* xlvii. 9.

1. HOW weary and how worthless this life at
        times appears !
    What days of heavy musings, what hours of
        bitter tears !
    How dark the storm-clouds gather across the
        wintry skies !
    How desolate and cheerless the path before us
        lies !

2. And yet these days of dreariness are sent us
   from above,
   They do not come in anger, but in faithfulness and love ;—
   They come to teach us lessons which bright
   ones could not yield ;
   And to leave us blest and thankful when
   their purpose is fulfilled.

3. They come to draw us nearer our Father and
   our God,
   More earnestly to seek His face, and listen to
   His word,
   And to feel, if now around us a desert land
   we see,
   Without the star of promise, what would its
   darkness be ?

4. They come to lay us lowly and humbled in
   the dust,
   All self-deception swept away, all creature-
   hope and trust,
   Our helplessness, our vileness, our guilt to
   make us own,
   And flee for hope and refuge to Jesus Christ
   alone.

5. They come to break the fetters, which here
   detain us fast,
   And force our long-reluctant hearts to rise to
   heaven at last,
   And brighten ev'ry prospect of that eternal
   home,
   Where grief, and disappointment, and fear
   can never come.

6. Then turn not in despondence, poor weary
   heart, away,
   But meekly journey onwards, through the
   dark and cloudy day ;
   E'en now the bow of promise is above thee
   shining bright,
   And soon a joyful morning shall dissipate
   the night.

7. Thy God hath not forgot thee, and when He
   sees it best,
   Will lead thee into sunshine, will give thee
   hours of rest ;
   And all thy pain and sorrow, when the pilgrimage is o'er,
   Shall end in heavenly blessedness, and joys
   for evermore.

251.   *Psalm* xxvii. 14.

1.   IN days of trouble and of care,
       I sought a message from above,
    Brief was the answer to my prayer,
      Few were the words, but full of love—
    Ye who mourn an adverse fate,
    Hear the message—" Pray and wait."

2.   Pray, the Lord is ever nigh,
      Ready still with open ear ;
    Wait—and He will yet supply
      Hope and strength, for every fear.
    Pilgrim, weeping at the gate,
    Hear His message—" Pray and wait."

3.   Pray, He knows thy ev'ry thought—
      Understands thy secret grief ;
    Wait,—He sends it not for nought,
      He will surely bring relief.
    Seeing all thy troubled state,
    Still He whispers—" Pray and wait."

4.   Does the way seem long and drear
      To thy sad bewilder'd sight ?
    Pray, and thou wilt see Him near,
      Wait,—He 'll lead thee to the light.
    Seek Him early, seek Him late ;
    Fear not, doubt not—" Pray and wait."

5.   Dost thou long the day to see,
      When thy Saviour shall appear?
   Pray, that thou may'st watchful be;
      Wait, the day is drawing near.
   Joyfully thou 'lt then relate,
   'T was not in vain to—" Pray and wait."

6:    Weeping prayers are heard no more
      From that home of endless joy;
   Days of waiting all are o'er,
      Songs of praise each tongue employ;
   They who enter Zion's gate,
   Need no more to—" Pray and wait."

---

252.   *Matthew* viii. 26.

1.   CALM me, my God, and keep me calm,
      While these hot breezes blow;
   Be like the night dew's cooling balm
      Upon earth's fever'd brow.

2.   Calm me, my God, and keep me calm,
      Soft resting on Thy breast,
   Soothe me with holy hymn and psalm,
      And bid my spirit rest.

3. Yes! keep me calm, though loud and rude
   The sounds my ear that greet;
Calm in the closet's solitude;
   Calm in the bustling street;—

4. Calm in the day of buoyant health;
   Calm in my hour of pain;
Calm in my poverty or wealth;
   Calm in my loss or gain;—

5. Calm in the sufferance of wrong,
   Like Him who bore my shame;
Calm 'mid the threatening, taunting throng,
   Who hate Thy holy name;—

6. Calm when the great world's news with power
   My listening spirits stir,—
Let not the tidings of the hour
   E'er find too fond an ear;—

7. Calm as the ray of sun or star
   Which storms assail in vain,
Moving unruffled through earth's war,
   Th' eternal calm to gain.

                              BONAR

253.   *James* i. 2.

1.   I THINK of Thee, O Saviour,
     And count affliction gain,
  If aught of suffering aid me
     To realize Thy pain.

2.   I think of Thee, O Saviour,
     And bless the chastening rod,
  Conforming to Thine image,
     Thou chasten'd Son of God.

3.   My sufferings no atonement
     For sin could make to God;
  Alone, of all the people,
     Thou hast the winepress trod.

4.   So there is nought of anger
     In this my Father's stroke;
  He is but gently teaching
     My neck to bear the yoke.

5.   And it is joy, my Saviour!
     A blessed joy to think,
  The cup I am but tasting
     Thou didst vouchsafe to drink.

6.   I would press closer to Thee,
     A heavier cross to bear,

So I might better know Thee,
And more Thy spirit share.

7.   Soon, as Thou overcamest,
        I too shall overcome ;
     And bless the love which kept me
        So long away from home.

8.   I had been lost for ever,
        Had 'st Thou not thought on me ;
     Cold is my heart and selfish ;—
        Yet, Lord, I think on Thee.

———

254.   2 *Corinthians* vii. 10.

1. REJOICE,—'t is not in sorrow
        To dim that fund of joy ;
    No darkening to-morrow
    Its brightness can destroy.
    For in the Christian's heart is found
    One little spot of sacred ground,—
    The waves may beat, the winds increase,
    They cannot reach that spot of peace.

2.   Rejoice when thou art feeling
     The keenest earthly smart,
     For then thy Lord is sealing
     His name upon thy heart.

For often through the glare of day
A cloudy pillar marks the way,
But in the dark and starless night
It changes to a shining light.

3. Rejoice, though thou art waging
A truceless war within,
With evil spirits raging,
And a heart prone to sin.
For He who leads thee through the fray,
Has fought the fight—has won the day;
His strength thy shield, thy guide His voice,
Sorrowful Christian, still rejoice.

255.　　　　*Revelation* ii. 10.

1. BE faithful to the end !
Let not danger nor distress
Make thy heart love Jesus less.
Until death trust thou that Friend !
Ah ! the suffering of this earth,
All the glory is not worth
Which Thy Lord will give to thee,
When up yonder thou shalt be.

2. Be faithful in thy grief !
Let not storms from Christ divide,

Let not weeping Jesus hide.
    Murmur not, to get relief;
For impatience makes thy care
Heavier much for thee to bear,
Happy he, who childlike will
Let God lead him up the hill!

3. Be faithful in thy faith !
Let not any robber bold
Take it from thy heart's stronghold ;
    Keep thy covenant till death.
Then in the o'erflowing wave
God is with thee, strong to save.
Ah ! thou goest there forlorn,
When thou art to Him forsworn !

4. Be faithful in thy love !
See the love God has for thee !
Love thy neighbour, e'en when he
    Lays more cares, thy care above.
Think how Jesus prayed for those,
By whose hands His cross arose.
E'en as God doth thee forgive,
So let mercy in thee live.

5· And in thy hope stand true !
Trust thou firmly in God's word !
Is thy cry in trouble heard,
    Comes He not to help thee through ?

Hope thou in Him firmly yet,
For the Lord doth not forget ;
Even now is help proclaim'd ;
Hope can never make ashamed

6. Then forward ! steadfast be,
In faith, love, hope, for ever !
Lord, I hear, and I will never
        Leave my God, who leaves not me.
He is my soul's rejoicing still,
Griefs no more my joy can kill.
Reach forth Thy hand, O God, my Friend !
Make me faithful to the end.

---

256.   *Micah* vi. 6.

1. HOW shall I meet my Saviour ?
        How shall I welcome Thee ?
What manner of behaviour
    Is now required of me ?
I wait for Thy salvation ;
    Grant me Thy Spirit's light,
Thus will my preparation
    Be pleasing in Thy sight.

2. While with her sweetest flowers
    Thy Zion strews Thy way,

I'll raise with all my powers
  To Thee a grateful lay;
To Thee, the King of glory,
  I'll tune a song divine,
And make Thy love's bright story
  In graceful numbers shine.

3. What hast Thou not performed,
      Lord to retrieve my loss,
    Whilst I was so deformed
      By sin and nature's dross!
    Thou raised'st me to glory,
      Endowed'st me with bliss,
    Which is not transitory,
      As worldly grandeur is.

4. No sinful man's endeavour,
      Nor any mortal's care,
    Could draw Thy sovereign favour
      To sinners in despair;
    Uncall'd thou cam'st with gladness,
      Us from the fall to raise,
    And change our grief and sadness
      To songs of joy and praise.

5. Ye, who with deep contrition
      Bemoan your sinful state,

32*

Fear not,—Christ gives remission
  Of sins, however great.
He comes, repenting sinners
  With life and love to crown,
And make them happy winners
  Of glory like His own.

———

257.   1 *Peter* ii. 21.

1. HE suffer'd !   And wilt thou repine
      In this thy Master's lot to join ?
    He died for thee !   And wouldst not thou
    Die to the world's seducing show ?
    He prayed for *thee !*   Wilt thou be slow
    To seek the grace He can bestow ?

2. He lived for thee !   Wilt thou not strive
    Henceforth to Him alone to live ?
    He bore God's curse thy soul to save !
    And fearest thou man's wrath to brave ?
    He bore the cross !   Wilt thou refuse
    To bear the cross His love shall choose ?

3. He rose for thee !   From earth arise,
    And fix thy gaze upon the skies !
    He loves thee !   Wilt thou turn away ?
    He calls thee on !   Wilt thou delay ?

Thou, whom He suffer'd to redeem,
Brother, make haste to follow Him.

E. Z. B.

---

258.   *John* i. 35.

1. MASTER, where abidest Thou ?
        Lamb of God, 't is Thee we seek ;
    For the wants which press us now,
        Other aid is all too weak.
    Can'st Thou take our sins away ?
        Can we find repose in Thee ?
    From Thy gracious lips to-day,
        As of old, breathes, " Come and see."

2. Master, where abidest Thou ?
        How shall we Thine image best
    Bear without upon our brow,
        Stamp within upon our breast ?
    Still a look is all our might ;
        Looking draws the heart to Thee,
    Sends us from th' absorbing sight
        With the message, " Come and see."

3. Christian, tell it to thy brother,
        From life's dawning to its end :
    Every hand may clasp another,
        And the loneliest bring a friend ;

Till the veil is drawn aside,
   And from where her home shall be,
Bursts upon the enfranchised bride,
   The triumphant, " Come and see."

---

259.   *Ezekiel* xxxvii. 9.

1.   SPIRIT of everlasting grace,
   Infinite source of life, come down !
These tombs unlock, these dead upraise,
Thy glorious power and love make known.

2.   Breathe o'er the valley of the dead,
   Send forth Thy quickening might abroad,
   Till, rising from their tombs, they spread
   In full array,—the host of God !

3.   Thy heritage lies desolate,
   And all Thy pleasant places mourn ;
   O look upon our low estate ;
   In loving-kindness, Lord, return !

4.   Now let Thy glory be revealed ;
   Now let Thy presence with us rest ;
   O heal us, and we shall be healed !
   O bless us, and we shall be blest !

260.   *Psalm* xviii. 46.

1. GOD liveth ever!
    Wherefore, soul, despair thou never!
    Our God is good; in ev'ry place
    His love is known, His help is found;
    His mighty arm, and tender grace,
    Bring good from ills that hem us round.
    Easier than we think can He
    Turn to joy our agony;
    Soul, remember 'mid thy pains,
    God o'er all for ever reigns!

2. God liveth ever!
    Wherefore, soul, despair thou never!
    Say, shall He slumber, shall He sleep,
    Who gave the eye its power to see?
    Shall He not hear his children weep
    Who made the ear so wondrously?
    God is God; He sees and hears
    All our troubles, all our tears.
    Soul, forget not 'mid thy pains,
    God o'er all for ever reigns!

3. God liveth ever!
    Wherefore, soul, despair thou never!
    He who can earth and heaven control,
    Who spreads the clouds o'er sea and land,

Whose presence fills the mighty whole,
In each true heart is close at hand.
Love Him : He will surely send
Help and joy that never end.
Soul, remember in thy pains,
God o'er all for ever reigns !

4. God liveth ever !
Wherefore, soul, despair thou never !
Scarce canst thou bear thy cross ?   Then fly
To Him where only rest is sweet.
God is great ; His mercy nigh,
His strength upholds the tottering feet.
Trust Him, for His grace is sure,
Ever doth His truth endure.
Soul, forget not in thy pains,
God o'er all for ever reigns !

5. God liveth ever !
Wherefore, soul, despair thou never !
When sins and follies long forgot
Upon thy tortured conscience prey,
O come to God, and fear Him not,
His love shall sweep them all away.
Pains of hell, at look of His,
Change to calm content and bliss.
Soul, remember in thy pains,
God o'er all for ever reigns !

6. God liveth ever!
    Wherefore, soul, despair thou never!
    Those whom the thoughtless world forsakes,
    Who stand bewilder'd with their woe,
    God gently to His bosom takes,
    And bids them all His fulness know.
    In thy sorrow's swelling flood
    Own His hand who seeks thy good.
    Soul, forget not in thy pains,
    God o'er all for ever reigns!

7. God liveth ever!
    Wherefore, soul, despair thou never!
    Let earth and heaven outworn with age,
    Sink to the chaos whence they came;
    Let angry foes against us rage,
    Let hell shoot forth its fiercest flame;
    Fear not death, nor Satan's thrusts,
    God defends who in Him trusts;
    Soul, remember in thy pains,
    God o'er all for ever reigns!

8. God liveth ever!
    Wherefore, soul, despair thou never!
    What though thou tread with bleeding feet
    A thorny path of grief and gloom,
    Thy God will choose the way most meet
    To lead thee heavenwards—lead thee home.

For this life's long night of sadness,
He will give thee peace and gladness.
Soul, remember in thy pains,
God o'er all for ever reigns!

FROM LYRA GERMANICA.

---

261.   *Hebrews* xi. 14.

1.   I AM bound for the kingdom! Tempt me
            not
     My spirit to delay ;
   In this wide world there's not a spot
     Where I would wish to stay.

2.   I am bound for the kingdom! Hopes are mine
            mine
     Brighter than all below ;
   I go where the glorious angels shine,
     And saints made perfect glow.

3.   I go where is waving the ever-green,
     And life-bestowing tree ;
   No flashing sword shall intervene
     To bar its fruit from me.

4.   I go where every sound is sweet,
     And every sight is fair ;

My longing heart and soul shall meet
  Full satisfaction there.

5. I am bound for the kingdom !   Not a spot
      On earth can tempt my stay ;
    Ye friends beloved ! will ye not
      With me too come away ?

E. W.

---

262.   *Psalm* xxxvii. 7.

1. BE still, my soul, Jehovah loveth thee ;
      Fret not, nor murmur at thy weary lot ;
    Though dark and lone thy journey seems to
          be,
      Be sure that thou art ne'er by Him forgot.
    He ever loves ; then trust Him, trust Him
          still ;
    Let all thy care be this—the doing of His
          will ;

2. Thy hand in His, like fondest, happiest child,
      Place thou, nor draw it for a moment
          thence ;
    Walk thou with Him, a Father reconciled,
      Till in His own good time He calls thee
          hence.

Walk with Him now,—so shall thy way be
  bright,
And all thy soul be fill'd with His most glorious light.

3. Fight the good fight of faith, nor turn aside
      Through fear of peril from or earth or hell;
    Take to thee now the armour proved and
      tried.
        Take to thee spear and sword ;—oh ! wield
          them well.
    So shalt thou conquer here, to win the day,
    To wear the crown when this hard life has
      passed away.

4. Take courage, faint not, tho' the foe be strong,
      Christ is thy strength ! He fighteth on thy
        side ;
    Swift be thy race ; remember 't is not long, ·
      The goal is near; the prize He will provide.
    And then from earthly toil thou restest ever ;
    Never again to toil, or fight, or fear :—oh !
      never.

5. He comes, with His reward ; 't is just at
      hand ;
      He comes in glory to His promised throne ;

My soul rejoice ; ere long thy feet shall stand
   Within the city of the Blessed One, —
Thy perils past, thy heritage secure,
Thy tears all wiped away, thy joy for ever
    sure.

----

263.   *Job* vii. 3.

(FOR AN INVALID.)

1. LORD, a whole long day of pain
      Now at last is o'er !
Ah ! how much we can sustain
  I have felt once more ;
Felt how frail are all our powers,
  And how weak our trust ;
If Thou help not, these dark hours
  Crush us to the dust.

2. Could I face the coming night,
    If Thou wert not near ?
Nay, without Thy love and might
  I must sink with fear.
Round me falls the evening gloom,
  Sights and sounds all cease,
But within this narrow room
  Night will bring no peace.

3.   Other weary eyes may close,
     All things seek their sleep,
     Hither comes no soft repose,
     I must wake and weep.
     Come then, Jesus, o'er me bend,
     Give me strength to cope
     With my pains, and gently send
     Thoughts of peace and hope.

4.   Draw my weary heart away
     From this gloom and strife,
     And these fever-pains allay
     With the dew of life.
     Thou canst calm the troubled mind,
     Thou its dread canst still,
     Teach me to be all-resign'd
     To my Father's will.

———

264.   *Isaiah* xxvi. 4.

1.   TRUST on, trust on, believer!
       Though long the conflict be,
     Thou yet shalt prove victorious,
     Thy God shall fight for thee.

2.   Trust on, trust on! thy failings
     May bow thee to the dust;

Yet in thy deepest sorrow
Oh, give not up thy trust.

3. Trust on ! the danger presses ;
Temptation strong is near ;
Over life's dangerous rapids
Who shall thy passage steer ?

4. Jesus is strong to save thee !
He is a faithful friend,
Trust on, trust on, believer !
Trust Jesus to the end.

E. W.

---

265.   *Psalm* cvii. 26.

1. LORD ! the waves are breaking o'er me and
   around ;
Oft of coming tempest I hear the moaning
   sound ;
Here there is no safety rocks on either hand ;
'T is a foreign roadstead, a strange and hostile land.
Wherefore should I linger ?   Others gone
   before
Long since safe are landed on a calm and
   friendly shore.

33*

Now the sailing orders, in mercy, Lord, be-
    stow,—
  Loose the cable, let me go !

2. Lord ! the night is closing round my feeble
        bark ;
    How shall I encounter its watches long and
        dark ?
    Sorely worn and shatter'd by many a billow
        past,
    Can I stand another rude and stormy blast ?
    Ah !. the promised haven I never may attain,
    Sinking and forgotten amid the lonely main ;
    Enemies around me, gloomy depths below.
        Loose the cable, let me go !

3. Lord ! I would be near Thee, with Thee where
        Thou art,—
    Thine own word hath said it, " 't is better to
        depart,"
    There to serve Thee better, there to love Thee
        more,
    With Thy ransom'd people to worship and
        adore.
    Ever to Thy presence Thou dost call Thine
        own—
    Why am I remaining helpless and alone ?

Oh ! to see Thy glory, Thy wondrous love to
  know !
    Loose the cable, let me go !

4. Lord ! the lights are gleaming from the dis-
      tant shore,
    Where no billows threaten, where no tem-
      pests roar ;
    Long beloved voices, calling me, I hear,—
    Oh ! how sweet their summons falls upon
      mine ear !
    Here are foes and strangers, faithless hearts
      and cold,
    There is fond affection, fondly proved of old !
    Let me haste to join them ! may it not be so ?
      Loose the cable, let me go !

5. Hark ! the solemn answer ! Hark ! the pro-
      mise sure !
    " Blessed are the servants who to the end
      endure !"
    Yet a little longer, tarry and hope on,—
    Yet a little longer, weak and weary one !
    More to perfect patience, to grow in faith
      and love,
    More *My* serength and wisdom and faithful-
      ness to prove ;

Then the sailing orders the Captain *shall*
   bestow,—
     Loose the cable, let thee go.

---

266.   *John* xiv. 27.

1.   LET not your hearts be faint ;
     My peace I give to you,
  Such peace as reason never plann'd,
    As worldlings never knew.

2.   'T is not the stilly calm
     That bodes a tempest nigh,
  Or lures the heedless mariner
    Where rocks and quicksands lie.

3.   It is not nature's sleep,
     The stupor of the soul,
  That knows not God, nor owns His hand,
    Tho' wide His thunders roll.

4.   It speaks a ransomed world,
     A Father reconciled,
  A sinner to a saint transformed,
    A rebel to a child.

5.   It tells of joys to come,
     It soothes the troubled breast,

It shines a star amid the storm,
   The harbinger of rest.

6. Then murmur not, nor mourn,
   My people faint and few,
Tho' earth to its foundation shake,
   My peace I leave with you.

———

267.   *Acts* xi. 23.

1. CLING to the Mighty One,
     Cling in thy grief;
Cling to the Holy One,
     He gives relief;
Cling to the Gracious One,
     Cling in thy pain:
Cling to the Faithful One,
     He will sustain.

2. Cling to the Living One,
     Cling in thy woe;
Cling to the Loving One,
     Through all below;
Cling to the Pard'ning One,
     He speaketh peace;
Cling to the Healing One,
     Anguish shall cease

3.   Cling to the Bleeding One,
            Cling to His side;
      Cling to the Risen One,
            In Him abide.
      Cling to the Coming One,
            Hope shall arise;
      Cling to the Reigning One,
            Joy lights thine eyes.

---

268.   *Judges* viii. 4.

1.   I DO not doubt my safety—that Thy hand
          Will still uphold me, even to the last,
      And that my feet on Canaan's hill shall stand,
          When the long wilderness is overpast;
      But often faith is weak, and hope is low;
      Forward, indeed, but faint and wearily I go.

2.   I do not doubt Thy love, my Lord and God,
          The love which suffer'd and which died
              for me,
          The love that sought me on the downward
              road,
          Unclasp'd the fetters, set the captive free!
      But mine seems now so languid, dull and
              cold—
      O for the blissful hours which I have known
              of old!

3.   I do not doubt, unworthy though I be,
        Thy worthiness, my Saviour, is my own !
    One of Thy many mansions is for me,
        In the good land where sorrow is unknown ;
    But often clouds obscure the distant scene,
    And from the flood I shrink, which darkly
        rolls between.

4.   Lord ! at the evening time let there be light ;
        Unveil Thy presence, bid all darkness fly ;
    Surely, ere now, far spent must be the night,
        The morning comes, the journey's end is
        nigh ;
    Renew my strength, what yet remains to run,
    Till glory crown the work which grace has
        here begun.

---

269.   *Hebrews* xiii. 5.

1.   Be thou content ; be still before
        His face, at whose right hand doth reign
    Fullness of joy for evermore,
        Without whom all thy toil is vain.
    He is thy living spring, thy sun, whose rays
    Make glad with life and light thy dreary days.
        Be thou content.

2. In Him is comfort, light, and grace,
        And changeless love beyond our thought;
    The sorest pang, the worst disgrace,
        If He is there, shall harm thee not.
    He can lift off thy cross, and loose thy bands,
    And calm thy fears, nay, death is in His
        hands.
                    Be thou content.

3. Or art thou friendless and alone,
        Hast none in whom thou canst confide?
    God careth for thee, lonely one,
        Comfort and help will He provide.
    He sees thy sorrows, and thy hidden grief,
    He knoweth when to send thee quick relief.
                    Be thou content.

4. The heart's outspoken pain He knows,
        Thy secret sighs He hears full well,
    What to none else thou dar'st disclose
        To Him thou may'st with boldness tell.
    He is not far away, but ever nigh,
    And answereth willingly the poor man's cry.
                    Be thou content.

5. Be not o'er-mastered by thy pain,
        But cling to God, thou shalt not fall;
    The floods sweep over thee in vain,
        Thou yet shalt rise above them all;

For when thy trial seems too hard to bear,
Lo! God, thy King, hath granted all thy
    prayer.
            Be thou content.

6. Why art thou full of anxious fear
    How thou shalt be sustain'd and fed?
He who hath made, and placed thee here,
    Will give thee needful daily bread.
Canst thou not trust His rich and bounteous
    hand,
Who feeds all living things on sea and land?

7. He who doth teach the little birds
    To find their meat in field and wood,
Who gives the countless flocks and herds
    Each day their needful drink and food,
Thy hunger too will surely satisfy,
And all thy wants in His good time supply.
            Be thou content.

8. Say'st thou, I know not how or where,
    No help I see, where'er I turn;
When of all else we most despair,
    The riches of God's love we learn.
When thou and I His hand no longer trace,
He leads us forth into a pleasant place.
           Be thou content.

34

9. Though long His promised aid delay,
    At last it will be surely sent :
Though thy heart sink in sore dismay,
    The trial for thy good is meant.
What we have won with pains, we hold most
      fast,
What tarrieth long, is sweeter at the last.
              Be thou content.

10. Lay not to heart, whate'er of ill
    Thy foes may falsely speak of thee,
Let man defame thee as he will,
    God hears, and judges righteously.
Why should'st thou fear, if God be on thy
      side,
Man's cruel anger or malicious pride ?
              Be thou content.

11. We know for us a rest remains,
    When God will give us sweet release
From earth and all our mortal chains,
    And turn our sufferings into peace.
Sooner or later death will surely come
To end our sorrows and to take us home.
              Be thou content.
              LYRA LYRA GERMANICA.

270 *Genesis* **xxviii. 15.**

1. GOD doth not leave His own !
    The night of weeping for a time may last,
    Then, tears all past,
    His going forth shall as the morning shine,
    The sunrise of His favour shall be thine—
    God doth not leave His own !

2. God doth not leave His own !
    Tho' few and evil all their days appear,
    Tho' grief and fear
    Come in the train of earth and hell's dark
    crowd—
    The trusting heart says, even in the cloud,
    God doth not leave His own !

3. God doth not leave His own !
    This sorrow in their life He doth permit—
    Yea, chooseth it.
    To speed His children in their heavenward
    way,
    He guides the winds ;—faith, hope, and love
    all say,
    God doth not leave His own !

271.   *John* xii. 21.

1. " WE would see Jesus "—for the shadows
           lengthen
     Across this little landscape of our life :
     We would see Jesus, our weak faith to
        strengthen,
        For the last weariness—the final strife.

2. " We would see Jesus "—for life's hand hath
        rested
        With its dark touch upon both heart and
           brow;
     And though our souls have many a billow
        breasted,
        Others are rising in the distance now.

3. " We would see Jesus "—the great rock foun-
        dation,
     Whereon our feet we've set by sovereign
        grace ;
     Not life nor death, with all their agitation,
        Can thence remove us, if we see His face.

4. " We would see Jesus"—other lights are
        paling,
        Which for long years we have rejoiced to
           see ;

The blessings of our pilgrimage are failing,
    We would not mourn them, for we go to
        Thee.

5. " We would see Jesus"—yet the spirit lingers
    Round the dear objects it has loved so long.
And earth from earth can scarce unclasp its
    fingers.—
    Our love to Thee makes not this love less
    strong.

6. " We would see Jesus "—sense is all too
    binding,
    And heaven appears too dim—too far away;
We would see Thee, to gain a sweet remind-
    ing,
    That Thou has promised our great debt to
    pay.

7. " We would see Jesus "—this is all we're
    needing,—
    Strength, joy, and willingness come with
    the sight .
" We would see Jesus," dying, risen, plead-
    ing ;—
    Then welcome day, and farewell mortal
    night !

34*

272.   *Philippians* i. 23.

1. I JOURNEY forth rejoicing,
       From this dark vale of tears,
    To heavenly joy and freedom,
       From earthly bonds and fears;
    Where Christ our Lord shall gather
       All His redeem'd again,
    His kingdom to inherit ;—
          Good night till then !

2. Go to thy quiet resting,
       Poor tenement of clay !
    From all thy pain and weakness
       I gladly haste away ;
    But still in faith confiding
       To find Thee yet again,
    All glorious and immortal ;
          Good night till then !

3. Why thus so sadly weeping,
       Belov'd one of my heart ?
    The Lord is good and gracious,
       Tho' now He bids us part.
    Oft have we met in gladness,
       And we shall meet again,
    All sorrows left behind us ;—
          Good night till then !

4. I go to see His glory,
      Whom we have lov'd below;
    I go the blessed angels,
      The holy saints, to know;
    Our lovely ones departed,
      I go to find again,
    And wait for you to join us;—
          Good night till then!

5. I hear the Saviour calling;
      The joyful hour has come:
    The angel-guards are ready
      To guide me to our home;
    Where Christ our Lord shall gather
      All His redeem'd again,
    His kingdom to inherit;—
          Good night till then! ·
          HYMNS FROM THE LAND OF LUTHER.

---

273.   *Hebrews* iv. 3.

1. REST, weary soul!
      The penalty is borne, the ransom paid,
    For all thy sins full satisfaction made;
    Strive not thyself to do what Christ has done;

Claim the free gift and make the joy thine
  own ;
No more by pangs of guilt and fear distrest,
    Rest, sweetly rest !

2. Rest, weary heart !
From all thy silent griefs and secret pain,
Thy profitless regrets and longings vain ;
Wisdom and love have ordered all the past ;
All shall be blessedness and bright at last ;
Cast off the cares that have so long opprest,
    Rest, sweetly rest !

3. Rest, weary head !
Lie down to slumber in the peaceful tomb,
Light from above has broken through its
  gloom ;
Here in the place where once thy Saviour lay,
Where He shall wake thee on a future day,
Like a tired child upon its mother's breast,
    Rest, sweetly rest!

4. Rest, spirit, rest !
In the green pastures of the heavenly shore,
Where sin and sorrow can approach no more,
With all the flock by the Good Shepherd fed,
Beside the streams of life eternal led,
For ever with thy God and Saviour blest,
    Rest, sweetly rest !

274. *Luke* xxi. 19.

1. BE still, my soul! the Lord is on thy side,
     Bear patiently the cross of grief and pain,
   Leave to thy God to order and provide,
     In every change He faithful will remain.
   Be still, my soul! thy best, thy heavenly
     Friend,
   Thro' thorny ways leads to a joyful end.

2. Be still, my soul! thy God doth undertake
     To guide the future, as He has the past:
   Thy hope, thy confidence, let nothing shake,
     All now mysterious shall be bright at last.
   Be still, my soul! the waves and winds still
     know
   His voice who ruled them while He dwelt
     below.

3. Be still, my soul! when dearest friends depart,
     And all is darkened in the vale of tears;
   Then shalt thou better know His love, His
     heart,
   Who comes to sooth thy sorrow and thy
     fears.
   Be still, my soul! thy Jesus can repay
   From His own fulness all He takes away.

4. Be still, my soul ! the hour is hastening on,
     When we shall be for ever with the Lord ;
  When disappointment, grief, and fear, are
       gone,
     Sorrow forgot, love's purest joys restored.
  Be still my soul ! when change and fears are
       past,
  All safe and blessed we shall meet at last.

5. Be still, my soul ! begin the song of praise
     On earth, believing, to the Lord on high ;
  Acknowledge Him in all thy works and ways,
     So shall He view thee with a well-pleas'd
       eye.
  Be still, my soul ! the sun of life divine
  Thro' passing clouds shall but more brightly
    shine.

HYMNS FROM THE LAND OF LUTHER.

275.   *John* xiv. 2.

  1.   GOING home ! and going quickly !
         'T is a thought to cheer the heart ;
       Should we suffer, be it meekly,
       Soon the world and we must part,
       Never more to meet again ;
       There 's an end of suffering then,

There's an end of all that grieves us;
How the thought of this relieves us!

2. Going home! How sweet and cheering!
Going to the place we love,
There in royal state appearing
Mid the shining court above:
There our Father lives and reigns,
Greater He than fancy feigns;
There His people live for ever,
There's a portion failing never.

3. Going home! There's nothing dearer
To the pilgrim's heart than home,
Drawing nearer still and nearer
To the place where pilgrims come:
Much he thinks of what will be,
Much of what he hopes to see,
Thinks of kindred, friends, and brothers,
But of Christ above all others.

4. 'T is the blessed hope of seeing
Him he loves in glory there,
Blessed hope of ever being
With the Lord, His joys to share;
'T is the hope which lightens toil,
And in sorrow makes him smile,
Cheers him in the midst of strangers,
Keeps him when beset with dangers.

5. Going home! Then it behoves us
   Here to live as strangers do ;
   When the trial comes, it proves us,
   Proves if we have faith or no ;
   Let us make the promise sure,
   Let us to the end endure,
   In the Saviour's love abiding,
   In the Saviour's strength confiding.

276　　　　　*Luke* xii. 32.

1. A LITTLE flock ! so calls He thee,
   Who bought thee with His blood ;
   A little flock, disowned of men,
   But owned and loved of God.

2. A little flock ! yea even so,
   A handful among men,
   Such is the purpose of Thy God ;
   So willeth He ; Amen !

3. Not many rich and noble called,
   Not many great and wise ;
   They whom He makes His kings and priests,
   Are poor in human eyes.

4. Church of the everlasting God,
   Our Father's gracious choice

Amidst the voices of this earth,
  How feeble is Thy voice!

5. But the chief Shepherd comes at length,
    Thy feeble days are o'er;
No more a handful in the earth,
    A little flock no more.

6. No more a lily among thorns,
    Weary, and faint, and few;
But countless as the stars of heaven,
    Or as the early dew.

7. When entering th' eternal hall
    In robes of victory,
That mighty multitude shall keep.
    A joyous jubilee.

BONAR.

---

277.   *Psalm* vi. 8.

1. WEEP not,—Jesus lives on high,
    Oh! sad and wearied one!
If thou with the burden sigh
    Of grief thou cans't not shun,
      Trust Him still;—
      Soon there will
Roses in the thicket stand,
Goshen smile smile in Egypt's land.

35

2.   Weep not,—Jesus thinks of thee,
    When all beside forget,
And on thee so lovingly
    His faithfulness has set,
      That tho' all
      Ruined fall,
Everything on earth be shaken,
Thou wilt never be forsaken.

3.   Weep not,—Jesus heareth thee,
    Hears thy moanings broken,
Hears when thou right wearily
    All thy grief has spoken.
      Raise thy cry,
      He is nigh ;
And when waves roll full in view,
He shall fix their " Hitherto."

4.   Weep not,—Jesus loveth thee,
    Tho' all around may scorn,
And tho' poisoned arrows be
    Upon thy buckler borne.
      With His love,
      Nought can move ;
All may fail,—yet only wait,
He shall make the crooked straight.

5.   Weep not,—Jesus cares for thee,
    Then what of good can fail ?

Why shouldest thou thus gloomily
At thought of trouble quail.
    He will bear
    All thy care;
And if He the burden take,
He will all things perfect make.

6. Weep not,—Jesus comforts thee;
    He yet shall come and save,
And each sorrow thou shalt see
    Lie buried in thy grave.
      Sin shall die,
      Grief shall fly;
Thou hast wept thy latest tears,
When the Lord of life appears.

R. SCHMOLK.

---

278.   *Hebrews* ii. 10.

1. PERFECT through suffering! Is this the
      path
    My Saviour trod?
And shall I shrink to follow Thee,
    Thou Lamb of God?

2. Perfect through suffering! The heart may
      faint
    Upon the road,

And flesh and spirit both may fail ; —
     Yet hope in God.

3.   Perfect through suffering !   The gold refined,
          No dross remains,
      And o'er the furnace watcheth One,
          To guide the flames.

4.   Perfect through suffering !   A bright reward
          Before thee lies,
      Gird up thy loins to run the race ;—
          Then seize the prize.

5.   Perfect through suffering !   The countless
          throng
              Of saints in light,
      Through tribulations great have come,
              Afflictions, fight.

6.   Perfect through suffering !   Their robes made
          white
              In Jesus' blood,
      The tears from ev'ry eye are wiped,
              They reign with God.

7   Perfect through suffering !   The conflict o'er,
              The race well run,
      A crown of immortality
              And joy is won.

8. Perfect through suffering ! Is this the path
      My Saviour trod ?
  Then welcome be its fiery cross ;
      It leads to God.

---

279.   2 *Corinthians* v. 17.

1. WE praise and bless Thee, gracious Lord,
      Our Saviour kind and true,
  For all the old things pass'd away,
      For all Thou hast made new.

2. The old security is gone,
      In which so long we lay ;
  The sleep of death Thou hast dispelled,
      The darkness rolled away.

3. New hopes, new purposes, desires,
      And joys, Thy grace has given ;
  Old ties are broken from the earth,
      New ones attach to heaven.

4. But yet how much must be destroyed
      How much renew'd must be,
  Ere we can fully stand complete,
      In likeness, Lord, to Thee !

5. Ere to Jerusalem above,
   The holy place, we come,
   Where nothing sinful or defiled
   Shall ever find a home.

6. Thou, only Thou, must carry on
   The work Thou hast begun ;
   Of Thine own strength Thou must impart,
   In Thine own ways to run.

7. Ah ! leave us not ! From day to day
   Revive, restore again ;
   Our feeble steps do Thou direct,
   Our enemies restrain.

8. Whate'er would tempt the soul to stray,
   Or separate from Thee,
   That, Lord, remove, however dear
   To the poor heart it be !

9. When the flesh sinks, then strengthen Thou
   The spirit from above ;
   Make us to feel Thy service sweet,
   And light Thy yoke of love.

10. So shall we faultless stand at last
    Before Thy Father's throne,

The blessedness for ever ours,
  The glory all Thine own !

HYMNS FROM THE LAND OF LUTHER.

---

280.   *Hebrews* xi. 16.

1. MY days are gliding swiftly by,
      And I, a pilgrim stranger,
    Would not detain them as they fly—
      These hours of toil and danger.
    For O we stand on Jordan's strand,
      Our friends are passing over,
    And just before the shining shore
      We may almost discover.

2. We'll gird our loins, my brethren dear,
      Our distant home discerning ;
    Our absent Lord has left us word,
      Let ev'ry lamp be burning.
              For oh ! we stand, &c.

3. Should coming day be cold and dark,
      We need not cease our singing,
    That perfect rest none can molest,
      Where golden harps are ringing.
              For oh ! we stand, &c,

4.   Let sorrow's rudest tempest blow,
        Each chord on earth to sever ;
     Our King says " Come,"—and there 's a home,
        For ever, oh ! for ever !
                For oh ! we stand, &c.

———

281.   *John* iii. 2.

1.   WHAT shall I be ? my Lord, when I be-
                hold Thee
        In awful majesty at God's right hand ;
     And 'mid th' eternal glories that enfold me,
        In strange bewilderment, O Lord, I stand.
     What shall I be ? these tears—they dim my
                sight ;
     I cannot catch the blissful vision right.

2.   What shall I be ? Lord, when Thy radiant
                glory,
        As from the grave I rise, encircles me ;
     When brightly pictured in the light before
                me,
        What eye hath never seen, my eye shall see.
     What shall I be ?   Ah ! blessed and sublime
     Is the dim prospect of that glorious time !

3.   What shall I be? when days of grief are
      ended,
   From earthly fetters set for ever free;
When from the harps of saints and angels
      blended,
   I hear the burst of joyful melody!
What shall I be, when risen from the dead,
Sin, death, and hell I never more shall dread?

4.   What shall I be? when all around are throng-
      ing,
   The loved of earth, where I have come to
      dwell;
When all is joy and praise—no anxious long-
      ing,
   No bitter parting, and no sad farewell.
What shall I be? Ah, how the streaming
      light
Can lend a radiance to this dreary night!

5.   Yes! Faith can never know the full salvation,
   Which Jesus for His people will prepare;
Then will I wait in peaceful expectation,
   Till the good Shepherd comes to take me
      there.
My Lord, my God, a blissful end I see,
Tho' now I know not what I yet shall be!

    HYMNS FROM THE LAND OF LUTHER.

282.　　　　*Psalm* xcv. 1.

1. JOYFULLY, joyfully, onward we move,
   Bound to the land of bright spirits
      above ;
   Jesus, our Saviour, in mercy says, " Come,"
   Joyfully, joyfully, haste to your home.
   Joyfully, joyfully, onward we move,
   Bound to the land of bright spirits above.

2. Soon will our pilgrimage end here below,
   Soon to the presence of God we shall go ;
   Then if to Jesus our hearts shall be given,
   Joyfully, joyfully, rest we in heaven.
      Joyfully, joyfully, onward, etc.

3. Teachers and kindred have pass'd on before.
   Waiting, they watch us approaching the
      shore,
   Singing to cheer us while passing along—
   Joyfully, joyfully, haste to your home.
      Joyfully, joyfully, onward, etc.

4. Sounds of sweet music there ravish the ear,
   Harps of the blessed, your strains we shall
      hear,
   Filling with harmony heaven's high dome ;
   Joyfully, joyfully, Jesus we come.
      Joyfully, joyfully, onward, etc.

5. Death, with its arrow, may soon lay us low;
Safe in our Saviour, we fear not the blow:
Jesus hath broken the bars of the tomb —
Joyfully, joyfully, we will go home.
     Joyfully, joyfully, onward, etc.

6. Bright will the morn of eternity dawn;
Death shall be conquered, its sceptre be gone;
Over the plains of our Canaan we'll roam,
Joyfully, joyfully, safely at home.
     Joyfully, joyfully, onward, etc.

---

283.   *Psalm* xxxvii. 5.

1. COMMIT thy way to God;
    The weight which makes thee faint—
Worlds are to Him no load!
    To Him breathe thy complaint.
He who for winds and clouds
    Maketh a pathway free,
Through wastes or hostile crowds
    Can make a way for thee.

2. Hope, then, tho' woes be doubled,
    Hope, and be undismayed;
Let not thine heart be troubled,
    Nor let it be afraid.

This prison where thou art,
   Thy God will break it soon,
And flood with light thy heart,
   In His own blessed noon.

3.   Up, up, the day is breaking,
    Say to thy cares, Good night!
Thy troubles from thee shaking
    Like dreams in day's fresh light.
Thou wearest not the crown,
    Nor the best course can'st tell;
God sitteth on the throne,
    And guideth all things well.

4.   Trust Him to govern, then:
    No king can rule like Him.
How wilt thou wonder when
    Thine eyes no more see dim,
To see those paths which vex thee,
    How wise they were and meet;
The works which now perplex thee,
    How beautiful, complete!

5.   Faithful the love thou sharest;
    All, all is well with thee;
The crown from hence thou bearest
    With shouts of victory.

In thy right hand to-morrow
   Thy God shall place the palms.
To Him who chased thy sorrow,
   How glad will be thy psalms!

PAUL GERHARDT.

---

284.   *Philippians* i. 21.

1. PRECIOUS Saviour, may I live
           Only for Thee.
  Spend the powers Thou dost give,
           Only for Thee.

2. Be my spirit's deep desire
           Only for Thee.
  May my intellect aspire
           Only for Thee.

8. In my joys may I rejoice
           Only for Thee.
  In my choices make my choice
           Only for Thee.

4. Meekly may I suffer grief
           Only for Thee.
  Gratefully accept relief
           Only for Thee.

5. Be my smiles and be my tears
    Only for Thee.
Be my young and riper years
    Only for Thee.

6. Be my singing and my sighing
    Only for Thee.
Be my sickness and my dying
    Only for Thee.

7. Be my rising, be my glory
    Only for Thee.
Be my whole eternity
    Only for Thee.

           E. W.

---

285.   *Psalm* cxvi. 7.

1. CEASE, my soul thy strayings!
  Have they brought thee peace?
Come, no more delayings,
  Cease thy wanderings, cease.
    These vanities how vain!
    Wander not again.

2. Thou hast found thy centre,
  There, my soul, abide,

Never more adventure
   Now to swerve aside.
      These vanities how vain !
      Wander not again.

3. Thou hast reach'd thy dwelling,
    Safe, sure anchorage,
  From the perilous swelling
    Of the tempest's rage.
      These vanities how vain !
      Wander not again.

4. Tranquil hours now greet thee
    In thy calm abode ;
  Gracious looks now meet thee
    From thy loving God.
      These vanities how vain !
      Wander not again.

5. Pierce these mists that blind thee,
    Press to yonder prize,
  Break the bonds that bind thee :
    Rise, my soul arise !
      These vanities how vain !
      Wander not again.

                                BONAR.

286.   *Isaiah* lvii. 19.

1.   ARE your souls the Saviour seeking ?
            Peace, peace, be still ;—
      T' is the Lord Himself is speaking,
            Peace, peace, be still.
      For before the world's foundation,
      God secured a full salvation,—
    · Happy people, chosen nation !
            Peace, peace, be still.

2.   'T is the blood of Christ hath spoken,
            Peace, peace, be still ;
      The destroyer sees the token,
            Peace, peace, be still.
      On God's word we boldly venture,
      All our hopes in Jesus centre ;—
      Into rest our souls can enter,—
            Peace, peace, be still.

3.   Great the calm the Saviour spreadeth,
            Peace, peace, be still ;
      Whatsoe'r your spirit dreadeth,
            Peace, peace, be still.
      Though with mighty foes engaging,
      War with sin and Satan waging,
      Storms of trial fiercely raging,
            Peace, peace, be still.

4. Ye who love the Lord's appearing,
      Peace, peace, be still ;
Day and night through faith unfearing,
      Peace, peace, be still.
Though approaching judgments thunder,
Filling all men's hearts with wonder,
Though earth's ties are rent asunder,
      Peace, peace, be still.

5. Jesus walks upon the ocean,
      Peace, peace, be still ;
He shall hush its loud commotion,
      Peace, peace, be still.
Soon shall end our days of sighing,
Pain and sorrow, death and crying,
Till that hour on God relying,—
      Peace, peace, be still.

---

287.   1 *John* iii. 2.

1. WE speak of the realms of the blessed,
      That country so bright and so fair ;
And oft are its glories confessed ;
      But what must it be to be there !

2. We speak of its pathways of gold,
      Its walls deck'd with jewels so rare ;
36*

Its wonders and pleasures untold—
But what must it be to be there !

3.   We speak of its peace and its love,
The robes which the glorified wear,
The songs of the blessed above—
But what must it be to be there !

4.   We speak of its freedom from sin,
From sorrow, temptation, and care,
From trials without and within—
But what must it be to be there !

5.   Do Thou, Lord, midst pleasure or woe,
For heaven our spirits prepare ;
That shortly we also may *know*
And *feel* what it is to be there !

---

288.   1 *Peter* ii. 7.

1.   MY Saviour ! Thou art precious, more dear
than life to me,
Ah ! whom have I in heaven above, or whom
on earth but Thee ?
And while Thy works reviewing, I wonder
and adore,
I love Thee for Thy tender love, still more,
and more, and more.

2. I see Thy form of beauty reflected in the
        deep,
    When sunny beams, like chains of gold,
        across the billows sweep ;
    And when I cannot number, like waves, Thy
        mercies o'er,
    I love Thee for Thy tender love, still more
        and more, and more.

3. To earth Thou art returning, and this fair
        world shall be
    A holy temple, Lord, at last, whence praise
        shall rise to Thee ;
    Then all Thy rule obeying, shall all Thy grace
        adore,
    And love Thee for Thy tender love, still more,
        and more, and more.

4. 'T is sweet, tho' oft in sorrow, to call my Lord
        my own,
    And bend in heartfelt silent praise before
        Thy heavenly throne ;
    But soon, each cloud of sadness, each fear,
        each danger o'er,
    The endless sunshine of Thy love shall bless
        me more and more.

5. To fairer, purer regions, my soul shall soar
       away,
   And e'er behold Thee as Thou art, in all Thy
       bright array;
   Yet while, in wonder gazing, Thy glories I
       explore,
   Thy love shall claim my ceaseless song, still
       more, and more, and more.

6. To faith Thou art revealing Thyself, while
       absent, Lord,
   By Thine indwelling Spirit's power, and by
       Thy written word,
   But soon the breaking morning her streams
       of light shall pour,
   And faith and hope shall yield the palm to
       love for evermore.

C. A. H.

---

289.   *Ecclesiastes* xi. 4.

1. SOW ye beside all waters,
       Where the dew of heaven may fall;
   Ye shall reap if ye be not weary,
   For the Spirit breathes o'er all.
   Sow, though the thorn may wound thee,
   One wore the thorn for thee;

And though the cold world scorn thee,
Patient and hopeful be.

2. Sow ye beside all waters,
    With a blessing and a prayer;
    Name Him whose hands uphold thee,
    And sow ye everywhere.
    Sow where the sunlight sheddeth
    Its warm and cheering ray,
    For the rain of heaven descendeth
    When the sunbeams pass away.

3. Sow when the tempest lowers,
    For calmer days may break;
    And the seed in darkness nourished,
    A goodly plant may make.
    Sow when the morning breaketh
    In beauty o'er the land:
    And when the evening falleth
    Withhold not thou thine hand.

4. Sow, though the rock repel thee,
    In its cold and sterile pride;
    Some clift there may be riven,
    Where the little seed may hide.
    Fear not, for some will flourish,
    And though the tares abound,
    Like the willows by the waters,
    Will the scattered grain be found

5. Work while the daylight lasteth,
    Ere the shades of night come on,
    Ere the Lord of the vineyard cometh,
    And the labourer's work is done.
    Watch not the clouds above thee,
    Let the wild winds round thee sweep ;
    God may the seed-time give thee,
    But another hand may reap.

6. Have faith, though ne'er beholding
    The seed burst from its tomb ;
    Thou know'st not which may perish,
    Or what be spared to bloom.
    Room on the narrowest ridges
    The ripen'd grain will find ;
    That the Lord of the harvest coming,
    In the harvest sheaves may find.

————

290.   *Luke* xxiv. 29.

1. ABIDE with me ! fast falls the eventide ;
        The darkness thickens ; Lord, with me
            abide ;
    While other helpers fail, and comforts flee,
    Help of the helpless, oh ! abide with me.

2. Swift to its close ebbs out life's little day ;
Earth's joys grow dim, its glories pass away;
Change and decay in all around I see,
Oh ! Thou, who changest not, abide with me.

3. Come not in terrors as the King of kings,
But kind and good, with healing in Thy
wings,—
Tears for all woes, a heart for ev'ry plea,
Come, Friend of sinners, thus abide with me.

4. Thou on my head in early youth did'st smile,
And, though rebellious and perverse mean-
while,
Thou hast not left me, oft as I left Thee ;—
Oh ! to the close, oh ! Lord, abide with me.

5. I fear no foe with Thee at hand to bless,
Ills have no weight, and tears no bitterness ;
Where is death's sting ? Where, grave, thy
victory ?
I triumph still if Thou abide with me.

6. Hold Thou Thy cross before my closing eyes,
Shine through the gloom, and point me to
the skies ;
Heaven's morning breaks, and earth's vain
shadows flee !
In life, in death, oh ! Lord, abide with me.

291.   *Acts* iv. 12.

1. CHRIST alone—Christ alone--
        Is the Christian's watchword here;
    Only Jesus will he own,
    Him proclaiming far and near.

2. Christ alone—Christ alone--
    Lisps the new-born child of God,
    When the Saviour first is known,
    And he feels the sprinkled blood.

3. Christ alone—Christ alone—
    Is the faithful watchman's cry,
    Midst the foes of Jesus' throne,
    Who His name and truth deny.

4. Christ alone—Christ alone—
    Is the noble martyr's song,
    Till his spirit home has flown,
    Gather'd to the white-robed throng.

5. Christ alone—Christ alone—
    Shout the glorious hosts above,
    Standing round the Father's throne,
    Worshipping in perfect love.

6. Christ alone—Christ alone—
    Echo back, my soul, the words;

Thy redeeming Saviour crown—
King of kings and Lord of lords.

---

292.   *Isaiah* xliv. 22.

1. RETURN, O wanderer, to thy home ;
        Thy Father calls for thee ;
No longer now an exile roam
    In guilt and misery.
                Return ! return !

2. Return, O wanderer, to thy home ;
        'T is Jesus calls for thee ;
The Spirit and the Bride say come—
    Oh now for refuge flee !
                Return ! return !

3. Return, O wanderer, to thy home ;
        'T is madness to delay ;
There are no pardons in the tomb,
    And brief is mercy's day.
                Return ! return !

---

293.   *Luke* xxiv. 49.

1. COME, Holy Ghost, our souls inspire,
        Let us Thine influence prove,

35

Source of the old prophetic fire,
Fountain of life and love.

2. Open the hearts of all who hear,
To make the Saviour room ;
Now let us find redemption near,
Let faith by hearing come.

3. Thou art the only Comforter
In all our soul's distress ;
Thou showest us our unbelief,
And Christ's redeeming grace.

4. Arise, and strengthen us, O Lord,
Thou know'st we all are frail ;
Grant neither Satan, world, nor flesh
May o'er Christ's flock prevail.

5. Cause all disharmony and strife
In Christendom to cease ;
And give to all the flocks of Christ
Love, union, truth, and peace.

——————

294.   *Genesis* xxvii. 34.

1. LORD, I hear of showers of blessing
Thou art scattering full and free,

Showers the thirsty land refreshing ;
Let some droppings fall on me,—
     Even *me.*

2.   Pass me not, O God my Father,
    Sinful though my heart may be ;
Thou might'st leave me, but the rather
    Let Thy mercy light on me,—
     Even *me.*

3.   Pass me not, O gracious Saviour ;
    Let me live and cling to Thee ;
Fain I'm longing for Thy favour ;
    While Thou 'rt calling, calling me,—
     Even *me.*

4.   Pass me not, O mighty Spirit ;
    Thou can'st make the blind to see ;
Witnesser of Jesus' merit,
    Speak the word of power to me,—
     Even *me.*

5.   Have I long in sin been sleeping--
    Long been slighting, grieving Thee ?
Has the world my heart been keeping ?
    Oh ! forgive, and rescue me,—
     Even *me.*

6. Love of God, so pure and changeless !
      Blood of Christ, so rich and free !
    Grace of God, so strong and boundless !—
      Magnify it all in me,—
            Even *me.*

7. Pass me not—Thy lost one bringing,
      Bind my heart, O Lord, to Thee;
    Whilst the streams of life are springing,
      Blessing others, oh ! bless me,—
            Even *me.*

---

295.   1 *Corinthians* i. 18.

1. I SAW the cross of Jesus
      When burden'd with my sin,
    I sought the cross of Jesus
      To give me peace within :
    I brought my sin to Jesus;
      He cleans'd it in His blood ;
    And in the cross of Jesus
      I found my peace with God.

2. I love the cross of Jesus,
      It tells me what I am ;
    A vile and guilty creature,
      Saved only through the Lamb

No righteousness, no merit,
　No beauty can I plead;
Yet in the cross I glory,
　My title there I read.

3.　I clasp the cross of Jesus
　　In ev'ry trying hour,
My sure and certain refuge,
　My never failing tower.
In every fear and conflict,
　I more than conqueror am;
Living I'm safe, or dying,
　Through Christ the risen Lamb.

4.　Sweet is the cross of Jesus!
　　There let my weary heart
Still rest in perfect peace
　Till life itself depart.
And then in strains of glory
　I'll sing Thy wond'rous power,
Where sin can never enter,
　And death is known no more.

　　　　　　　　　F. WHITFIELD.

――――――

296.　　　*Matthew* xxviii. 20.

1.　" LO! I am with thee!" bid thy fears
　　　And anxious sorrows cease;

35*

My hands shall dry thy bitter tears,
My lips shall whisper peace.

2. " Lo ! I am with thee," when the tomb
    Thy loved ones calls away,
    My voice shall cheer the valley gloom
    With thoughts of endless day.

3. " Lo ! I am with thee;"—-What the loss
    Of all thou can'st deplore,
    When placed beside the awful cross,
    Which once for thee I bore !

4. " Lo ! I am with thee," when the bed
    Of languishing is thine ;
    Thou shalt repose thine aching head
    Upon my love divine.

5. " Lo ! I am with thee," when the knell
    Of closing hours shall ring ;
    Mine arm the fatal foe shall quell,
    And crush his vanquished sting.

6. " Lo ! I am with thee," still the same
    Through endless years above ;
    'Mid brighter worlds I shall proclaim,
    My changeless, deathless love !

MACDUFF.

297. *Matthew* vi. 6.

1. A LONE with Thee, my God! alone with
   Thee !
   Thus would'st Thou have it still—thus let it
   be.
   There is a secret chamber in each mind,
   Which none can find,
   But He who made it—none beside can know
   Its joy or woe.
   Oft may I enter it oppressed by care,
   And find Thee there ;
   So full of watchful love, Thou know'st the
   why
   Of ev'ry sigh.
   Then all Thy righteous dealing shall I see,
   Alone with Thee, my God! alone with Thee !

2. The joys of earth are like a summer day,
   Fading away ;
   But in the twilight we may better trace
   Thy wondrous grace.
   The homes of earth are emptied oft by death
   With chilling breath ;
   The loved departed guest may ope no more
   The well-known door.
   Still in that chamber seal'd, Thou 'lt dwell
   with me,
   And I with Thee, my God, alone with Thee.

3. The world's false voice would bid me enter
      not
    That hallow'd spot ;
    And earthly thoughts would follow on the
      track,
    To hold me back,
    Or seek to break the sacred peace within,
    With this world's din.
    But by Thy grace, I'll cast them all aside,
    Whate'er betide,
    And never let that cell deserted be,
    Where I may dwell alone, my God, with Thee.

4. The war may rage ;—keep Thou the citadel,
    And all is well.
    And when I learn the fulness of Thy love
    With Thee above—
    When ev'ry heart oppressed by hidden grief
    Shall gain relief ;
    When ev'ry weary soul shall find its rest
    Amidst the blest,
    Then all my heart, from sin and sorrow free,
    Shall be a temple meet, my God, for Thee.

---

298.   *Matthew* xxviii. 6.

1. THOU hast stood here, Lord Jesus,
        Beside the still cold grave ;

And proved Thy deep compassion.
And mighty power to save.
Thy tears of tender pity,
  Thine agonizing groan,
Teach how for us Thou feelest,
  Now seated on Thy throne.

2. Thou hast lain here, Lord Jesus,
      Thyself the victim then ;
    The Lord of life and glory,
      Once slain for wretched men.
    From sin and condemnation
      When none but Thou could'st save,
    Thy love than death was stronger,
      And deeper than the grave.

3. Thou hast been here, Lord Jesus,
      But Thou art here no more ;
    The terror and the darkness,
      The night of death are o'er.
    Great Captain of salvation,
      Thy triumphs now we sing ;
    O grave ! where is thy victory ?
      O death ! where is thy sting ?

4. We wait for Thine appearing,
      We weep, but we rejoice ;

In all our depths of sorrow,
　We still can hear Thy voice;—
" I am the resurrection;
　I live, who once was slain;
Fear not, thy friend and brother
　Shall rise with Me and reign."

299.　　　　*2 Timothy* iv. 7, 8.

A DYING MARTYR'S HYMN.

1.　SING with me! sing with me!
　　　Weeping brethren, sing with me!
For now an open heaven I see,
And a crown of glory laid for me:
How my soul this earth despises!
How my heart and spirit rises!
Bounding from the flesh I sever!
World of sin, adieu, for ever!

2.　Sing with me! sing with me!
　　Friends in Jesus, sing with me!
All my sufferings, all my woe,
All my griefs I here forego.
Farewell terrors, sighing, grieving,
Praying, hearing, and believing,
Earthly trust, and all its wrongings,
Earthly love, and all its longings.

3. Sing with me ! sing with me !
Blessed spirits, sing with me !
To the Lamb our songs shall be,
Through a glad eternity !
Farewell, earthly morn and even,
Sun and moon, and stars of heaven ;
Heavenly portals, ope before me,
Welcome Christ, in all His glory !

---

300. *Revelations* **xxi. 4.**

1. BEYOND the smiling and the weeping,
   I shall be soon ;
Beyond the waking and the sleeping,
Beyond the sowing and the reaping,
   I shall be soon.
   Love, rest, and home !
   Sweet hope !
   Lord, tarry not, but come.

2. Beyond the blooming and the fading,
   I shall be soon ;
Beyond the shining and the shading,
Beyond the hoping and the dreading,
   I shall be soon.
   Love, rest, and home ! &c., &c.

3.   Beyond the rising and the setting,
            I shall be soon ;
    Beyond the calming and the fretting,
    Beyond remembering and forgetting,
            I shall be soon.
        Love, rest, and home ! &c., &c.

4.   Beyond the gathering and the strowing,
            I shall be soon ;
    Beyond the ebbing and the flowing,
    Beyond the coming and the going,
            I shall be soon.
        Love, rest, and home ! &c., &c.

5.   Beyond the parting and the meeting,
            I shall be soon ;
    Beyond the farewell and the greeting,
    Beyond the pulse's fever-beating,
            I shall be soon.
        Love, rest, and home ! &c., &c.

                                BONAR.

                    END.

www.ingramcontent.com/pod-product-compliance
Lightning Source LLC
Chambersburg PA
CBHW030955110726

47900CB00004B/1286